MURDER CAN'T BE HIDDEN

"The murder knife," Mother said. "It belongs to your brother Larry. Do you want him to go to the chair? You'll have to get rid of it, Judy!"

I took a handkerchief and wrapped the thing in it. I slipped out of the house into the darkness. I'd decided to bury the knife under the hemlock trees, and when I reached the place, I slipped it from under my coat and began digging a hole with it.

I never finished it.

There was a sudden flash of white light that almost blinded me, and immediately after a man's voice spoke, from close beside me.

"I'll take that, sister," it said.

EPISODE OF THE WANDERING KNIFE

MARY ROBERTS RINEHART

ZEBRA BOOKS
KENSINGTON PUBLISHING CORP.

ZEBRA BOOKS

are published by

Kensington Publishing Corp.
475 Park Avenue South
New York, NY 10016

First Zebra Books printing: January, 1990

Printed in the United States of America

Contents

Episode of the Wandering Knife

I

The night it happened Mother was giving a dinner party for the Mayor. I had no idea why she was giving a party for the Mayor. So far as I knew she had never even seen the man. But I knew what nobody else did that night. It was what you might call her last fling. Although the news wasn't out, she had offered the place to the government for a convalescent home, and after six months it had been accepted.

Mother is just Mother, and my brother Larry and I let it go at that. She has her own idea of how to amuse herself. Once I remember she brought out a part of the circus for a charity benefit, and it took three years to repair the lawns.

I must say the farewell party was quite in character. We managed to seat two hundred people hither and yon, and when a mounted policeman took his place in the driveway and the Mayor drove up with a screaming escort of motorcycle officers, there was a whole battery of photographers outside the gates. They had not been allowed inside, and from a distance it looked like summer lightning, all flash and no noise.

That was the point of the whole business. Nobody was allowed inside the grounds without being identified, and Alma Spencer, Mother's friend, companion, secretary and general watchdog, checked the guests off her lists as they entered the house. It appeared that the Mayor had been threatened with assassination or something of the sort, and he was making the most of it. The result was a policeman at all the doors except the front one, and the mounted policeman was to keep an eye on that.

Not that the Mayor was assassinated. He is still alive and running for office again. But I just want to point out that the house was a fortress that night.

Well, the party ended, as everything must eventually. I had loathed it from start to finish. Larry had been frankly bored, and only Mother seemed her usual self. I can still see her, standing in the wreck of the house after the sirens had shrieked away and the last guest had gone. It was a warmish October night, and she was in the marble rotunda which the architect playfully called our hall. Someone had had the idea of dipping the goldfish out of the basin around the fountain with a soft hat and putting them in a champagne bucket. I remember rescuing them, torpid from the melted ice but still alive.

Mother had stepped out of her slippers, which let her down to her normal five feet two inches, and she had taken off her diamond collar, which has been too tight for the last ten years, and was holding it in her hand.

"I think it went pretty well," she said complacently.

Alma was beside her. She had the usual pad in her hand, and she looked exhausted. Somewhere the caterer's men were folding up tables and extra chairs, and she jumped at every bang. Larry was in the men's room, looking for his hat.

"There has been some breakage," Alma said. "That drunken waiter dropped a tray of cocktails. But the silver is all here."

"What on earth did you expect?" Mother inquired sharply. "I don't invite people who steal spoons."

Alma raised her eyebrows. She had rather handsome eyebrows. And I remember I laughed. Matters were not helped either by Larry, who came back scowling from the men's room. He hadn't found his hat, and he pounced on the one by the fountain.

"Well, for God's sake!" he said. "If that's mine . . ."

It wasn't, however. He picked it up and looked at it. It was a dreadful hat. It had been a poor thing even before it had been wet. It had no sweatband in it, and now it smelled of fish. Larry put it down distastefully. But Mother wasn't interested in hats at the moment.

"Where was Isabel tonight, Larry?" she said.

Larry grinned at her.

"You know she never comes to your brawls, Mother."

Mother stiffened.

"I resent that word," she told him indignantly.

But she is never really angry with Larry. He is tall and very good-looking, especially in full evening dress as he was then.

He stooped over and kissed her. "Sorry," he said. "She didn't feel well. I told Alma in plenty of time. Isabel hasn't been up to much for the last week or two."

Mother glanced at him hopefully. She has always thought she would like a grandchild to dandle on her knee, but personally I thought she would be bored to death with one. Larry however was not looking at her. He went back to look for his hat again, and Mother sat down. The house was quieter by that time. As it is about the size of the White House in Washington there was a lot of it to be quiet. I watched the goldfish. They were beginning to recover.

"I do think Isabel might have made an effort," Mother said rather plaintively. "After all I've done for her and Larry."

Well, of course it hadn't been necessary for her to do anything for either of them. Isabel had a lot of money of her own, and so had Larry. I have always thought that the reason she built them a house on our grounds was to keep Larry close at hand. But she had built the house, and that is the story. Not that she was jealous of Isabel. Deep in her heart she was proud of her. It was not only that she was lovely to look at. I had disappointed Mother in that, having only the usual assortment of features. But Isabel had been a Leland, and to be a Leland meant something.

It meant belonging to the conservative group in town, the people who lived elegantly but quietly in their hideous old red-brick houses, exchanged calls, gave stuffy dinners with wonderful food and—at least until the war—drove about in ancient high limousines.

Not that Mother wasn't well born. She was, but our money had come from trade, and to the Lelands trade was simply out. Not even Strathmore House, built on the edge of town on what once had been my grandfather's country place before the city grew up around it, had wiped out the smell of wholesale groceries years ago. It was just as well—Mother would rather have died than be conventional.

Larry did not find his hat, and came back scowling.

"Nice crowd you had here," he said. "Somebody traded in my new opera hat for that thing on the floor."

Alma looked unhappy.

"I'm sorry," she said. "I suppose it's my fault. I found it on the floor in a back hall and sent it to the men's room. It wasn't wet then, of course.

Larry picked it up gingerly.

"You owe me for a hat," he said to Mother. "I'll take this home to remind you of it. And to show Isabel what she missed!"

Mother yawned.

"She missed a good dinner," she said.

She had relaxed by that time. She put out her feet and inspected them. They looked small and swollen, and vaguely pathetic. Larry saw them, and leaning over patted her bare shoulder.

"All right, old girl," he said. "Forget it. Go to bed and get some sleep."

I went out with him. The driveway was empty now, and the early fall air felt cool. It was dark, because of the dimout. The only light was from the open door behind us. I remember leaning against a pillar, and Larry's putting an arm around me.

"Pretty bad, wasn't it?" he said.

"Awful."

"Don didn't come?"

"No. He's like Isabel. He doesn't like our brawls."

No use telling him I had called Donald Scott myself and asked him. No use telling him the night had been a total loss for me because Don had refused. Politely, of course. Don is always polite. Anyhow, Larry wasn't interested. He stood looking down toward his house, which stood not far from the gate at the foot of the lawn.

"Look, Judy," he said. "You and Isabel get along pretty well, don't you?"

"I like her. I don't know how well she likes me. She's

not demonstrative."

"Still, you do go around together."

"Oh, that. Yes. She likes Alma better, you know."

He seemed embarrassed. He got out a cigarette and gave me one.

"Have you noticed any change in her lately?" he asked. "I've thought she was looking tired. She doesn't say anything. You know the Lelands. They don't talk about themselves. But there's something wrong."

"She's thinner. I've noticed that. I'm like Mother. I wondered if she was going to have a baby."

He shook his head.

"It's not that," he said. "I wish to God she'd talk to me if anything is bothering her."

He went off down the drive and I went inside. Patrick, the butler, was reporting when I got back. He looked old, tired, and disapproving. He said there was a hole burned in the Aubusson carpet in the Reynolds room, and someone had spilled a cocktail in the piano. Luckily he had got rid of the drunken waiter without trouble. What he meant, I gathered, was that he hadn't been so lucky with some of the guests.

Like Alma, he seemed exhausted. After all he has been with Mother for thirty years, from birth to brawl, as Larry put it, and he was fully seventy. But his dignity was unimpaired. He looked around at the wreckage of the big drawing room, much as Williams, the head gardener, had looked at his lawns after the circus, and he said much the same thing.

"After all, madam, with a crowd of people like that . . ."

Only Williams had said animals.

I sat down on the edge of the pool. I was a casualty too. Someone had stepped on the skirt of my white chiffon and torn it. But I didn't mention it. What was the use? For months I had been trying to get into the WAACS or the WAVES and I was expecting to be called any time. I supposed there would be hell to pay, but at least I was through with evening clothes. I looked at Mother. She was tired, but she somehow seemed even more complacent than usual. After Patrick had gone she spoke to me.

"I have something to tell you, Judy," she said. "And Alma

too. I hope you agree with me. I think you will. The fact is—"

She never finished that sentence. Patrick had left the front door open to air the hall, and we all heard someone running up the drive. It was Larry. When he got to the top of the steps he was staggering, and had to clutch the side of the doorway for support. He looked at us as if he had never seen us before.

"What is it, Larry?" Mother said. "Is something wrong?"

"Isabel!" he said. "She's dead."

Mother stood still. She was quite white under the liquid powder and rouge she insists on using, but her voice was calm.

"I'm sure you're wrong," she said. "She may have fainted. Get him a chair, Judy. And Alma, bring some brandy."

She asked no questions. She simply stood by Larry and waited until he had had the brandy. Even then she was calm, except that her plump small body was quivering. Then she said, "Can you tell me about it, son?"

"She's dead. That's all I can tell you." He got up, and looked around him wildly. "I've got to call the police."

"The police?"

"She's been murdered," he said, and staggered toward the library.

II

I thought I had seen Mother in action before. The time the boxing kangaroo she had brought for a children's party got excited and began knocking the kids over one by one, for instance. I was one of the kids, so I remember. Before I could speak she told Alma to look after him. Then she was out the front door and running down the driveway in her stocking feet. She almost beat me to Larry's house. I caught up to her finally and yelped at her to remember her blood pressure, and we entered the house together.

It is a pretty house. Mother's taste in people may be catholic, but in houses and furnishings she knows her stuff. And except that Larry had left the front door standing open it looked as quiet and orderly as ever. Mother gave one look around and then climbed the stairs. That is, she got almost up and stopped.

Isabel was lying on the landing, and there was no doubt that she was dead. She lay on her back, her arms outstretched, and except that one of her bedroom mules was off there was no sign of any struggle. Her lovely dark hair was spread over the carpet, making a frame for her face, and one arm was out of her dressing gown, as though she had been putting it on when she met her murderer.

Not that I noticed that then. All I could see was the small spot of blood on the front of her silk nightgown.

Mother stood very still, looking down at her. Then she reached down and touched the hand nearest to her. She drew back, and I knew Isabel really was dead. Neither of us said anything. Then Mother sank down on the stairs, as if she felt faint, and when Larry came pounding back she was still there. She wouldn't move to let him pass.

"There is nothing you can do," she said. "Go down and call the police. I'm here."

I went down to the porch with Larry. Alma was standing there, looking like death, and a few moments later I heard the siren. A police car swung in on two wheels and stopped with the engine still going. Two uniformed men leaped out. One of them touched his cap.

"Understand you've had some trouble here," he said.

Larry braced himself.

"We have. My wife . . ." He choked and did not finish.

They pushed past us and into the house, to see Mother sitting on the stairs. She was holding that wretched diamond collar. In her glittering gold-brocade dress and with her bright red hair she completely stopped them. They stood gazing up at her.

"My daughter-in-law is here," she said. "I'm afraid somebody has stabbed her."

"Is she badly hurt?"

"She is dead."

She let them pass then, but she stayed where she was. Behind me I heard Larry groan, and I turned and went back to him. I got him into the library, although he would not sit down. He paced the floor, looking like a wild man and saying over and over: "Who would do it? She had no enemies. Who would do it?" I think he didn't even know he was speaking, or that I was there.

It was only a minute or so before one of the officers came down the stairs to the telephone. He hung up and looked at Larry.

"Who found her?" he asked.

Larry tried to explain, but he made so bad a job of it that I took it over. I told about the party for the Mayor, the two hundred people, the orchestra, the forty extra waiters, even the Mayor's screaming escort. And I told about Larry's coming home to find Isabel dead. He looked bewildered.

"What you're saying, miss, is that close to three hundred

people were in and out of this property tonight. That right?"

"That's right."

"They all drove in at the gate out there?"

"That's the only way they could get in."

But the knowledge that the Mayor had been among them made him treat us both with more marked consideration.

"Anything missing in the house?" he inquired. "It might have been a burglar. If she woke up and was raising an alarm . . . Anything valuable around?"

The idea of a burglar at least gave Larry something to hold to. He said Isabel's jewels were in the house. In the safe in her room. He even listed them, while the officer wrote them down: her diamond and other earrings, her bracelets, her clips and her pearls—although pearls are worth a dime a dozen nowadays. But when the officer came back again he said the safe was closed and locked.

"Maybe if you'd come up and open it . . ." he suggested.

Larry however had taken all he could. He shook his head.

Mother was still on the stairs when the homicide squad arrived. They had to push past her. The Inspector came first, with his car jammed with detectives and a uniformed stenographer. Following him came another car with a photographer and fingerprint men, and soon after the captain of our local precinct, a youngish man who said he had been at a fire somewhere and been delayed. The hall and stairs were jammed, but Mother refused to move.

"She was my son's wife," she said. "I was fond of her. And some woman has to stand by her now. She's—helpless."

I had to take my hat off to her, tired as she was. She still had no slippers on her feet; she still hung on to her choker. But she never gave an inch, although she looked pretty sick.

"What I want," she said, "is to know who did this to her. And why?"

That was at half-past twelve on Thursday, the 15th of last October, or rather the early morning of the 16th. There were police all over the house by that time, and to add to the confusion I had a half-dozen hysterical women on my hands. The sirens had wakened the maids, and one or two of them fainted when they heard what had happened. The rest were crying, and I would have given a lot to have slapped some sense into them. As it was, all I could do was to force the cook to stop wailing and make coffee, and I took some myself. I was pretty jittery by that time. I was drinking it in the pantry when the photographer came and asked for a cup.

He was a tall thin young man. He looked tired, and I gave him the coffee quickly. I hardly noticed him, which seems queer now; but he eyed me with interest.

"So you're Judy Shepard," he said.

"Judith," I said. "My mother's answer to my father's wish that I be named for his sister Henrietta."

He gave me a pale sort of grin, as if he understood why I had to talk or go into shrieking hysterics.

"I'm Anthony King," he said. "Generally known as Tony." He seemed to think I might know the name. I didn't.

"Any ideas about this thing?" he asked. "See any weapon when you got here? Anybody hate your sister-in-law? No. Then do you mind if I sit down? I'm just getting over a spell in the hospital."

He sat down rather abruptly and drank his coffee. Then he reached into his pocket and pulled out a fine platinum chain with a small white silk tassel hung on it. I stared at it.

"Ever see it before?"

"Never."

"It was under the—under Mrs. Shepard. Kind of funny, isn't it? I mean, do women hang tassels on chains?"

He let me take it and look at it. I suppose because there could be no fingerprints on a thing like that. The chain was the usual sort, but the tassel was not. It was ordinary enough in itself, but on the small solid top someone had made a cross in ink.

The King man had his eyes on me.

"Curious, isn't it?" he said.

I gave it back to him.

"I can't imagine her having a thing like that," I told him. "You'd better show it to the police."

"They know I have it," he said cryptically, and got up. "I'm just asking around."

He stopped in the doorway however and looked back at me.

"Look here," he said, "you can't do anything, you know.

Why not get out, for a while anyhow? Go home and get some rest. You may not know it, but you have a bad case of shock."

Well, I suppose I had, for the next thing I realized was that I was in a chair and he was pushing my head down between my knees.

"Take it easy," he was saying. "You're a big girl now, and big girls don't faint."

He didn't leave me until the pantry shelves had stopped whirling, dishes and all. Then he wandered back to see the women in the kitchen, and I carried coffee to Mother. She was still on the stairs, looking defiantly at the police as they trampled over and around her. I thought she wanted to say something to me, but there was no chance.

She never moved until at two o'clock the police ambulance came to take Isabel away. Larry was in the library with the Inspector, whose name turned out to be Welles, and a half-dozen detectives. Alma had been sent up to the house for the guest list of the dinner, and it was being checked over in the sun parlor. Other policemen were searching inside and out for the weapon, which the medical examiner had said was a knife. But they had not found it when the ambulance came.

Mother got up then. It was the first time she had moved since she saw the body. She came downstairs stiffly, to close the library door so that Larry would not see that awful basket being carried out. She looked very queer. Not shocked, exactly. If anything, she looked stealthy.

It seems queer, but it was not until then that we remembered the Lelands, and Larry finally roused enough to call them. As I have said, their house is still in the heart of town, one of those survivors of a past age before cars came and most people either evacuated the city or moved into apartments. It is a big square red-brick affair which has never compromised with the last quarter century. The Lelands were like that too. They belonged to the no-surrender group. The old lady, Isabel's grandmother, used a handsome pair of horses and a carriage for her daily outing until she died. Her spinster daughter, Eliza, had lived up to the family tradition, devoted herself to her mother and good works, and left Isabel a fortune in trust when she passed on, the Leland words for dying. Isabel's father, Andrew—always

Andrew, never Andy—still wore a small imperial and a stiff winged collar. He was a precise dapper little man usually, but there was nothing precise about him when, at three that morning, he stormed into Larry's house.

The first thing he saw however was Mother, and he stopped dead.

"What is all this?" he demanded. "What has happened? Where's Isabel?"

"I'm sorry, Andrew," Mother said. She had called him by his first name since the day Larry and Isabel were married, and he hated it. "I didn't think Larry was being clear. It's true."

"You mean that Isabel—"

"They've taken her away. The police, I mean. I tried to stop them, but—Andrew, this will be a shock. She didn't just die. She was—somebody killed her."

He took it very well. You have to say that for the Lelands of this world. They can take it. Pride or simply restraint, they can take it. And Andrew Leland, save that he sat down suddenly on one of the hall chairs, kept himself well in control. He shook his head when I brought him some brandy.

"Just a moment," he said. "I—I'm afraid I . . . It's a great shock." And after a minute: "Where is Lawrence? What does he know about this?"

"He found her," said Mother. "That's all he knows. He loved her and he found her. Just remember that, Andrew."

She looked almost dangerous. They can talk all they like about a lioness protecting her young, but a lioness has nothing on a woman like mother protecting her beloved son. She glared down at Andrew Leland, and he buried his face in his hands and groaned.

"God knows how I'm to tell Emily," he said, and got up. "Where is Lawrence?" he inquired, more steadily.

"In the library. The police are there."

He went in, not bothering to knock. The Inspector looked up, annoyed. Then he saw who it was and came forward.

"Very sorry about this, Mr. Leland," he said. "Very sorry indeed."

Andrew, however, was not looking at the Inspector. He was staring at Larry, sunk in a chair and looking collapsed.

"I would like to speak to Mr. Shepard alone," he said.

The Inspector did not like it.

"Perhaps I'd better tell you first all we know," he said. "If you'd care to sit down . . ."

I don't believe he would have, but Mother was beside him. She gave him a shove, and looking very surprised he found himself in a chair. The Inspector seemed gratified. I even thought he looked amused.

"These are the facts so far as we know them, Mr. Leland," he said. "At eight o'clock Mr. Shepard left this house for a dinner at his mother's. His wife had intended to go, but at the last moment complained of not feeling well, and Mr. Shepard suggested that she go to bed instead. This she did. Her personal maid reports that she was in bed at eight-thirty. She seemed nervous and upset.

"Between nine and ten the other servants all went to bed. But the personal maid, Anna Griffin, left the house by the kitchen door at nine o'clock and walked to Strathmore House. According to her story she was gone about an hour, leaving the kitchen door unlocked. She stopped and explained who she was to the mounted officer on duty in the driveway, and then went on to the house.

"She stayed there outside a window, looking in and listening to the music, for approximately one hour. Then she came back to this house and went to bed. She did not enter this part of the building at all. There was a bell from your daughter's room to her own, and the parlormaid, who was still awake and reading, reports that it did not ring.

"At eleven-thirty o'clock Mr. Shepard left his mother's house and came home. The front door was locked. He used his key to get in, and he found the lower hall dark. This, he says, surprised him, as a light is always left until he comes in. He did not bother to turn it on, and so"—here his voice became almost human—"he had the unfortunate experience of stumbling over his wife at the top of the stairs.

"I suppose we must make some allowance for the resulting delay. He did not call us at once. Instead he ran back to his mother's house and collapsed there. His mother and sister came here and he followed them almost immediately. He then notified us."

Andrew Leland looked up.

"That's *his* story," he said. "He could have left his mother's house earlier, couldn't he? There was a crowd of people. I understand half the undesirables in town were there."

"Don't be a fool, Andrew!" Mother snapped. "Just because you don't like me is no reason to accuse Larry. And if you want to know, the people I had tonight—"

The Inspector looked tired.

"Just what reason have you, Mr. Leland, for intimating that your son-in-law did this thing?"

"I said he could have. When did she . . . When did it happen?"

"Probably between nine and ten. The medical examiner may be able to set the time closer."

"We didn't finish dinner until almost ten," Mother broke in triumphantly.

But nobody was listening. Not even Larry. All this time he had not spoken. It was as though everything was unimportant except for the single fact that Isabel was dead. I think he hadn't even heard Mr. Leland's accusation. He stirred now, however.

"Why?" he said, out of a clear sky. "Why would anyone want to kill her? She never hurt anybody in her life."

The Inspector looked at him.

"I suppose you can account for your time, Mr. Shepard?"

"Not exactly. I didn't look at my watch."

"Did you leave the house at all during the evening? Your mother's house?"

Larry shrugged.

"I went outside after dinner was over," he said indifferently. "To get away from the noise. I lit a cigarette and walked down the drive a few yards. That's all."

"Did anyone see you?"

"I don't know. It was pretty dark. I heard the policeman's horse. I'm not sure he was on it. If he was he could have seen me. The outside lights were off on account of the dimout, but I left the hall door open."

"You didn't come down to your own house?"

"I wish to God I had."

"What about cars? Were there no chauffeurs around?"

"There were a few parked cars, but their lights were off too. The cars with chauffeurs had been told to stay outside in Linden Avenue until they were called."

The Inspector abandoned Larry for the minute. He picked up the platinum chain with its tassel and held it out.

"Do you recognize this, Mr. Leland?" he inquired.

Andrew Leland looked uncertain.

"I don't remember it. What about it?"

The Inspector explained, but he shook his head.

"I wouldn't know. Perhaps Emily—perhaps my wife will remember."

The thought of his wife seemed to overwhelm him. He got out a handkerchief and wiped his forehead, and I glanced at Mother. All at once I felt there was something queer about her. She nodded her head to me, but I couldn't understand what she meant. The Inspector was talking. There had been no robbery. Isabel's pearls were on her dressing table, as was her huge square-cut diamond engagement ring. Larry had given the police the combination of Isabel's safe, but her bracelets and other jewels were still there.

"That is not conclusive, of course," he said. "The man might have been scared off, perhaps by the maid's return. And we have not been able to find the weapon. It may have been thrown into the shrubbery, and we will find it in the morning. Mr. Shepard states that he saw no weapon by the body, and so does his mother."

"I wouldn't believe either one of them on oath," said Andrew Leland, and gave Larry a look of pure hatred.

That was when Mother did something she had never done before. She simply put her head back in her chair, closed her eyes, and sagged. Larry was on his feet in a second, yelling for water. But by the time he reached her she was over whatever it was. She looked up pathetically.

"I'm so tired, Larry," she said. "I'm too old for this sort of thing. Can't I go home and go to bed?"

I knew then that it was an act. In all her life Mother has never admitted age, and she has never wanted to go to bed until there was nothing left to stay up for. For some reason she wanted to get out of the house.

I played up as well as I could. "She's had a frightful day," I said. "And of course she is getting on, as she says." She gave me a nasty look from under her eyelids. "I can take her home, if you like. That is, if she can walk."

They wouldn't let her walk, however. They took her in one of the police cars, and one of my most vivid memories of that awful night is mother padding out in her stocking feet, holding to an officer's arm and giving everyone in the room but Andrew Leland a faint but winsome farewell nod.

I followed her out. I knew she wanted me to go with her, but I couldn't leave Larry. A man in the hall was sprinkling powder on the light switch there. He blew on it and then examined it with a magnifying glass. The man called Tony King was on his knees inspecting the stair carpet. When I looked out Mother was getting into the police car, and she was still putting on an act, crawling in as if she was too feeble to lift her legs.

Only it was not an act, as I learned later.

III

It must have been about four in the morning before the mounted policeman was brought in. Without his mount, of course. He was a tall young man, and he looked scared to death. Evidently he had been in bed, for his hair was still rumpled. He had put on his uniform, however, and he blinked in the light as he stood in the doorway.

The Inspector eyed him coldly.

"Officer Barnes?"

"Yes, sir."

"You were on duty here tonight?"

"Not here, sir. I was ordered to report outside the big house up the drive, to watch the traffic. The Mayor—"

"We know all that. Did you leave your post at any time during the evening?"

"No, sir. That is . . ."

He looked at me.

"Well, did you?" snapped the Inspector.

He gulped.

"Only once, sir. A call of nature. I . . ."

"All right," said the Inspector, rather hastily. "What I want to know is this. You were within sixty feet or so of the house. Did you see anyone leave that house at any time during the evening? Before the party broke up?"

"No, sir. I didn't."

Larry leaped to his feet, but the Inspector motioned for him to sit down again. He turned to Barnes, standing still and unhappy in front of him.

"Did you see a woman go up the drive and stand on the side terrace, looking in?"

Barnes looked more scared than ever, as if he wanted to bolt and run. He glanced around the room. Andrew Leland was watching him, as were all the others, including Larry, who was looking bewildered.

"If I could know what it's all about, sir," he began uneasily.

"Answer the question," the Inspector roared. "Did you or did you not see a woman go up the drive and onto the terrace?"

"Not that I remember," he mumbled. "She might have. I'm not saying she didn't. I was pretty tired, sir. I may have dozed a bit." He looked as though the idea had just occurred to him. He was sheepish but reassured. He even grinned a little. "I guess that's it, sir. I may have shut my eyes for a minute."

The Inspector looked back through his notes. He picked one out and examined it.

"I see. And in your sleep, when this woman told you she was going to look in a window and try to see the Mayor, you then replied: 'Atta girl, and to hell with him.'"

Barnes looked shocked and then absolutely terrified. It was some time before he even spoke. Then his voice was shaking.

"I never said anything of the sort. She's—she's lying."

"One of you is lying, that's certain," said the Inspector, and sent him out to another room under guard. When the door had closed behind them he looked at the captain of the local precinct.

"What about him?" he said. "What's scared him?"

"I don't know, sir. He's a decent sort. Has a wife and two children. Lives not far away. I don't get it."

I have often wondered since what would have happened had Barnes told his story that night. As it was they only confused and alarmed him. Perhaps he knew they would not have believed him. There was that fifty dollars to account for, and he had already given it to his wife. But they let him go eventually, on orders to report at the Inspector's office the next morning, and I took Larry home to get what sleep he could. Mr. Leland protested about their letting him go, but the Inspector was firm.

"We don't arrest on opportunity alone," he said, "and we have yet to find that there was even opportunity."

"That policeman was bribed. It stuck out all over him."

Even this resort to the vernacular, coming from a Leland as it did, failed to impress the Inspector. It merely annoyed him.

"You can leave that to me, sir," he said gruffly, and drove away.

Larry and I walked up to the house. There was no incentive to talk, even if we had wanted to, as one of the detectives went with us. He said good night quite civilly, however, when we got there, and, turning, went briskly down the drive. When we went in Patrick and James, the footman who valets Larry, were waiting. Alma had had a hysterical attack and gone to bed.

Larry fairly reeled when we got into the house, but the two men took charge of him. I waited until his door closed, then I went in to see Mother. The lights were all on, and it was evident she had sent her maid, Sarah, away and undressed herself. Her clothes were all over the room. She was sitting upright in bed, and she looked at me with an expression which was a nice mixture of grief and triumph.

"I just made it," she said. "That damned stocking of mine tore. Right in front of all those policemen too. That's why I fainted."

I eyed her.

"You didn't faint," I said. "I watched you."

"Of course not, but with you being completely dumb what could I do? I had to get away before it fell out."

I hope I was patient. She says now that I exhibited all my father's vicious temper plus the worst traits of Aunt Henrietta, who was the family harridan. But at last I got it out of her.

She had had the knife all along.

"What do you suppose kept me on the stairs?" she demanded. "There it was stuck under the edge of the carpet. What could I do but sit on it?"

"You might have given it to the police," I suggested.

"To the police? Larry's knife! Are you crazy?"

I could feel myself going cold all over. And it *was* Larry's knife. She had known it by the part of the handle she could see; the moth-eaten hairy handle of the old hunting knife that he had carted around with him on hunting trips for years. After he married he still kept it, in the room he called his gun room, downstairs in his own house. "Anyone could have got at it, of course. The glass doors of the closet were never locked. Just the same . . ."

"Don't be an idiot," Mother said sharply. "He didn't kill her. If he had, would he have used his own knife and left it there? That knife was meant to be found, and by the police. Anyhow, why should he? He liked her."

"Look, Mother," I said, lowering my voice, "what have you done with it?"

"I've hidden it," she said craftily.

"And how long will it stay hidden?" I inquired. "With servants all over the place, and as much privacy for us as canary birds."

Mother smirked. There is no other word for it.

"It's entirely safe," she said. "It's in the tank of the toilet in my bathroom."

"Look, Mother," I said patiently, "you never read crime books. You never read any books, for that matter. But toilet tanks are the universal hiding places for all lethal weapons. If they ever search this house—"

"Why on earth would they search this house?" she demanded indignantly. "Who do they think did it? We all have alibis. I sat beside that idiot of a Mayor for hours. Anyhow, who would come up here to my bathroom? If any one needed . . ."

I didn't say anything. What was the use? I went into her bathroom and lifted the porcelain top of the tank. The knife was there, and it was Larry's all right. I didn't touch it. I just put the lid back on. I felt dizzy.

"Nobody will find it there," Mother said, "and tomorrow we will get rid of it."

I don't remember saying anything. I had just seen Mother's stockings. They were lying on the floor, and one of them was torn to ribbons. I picked it up. There was a little blood on it from the knife; not much, but enough to make me shiver.

I knew right off that I had to do something about it. It looked simple enough, on the surface; just wash it out and let it go.

But you have to remember the way we lived. It was almost five in the morning, and Mother's early tea was brought in by Sarah at eight-thirty, no matter when she had gone to bed. I could see Sarah, whose life is entirely vicarious—meaning that our affairs are hers and hers are her own—picking up that torn wet stocking and holding it up.

"Whoever washed this stocking, madam? And torn as it is, too!"

I stood holding it and trying to think. There were no fires going, except in the furnaces in the cellar, and, anyway, Sarah knew every stitch of Mother's wardrobe. "Surely, madam," she'd say, "you couldn't have lost it. You can't lose a stocking." I couldn't fool her with one of mine, either. My feet are half again as big as Mother's. So I did the only thing I could think of. I picked up a nail file from the toilet table and before mother could open her mouth I had jerked down the covers and scratched her leg with it just above the knee.

She let out a howl and grabbed her leg.

"Are you crazy?" she yelped. "My own child! What on earth do you mean, attacking me like that?"

There was a drop of blood, fortunately, and I wiped it with the stocking. These days of tests for typing blood and so on certainly make it difficult even for the innocent. Then I explained to Mother, and to my relief she listened.

"All right," she said. "Only how am I to tell Sarah I got that scratch?"

I left her to work that out and went to my room across the hall. It was still dark, but I could see pinpricks of light through the grounds where the police were continuing their search for that wretched knife. I knew there was only one thing to do—go to them with it and tell the truth. After all nobody but a lunatic would leave the murder weapon—especially his own—where it would be certain to be found.

But I knew too that Mother would never agree. I couldn't even slip it out of her room, for she had locked the door behind me. Finally I went to bed, to lie in the dark and see Isabel lying dead at the foot of the stairs, and the King man on his knees examining the carpet. It was broad daylight when I finally dozed off.

At noon Alma wakened me, looking apologetic.

"I'm sorry, Judy," she said. "But there's a man downstairs to see your mother, and she won't see him. I'm afraid he's from the police."

I sat up in bed. In the strong light she looked devastated, and I remembered that she had really been closer to poor Isabel than any of us except Larry. She was older than Isabel, but from the time they first met they had been good friends.

She sat down while I took a shower and got into some clothes, and when she tried to light a cigarette I saw she was shaking.

"Emily Leland has sent for me," she said. "I suppose it's about the funeral. I don't know what to do."

"Better go," I told her. "You can't do anything here, Alma."

"I've tried to see your mother. She won't let me in."

"I wouldn't worry about that. She's had a dreadful shock. Where's Larry?"

"Downtown. And there are reporters swarming all over the place." She rose and, going to my dressing table, surveyed herself in the glass. "I look like the devil," she said. Then she turned. "Judy, what on earth are they looking for in the grounds? The police, I mean."

"They didn't find the knife—if it was a knife."

She went white. She was a good-looking woman, tall and slim, but under her make-up she was ghastly.

"I'm sorry," she gasped. "I'm afraid I'm going to be sick."

She rushed out of the room, leaving me uncertain whether to follow her or to leave her alone.

In the end I left her alone. I dressed and went downstairs, to find the King man in the lower hall. He was watching the fish in the pool, and this time he had no camera. James was watching him, and he looked annoyed. He didn't even say good morning.

"So people do live like this, in this day and age," he said.

"Until they're liquidated. What would you suggest?"

He shrugged and grinned.

"All right, sister," he said. "Is there a spot anywhere to talk, or do I whisper here?"

"We have a few odd corners," I told him.

Of course the house is outrageous, as I have said. The hall is circular, and is two stories high, with a gallery along the back of it. The big drawing room is the size of a ballroom, but thank heaven there are half a dozen other rooms where one can sit. I took Tony King to the library.

"Now," I said, when I had closed the door. "What do the police want with me? Isn't it enough they have my brother?"

"I don't belong to the police."

"You did last night."

He gave me a curious look.

"I just happened to be with the Inspector when the word came."

"You took pictures, didn't you?"

"The official photographer wasn't around. And I take pretty good pictures."

He offered me a cigarette and took one himself. I sat down. He didn't. He took a turn or two around the room before he spoke again. When he did I almost fell out of my chair.

"Look here," he said, "what have you done with it?"

"With what?"

"The knife." He was impatient. "That trick of your mother's didn't fool me any. She had sat for hours on the stairs and never blinked an eye. Then she gets into a good chair and faints, just when things were getting hot."

I pulled myself together as well as I could.

"I don't know what you are talking about. If you don't belong to the police you have no right to be here at all."

"Don't be a little fool," he said rudely. "You're on the spot, and your mother too. I examined that stair carpet. How long do you think it will be before they begin to wonder about your mother sitting there for all that time? If she has the knife do the right thing and turn it in. The truth never hurt anybody."

I knew that too. I knew perfectly well that the thing to do was to go upstairs, choke mother into insensibility, get the knife and give it to the police. I looked at Tony King, who apparently had been up all night and certainly needed a shave, and knew that he was right. But I never had a chance to answer him.

The door opened, and Donald Scott came in, looking

immaculate and well-tailored and with just the right degree of sympathy on his handsome face.

I saw the King man give him a long hard look.

"My poor girl!" Don said, holding out both hands. "I came as soon as I could."

Maybe I was just excited. Maybe I thought Tony King could stand seeing that not everybody thought I was a little fool, and conniving at murder at that. I remember screeching, "Darling!" and throwing myself into Don's arms, and the King man grinning as he more or less oozed out. And then, to my own astonishment, I was crying.

And not just crying. Practically shrieking. I suppose I had been more shocked by Isabel's death than I knew; that, and Mother sitting up in her bed keeping a watch on that wretched tank in her bathrom, and Larry downtown being interrogated, and the men in the grounds outside. As far as Don was concerned the dam had burst all over him, and he didn't like it any too well. He held me off until the flood was over. Then he patted me on the back and gave me his handkerchief. After which he took it back and carefully dried the lapel of his coat.

"I'm terribly sorry, Judy," he said. "Maybe I'd better come back later."

But I wasn't letting him go. Not until I knew why he was there, and not when I hadn't seen him for weeks. I suppose it happens sometimes that a bad case of calf love carries over even when people are old enough to know better. Anyhow it had been that way with me. But the very way he had wiped his coat when I had cried all over it should have taught me something. It didn't, of course.

I sat down and grinned feebly at him.

"It's all over," I said. "I suppose I had to burst on somebody, and it happened to be you. But the idea of anybody's thinking Larry did it!"

"Who thinks that?" he asked, eying me.

"They have him downtown."

"They have a lot of people," he said. "See here, Judy, are you afraid he did it, after all? Is that why you are scared?"

"I'm not scared, damn it," I said, shaking all over again. "He adored her. Ask Mother. No, don't ask Mother," I added hastily. "She's in no shape to be questioned. But it's true. They were really happy. You can ask the servants. You can ask . . ."

I suppose I would have babbled on indefinitely if I had not suddenly noticed his face. He looked shocked, like a man who has had a blow. I knew why, too. Six or seven years ago, when he was only a struggling young lawyer, he had been crazy about Isabel. I was at boarding school when I heard it, and I cried all night.

I looked at him that morning and felt as sick as he looked.

"I'm trying to help Larry," he said. "If it comes to that. Probably it won't." He walked over to the window and stood looking out. I remember the sun on his hair, and wanting just once to touch it. But when he turned I realized he didn't really see me. He had been seeing Isabel instead, lying dead at the top of the stairs in her house. He lit a cigarette and sat down. His face was under control again.

"I want to ask you something, Judy," he said. "Did you see the chain they found under her?"

"Yes. That man who just went out showed it to me last night. Why, Don?"

"Did she—did you ever see it before?"

"Never. But then she had a lot of things I never saw."

He drew a long breath.

"Look, Judy," he said. "I've got to tell you something, although God knows . . ." He stopped. "I gave her that chain, years ago," he said. "I saw it this morning at Headquarters. I had no idea she still had it."

I suppose I gasped, for he looked angry.

"Don't be an idiot," he said. "I didn't kill her. Everything between us was over long ago. But I'd given her a ring, and she wasn't allowed to wear it. The chain was to hang it on."

I managed to breathe again.

"Have you told them about it?" I asked.

"Not yet. What good would it do? But look, Judy, what about the thing that was strung on it. What is it? You're a woman. Haven't you any idea?"

I shook my head.

"Nobody wears things like that nowadays, Don."

"It must have meant something."

"Yes," I said dully. "It must have meant something. I don't know what."

He had a whiskey and soda before he left, and he began to look almost human. He even took the time to say that I looked like the wrath of God.

"Why don't you go to bed and get some rest?" he said.

"I would," I told him, "only Mother had the idea first."

For the first time that day he smiled, and I smiled back at him. I suppose he was just a nice blond young man who had pulled himself up by his bootstraps, but I had cherished him for a long time, and the smile simply broke me up.

"Poor Judy," he said. "It's just too damned bad, isn't it?"

For one idiotic moment I thought he meant to kiss me. He didn't, of course, and with the slam of his car door I had a queer feeling that he was going out of my life for good. Or that he had never been in it.

IV

Alma and I ate a silent lunch together, or pretended to. One of the tragedies of an establishment like ours is that there is always food. It comes and goes, whether it is wanted or not, and we go through the forms of eating it or pushing it away. Alma was in black, ready for the Lelands. She looked better, but she didn't eat.

"I don't know what's wrong with your mother," she said before she left. "She won't even allow me in her room. It isn't like her."

"She was fond of Isabel."

"That's no reason," she said tartly. "Somebody has to run this house. It doesn't run itself."

I watched her go. She was not really handsome, but she was always smartly dressed. Isabel had always given her clothes she was tired of or which didn't suit her, and she did miracles with them. She must have been thirty-five—we never did know her exact age—and Larry always maintained she still had the first dollar she ever earned. But we couldn't have done without her, and she knew it.

After she left I wandered up to see Mother. She was sitting in bed, surrounded by pillows, and I could see that she was still keeping an eye on the tank in her bathroom. Sarah was there, putting iodine on her leg, and looking disapproving and slightly suspicious.

"That's enough," Mother snapped. "Now get out of here and call the doctor. And I don't want to wait all day for him."

I waited until Sarah had gone. Then I went over and sat down on the bed.

"Why the doctor?" I asked. "That's only a scratch."

She gave me a cold look.

"Because I'm in a state of collapse," she said morosely. "I'm in a state of collapse until I can take my eyes off that sickening tank. That ought to keep the police out, too."

I advised her to remove some of her make-up if she meant to impress the doctor, and I told her it was silly to keep Alma out of the room.

"If you want her to suspect you, you're doing all right," I said. "And I'll tell you this. A man named King was here this morning. He suspects you of having the knife. In fact he's damned sure you have it."

"I do wish you wouldn't swear, Judy," she said. "What does he know anyhow? How could he know anything?"

"He examined the stair carpet last night. I don't think he has told the police yet. He wants you to go to them yourself."

But she was completely and utterly stubborn. She was saving Larry. All they needed for a case against him was that wretched knife, and she would guard it with her life. I could talk myself black in the face, she said. The police would never get it.

Then she looked pleading.

"Be a good girl, Judy," she said, "and get rid of it for me. I'm cross-eyed from watching it. It can't stay here."

"It will as far as I'm concerned," I said bitterly. "Don't bring me into it. And don't go pathetic on me, Mother. Here you are, all nicely tucked up in bed, while I have to tell all the lies, and maybe get arrested in the end."

"Of course you won't be arrested. Don't be silly, Judy," she said absently. "I've thought it all out. You can take it tonight and bury it in the grounds. Some place where the gardeners aren't working," she added vaguely.

"And where would that be?"

"Good heavens! With all this ground! You can look around this afternoon and pick a place. Then tonight, when every one else is in bed—"

"Little Judy will be in bed, too, Mother darling," I said firmly.

But of course she knew she had me. I'm fond of her, and when she tried to light a cigarette she was trembling so she almost set the bed on fire.

"All right," I told her. "Just remember when I'm arrested that my fingerprints will be all over it."

"You could wear gloves," she said hopefully.

I laughed.

"I'd like to try explaining why I'm wearing gloves in the rose garden at two A.M."

When I went downstairs there was a young woman waiting to see me. Patrick had put her in the red room, where he places visitors he is uncertain about. He said in a whisper that she had been crying, and he was right. She had not only been crying. She was still crying. She was a pretty young woman, rather nicely dressed, and she looked as if she had not slept for a week.

She stopped weeping when she saw me, however. In fact, she looked at me as if I were something to step on.

"You're Miss Shepard?" she asked.

I said I was, and waited. She was standing, and she remained standing.

"I want to know what they've done with Jim," she said. "I don't care what they say. They've got him locked up somewhere. As if he would kill anybody! Or even know about it! He's the kindest man I ever knew. As for your sister-in-law, he didn't even know her. He may have seen her driving about, but that's all."

"Who on earth is Jim?" I said puzzled.

"Jim Barnes."

"Barnes!" I said incredulously. "Do you mean he hasn't been home?"

"Oh, he came home all right," she said. "They took him away around half-past three this morning, and he came back before five. But he didn't sleep. He didn't even come up to bed. He looked like death. Then at six they came for him again. He hasn't been back since."

"I wouldn't worry too much," I said, as comfortingly as I

could. "Nobody thinks he had anything to do with my sister-in-law's death. But after all it is a murder."

"Why are they holding him, then?"

I hesitated. She was a pathetic figure, her eyes swollen, the hands pulling at the gloves she held showing hard work. I remembered, too, the children the police captain had mentioned, and that Barnes had been what he called a decent sort.

"It's rather hard to tell you," I said uncomfortably. "The fact is—well, I'm afraid they think he hasn't told quite all he knew about last night."

She was indignant. She flushed.

"He told all he knew," she said stubbornly. "It's easy enough for you to try to put something on him, to protect your brother. But all your money won't save him, if he did it."

I suppose that made me angry. Anyhow I told her the whole story, about his denying he had seen Anna on the drive, and Anna's insisting that he had. I even told her that he had said "to hell with the Mayor."

She looked shocked when I finished. Shocked and frightened. "That's ridiculous," she said. "No officer would say a thing like that. Not Jim, anyhow."

"Somebody said it," I told her. "Why would Anna Griffin invent such a thing? I felt like saying it myself last night, but not even I . . ."

She didn't wait for me to finish. She started for the door, and she was crying again. When I got to her and touched her arm she shook me off.

"You think it's a sort of game, don't you?" she said. "Well, it isn't. It's more than Jim's job that's at stake. It might be his life. I suppose you would laugh your silly head off if anything happened to him."

I didn't feel funny, however. I felt pretty sick, and it was not helped by finding Mother awake when I went upstairs. She was covered with a sort of whitewash, I suppose to make the doctor realize that she was pale and needed to stay in bed. It wouldn't have fooled anybody but a man with double cataracts, of course, but it was no use saying anything. She had fixed on the sunken garden as the place to bury the knife, which didn't help any.

I wandered down to the other house after that, more to see how the servants were getting along than for any other reason. The reporters had gone from the main gate on Linden Avenue, but one lone man in plain clothes was still working through the trees and shrubbery near-by, and a uniformed officer was on duty at the front door. He didn't know me, but he let me in when Mary, the parlormaid, identified me.

"Only don't disturb anything, miss," he said. "That's orders."

The house felt ghostly. There was a thin film of fingerprint powder on the stair rail as I went up, and a chalk outline where Isabel's body had lain on the landing. I shivered as I stepped over it. But her room was as she had left it, her bed turned down as she had slipped out of it, even the magazine she had been reading still on the silk blanket cover.

I still don't know why I lifted it. I hadn't meant to touch anything. But lift it I did, and a small snapshot fell out. It was the side view of a woman near a palm tree. She wore a plain white dress, and her profile was rather unusual, a short aquiline nose and a slightly retreating chin. Behind her and somewhat out of focus a group of children were playing in some sand.

It meant nothing to me. I carefully replaced it and put the magazine where I had found it.

The servants were huddled together in the kitchen when I went downstairs. They looked lost and unhappy, as they always do when something upsets their routine. Anna was there, sulky and resentful. She insisted that she had spoken to Barnes, and that he had said what she claimed he had.

"He was kind of laughing," she said. "I thought maybe he'd had a drink or two. Those chauffeurs out on the Avenue had a bottle." She gave me a sly look. "That hunting knife of Mr. Shepard's is missing, Miss Judy. Mary saw it in the closet yesterday. It's gone."

"And I suppose you couldn't wait to report that to the police?"

"Well, what were we to do?" she said defensively. "They were out here, counting the kitchen knives. Anyhow it was

Mary who told it. I didn't."

I looked them over, the cook preparing a tray of tea and fresh doughnuts for the officer at the door, the others watching me with furtive curiosity. In their own way they were enjoying it, I thought bitterly; the excitement, the pictures in the newspapers, even Larry's probable arrest. It was a change from the dull routine of their lives.

And now the knife. I knew then that we would have to get rid of it. It was too late to go to the police with Mother's story. I thought of the river. If I could get out that night and drop it from a bridge . . .

I was still planning what to do when the plainclothes man backed out of the shrubbery. When he straightened and turned I saw that he held something in his hand. It was a man's opera hat. I knew without looking again that it was Larry's. . . .

V

To my amazement Larry came home that night. Alma was still at the Lelands', and I had had dinner on a tray in Mother's room. He came in, looking exhausted, but Mother smiled like the angel she really is when she saw him. Her chin was trembling, though.

"So they had the sense to let you go," she said. "I thought perhaps the fools would try to hold you. Oh Larry, my own boy . . ."

Like me in the morning she burst into tears then, and Larry held her poor face against his coat and got covered with whitewash.

"Of course they didn't hold me, old girl," he said. "Of course not."

"I've been so scared, son."

"I loved her Mother. They know that."

She pulled herself together after that, and looked at the smear on his coat.

"Wipe him off, Judy," she said. "It's some of my night cream." Which of course was a shameless lie.

I waited for her to tell him about the knife, but of course it was too much to hope for. He knew about the hat, however. It puzzled him.

"It was mine," he said. "Only who would deliberately take it from here and hide it in a tree?" He smiled faintly. "I think that's why they let me go. They couldn't figure it out."

The tree, it appeared, was why it had not been found sooner.

It was in the center of one of our big evergreens, and it hadn't been thrown there. It had been deliberately hidden. I wondered—as I am sure Larry did—whether that was how Isabel's killer had got up the stairs to her; in an overcoat like his, perhaps, with the hall light dim and Larry's dark hat on his head.

I went with him to his old sitting room where Patrick had sent him a tray. But he wasn't hungry. He took some soup and pushed the tray away.

"What's the matter with Mother?" he asked. "She can't think I had anything to do with it."

"She didn't hear from you all day," I told him. "I think it upset her."

It seemed to satisfy him. At least he told me what he had been doing, talking in a queer detached voice, as though he had deliberately wiped away all feeling. The autopsy, he said, showed that Isabel had been killed between nine and ten o'clock the night before. It also showed that she had been stabbed twice. The first blow had apparently knocked her down. The second had been delivered from above, while she lay there helpless.

It was so cold-blooded that I shivered, and Larry looked sick.

"Why didn't she scream?" I said. "After all there must have been a second or two, Larry, when she saw whoever it was. With all those women in the house—"

"That's what the police are asking me," he said thinly. "It's the old story of why didn't the dog bark."

"But that policeman, Barnes, knows you didn't go down to your house."

"Barnes is missing," he said. I nodded, and he went on. "I've been wondering—Judy, did Isabel know Barnes? She had been meeting somebody in the park in town. We don't know who."

"His wife says he didn't know her. Even if he did . . ."

I sat still, thinking of his young wife that afternoon. "The kindest man she ever knew," she had said. And yet he had had the chance. He had been alone in the drive, and he had not seen Larry when he went out to smoke a cigarette and escape the noise.

Larry was pacing the floor by that time. He walked and talked, as though he were thinking out loud. He was free, he said, because of two things, his hat's being found where it was, and the man Isabel had been meeting in the park.

It seemed that MacIntrye, Isabel's chauffeur, had told about the man.

When he arrived that morning—he was a family man and slept at home—he had learned of the murder for the first time. Mac is a Scot, dour and uncommunicative. He listened to the excited women, and then went out in the garage and worked on Isabel's limousine as usual. After that he put on the soft hat he wears when off duty to show he is a man like other men, and drove his old Ford down to Police Headquarters. For a long time no one paid any attention to him. He sat on a bench outside the homicide office for what he considered a proper length of time. Then he simply got up, opened the door and walked in.

Larry had been taken out for a belated breakfast, but the Mayor was there, the Commissioner of Police, the District Attorney and half a dozen others. They stared at Mac.

"I've got something more to say," Mac announced bluntly. "I'm Mrs. Shepard's chauffeur."

His story was pretty incredible. Isabel had been meeting a man in the park downtown, a shabby sort of man. For the past month once or twice a week she had had Mac drive to one of the entrances and had gone into the park—for a walk, she said.

"But she was never one to walk much," Mac said, "so one day I left the car and took a walk myself. She was on a bench, talking to this fellow. They seemed to be arguing about something."

"Would you know the man again?"

Mac shook his head.

"I wasn't anywhere near," he told them. "I never did get anywhere near. But she met him often. Five or six times that I know of."

It was a break for Larry, of course. Mac was of the opinion that she was quarreling with the man, and once at least he thought she had been crying when she came back to the car.

Larry looked crushed when he told me. "They seem to think it might be blackmail," he said. "But who in God's name would try to blackmail Isabel?"

Some bright soul among them finally thought of Barnes. They sent for a photograph of him and showed it to Mac.

He shook his head. "Not the same guy," he said. "Other one was older and thinner."

So there they were, Isabel dead, Barnes missing, and some man meeting Isabel in the park and making her cry. An Isabel wrapped in furs on a park bench with a strange man in shabby clothes—not once, but five or six times. No wonder they thought of blackmail.

That was Friday night. The murder had been twenty-four hours before. Barnes was still missing, Mother and I were both going to attend the inquest the next morning, there were two hats in the safe at Headquarters, somewhere Don was probably puzzling over the platinum chain he had given Isabel, and I still had the knife to hide.

I hadn't told Larry about it, that it was missing, or that we had it. The police were probably keeping it as an ace in the hole, and he had enough to bear as it was. I did make an attempt to, however. He had insisted on sleeping in his own house, and I went downstairs with him. There was no one in the hall, and as he opened the door I stopped him.

I remember trying to light a cigarette, but my hands were not so good.

"Look, Larry," I said, "have they told you your knife is missing?"

"What knife?"

"Your old hunting knife."

He didn't say anything for a minute. He stood looking out into the darkness, his face stiff.

"I suppose that settles it," he said. "No. They didn't tell me." He turned suddenly and faced me. "See here, Judy, did you or Mother find it? Is that what's wrong with her? Because if she did it's bad business. It's about all they need."

"I don't see why."

"For God's sake!" he said roughly. "If my own people think I did it and hid the weapon—"

I had recovered, however.

"Nonsense," I told him lightly. "I never saw the thing. As for Mother, don't be silly. What would she have done with it. How could she had got it out of the house. She was in a low-cut dress, and that means low."

He let it go at that. Probably the picture of Mother in one of her evening gowns convinced him, Mother considering there is nothing shameful about good substantial human flesh. I couldn't tell him the truth, of course. I knew what he would do. He would take it straight to the police.

"I didn't kill my wife," he would say, "but here's the weapon. It belongs to me."

He didn't go at once. He stood there staring out at the grounds, dark and sinister in the dimout, and at the black hulk of his house.

"Who would kill her, Judy?" he said. "Why would she put on a dressing gown and stand there while her murderer came up the stairs? Why didn't she scream? Why didn't she run back to her room and lock the door?"

"She'd have let a policeman come in," I said. "They're not supposed to be human. Suppose Barnes came in, saying he'd found the kitchen door unlocked, and that he'd better look around to see if anyone had got in?"

"Why on earth would Barnes kill her?"

"I don't know," I said, deflated. "Only his being missing, and all that . . . But there are such people as homicidal maniacs. I suppose that's rather fantastic, isn't it? And there's the hat, too. Patrick thinks it may have belonged to the drunken waiter he had to throw out. If you could find that waiter . . . After all he was inside the gates. Nobody else was."

"She wouldn't have let a waiter up the stairs."

"He was in full dress. She mightn't have known who he was. And Anna had left the kitchen door open. He could have put on your hat, and Isabel would have thought it was you."

He considered that, still gazing out.

"Possible, but not probable," he said. He sighed. "Look,

Judy. Who was to know that Anna was to decide to see the party, and leave the kitchen door open? What outsider would know about my knife, or where I kept it? It won't wash, my dear."

I let him go at last. I had a queer feeling that as he walked down the drive, somebody leaped back into the trees. So I was not going to be able to get out and drop Larry's knife in the river. The police were still on the job.

Mother was reading in bed when I got upstairs. She had taken off the whitewash and put on her night cream and her chin strap, and now that Larry was back she looked so darned complacent that I wanted to scream. I went over to the bed and stood looking down at her.

"Look," I said, "they know that knife is missing. They probably know you have it. But they aren't going to search this house. They might as well try to search the British Museum. And if you think I'm going out in the middle of the night to dig a hole for that wretched thing . . ."

She put down her book and stared at me.

"I suppose you'd like to see Larry going to the chair," she said. "Your own brother! I can stay here in bed for days watching it, but you won't even lift a hand to help him."

Well, of course it was silly. She had had a perfectly good rest, and slept at least part of it. I was just about to tell her so when she moved to get out of bed.

"Very well," she said. "I'm not so old that I can't walk out in my own grounds and do it myself. Get me my dressing gown."

She knew she had me, of course. I couldn't let her go wandering around in the dark. She would sprain her ankle or do some other fool thing. I didn't trust her, either. She would probably use a flashlight, and after seeing that movement down the drive I had an idea that the police were still keeping an eye on the place. The police around, and mother working her way through the shrubbery giving a fine imitation of a bull elephant on the loose. It made me shudder.

So I stalked into her bathroom, got the knife out of the tank, dried it, and was stalking out again when she spoke.

"Do show some sense, Judy," she said. "Wrap it in a

handkerchief or something. Do you want it covered with your prints?"

"I thought the idea was that nobody would find it."

Nevertheless I took a handkerchief from an upper drawer and wrapped the thing in it. I hated to touch it, and I wasn't comforted when, as I closed the door, I heard Mother put out her reading lamp and knew she was going to sleep. I felt deserted, as though I were alone in a dark and dangerous world, and I wasn't so far wrong at that.

I didn't go at once. I had to wait for Alma to settle down, for one thing. I slipped on a dark dress with a coat over it, and thank heaven I put on my tennis shoes. Then I tried a crossword puzzle and waited. I've seen that puzzle since. I must have been out of my mind when I did it. At one o'clock I gave it up and went downstairs.

There is something rather dreadful in a house the size of ours at night, with all the lights off. Especially downstairs, with arches here and there instead of doors—Mother likes vistas, as she calls them—and every small sound echoing all through the place. I had always loathed the house anyhow, and I disliked it more than ever that night. Even the fountain in the hall sounded like a cataract, and when the kitchen cat—which is supposed to catch mice, but spends most of its nights trying for the goldfish in the pool—when the fool cat ran over my feet I almost dropped the knife.

I felt a little better when I got outside. Even with the dimout there was a faint glow over the city, enough to let me see the drive after my eyes got used to the darkness. I kept an eye out for any policeman who might be about, and I am certain I made no noise whatever. But one thing was sure. If the knife was ever found it would have to be where a murderer in a hurry to escape could have hidden it.

So I struck toward the gates on Linden Avenue and the trees and shrubbery inside them.

Larry's house on the other side of the drive was dark. For that matter everything was dark, and once under the trees I had to feel my way. I had decided on one of the hemlocks, as the branches grew close to the ground, and when I reached the place, I slipped the knife from under my coat and began digging a hole with it.

I never finished it.

There was a sudden flash of white light that almost blinded me, and immediately after a man's voice spoke, from close beside me.

"I'll take that, sister," it said.

VI

I was too shocked even to straighten. The light was gone, and I could see only his outline. Believe me, I was shaking.

"What do you mean?" I managed to say.

But he didn't reply. He took a step toward me, and with that my spinal cord—not my brain, never my brain—took automatic control of my legs, and I was running. I can run, thanks to tennis and golf and miles of dancing. Also I had an advantage over him. I knew the grounds. Not that he didn't make a darned good try. He pounded after me and almost got me, but for once I thanked heaven for Mother's sunken garden. Either he didn't know it was there, or he hadn't expected it so soon. He fell into it with a crash, and I made the front door and locked it.

I simply sat down on the cold floor inside and tried to get some air into my lungs. When I did I heard myself using language even I had not known I possessed. It was a trick, all of it. Because I knew who the man was. It was Tony King. He had laid a trap that morning, and calmly waited for me to fall into it; waited for me with a camera and a flash bulb. He didn't have the knife, but I was willing to bet that the picture showed me burrowing like a dog with a bone, and using the wretched thing to do it with.

After a while I managed to get up the stairs. Mother's room was dark, but she was not asleep. She stirred when I went in.

"Everything all right?" she asked.

I turned on the lights and walked over to her bathroom door.

"I've just been chased by an expert," I said. "Either by the police or by the man who killed Isabel."

"Oh, Judy!" she wailed. "Don't tell me—"

"Right the first time," I said. "We've still got the damned thing and in an hour or so the police will know it too."

I dropped it back in the tank. Mother was looking ghastly, but her mind was all right.

"Don't put the handkerchief in there," she said. "It will block the pipe. Didn't you see whoever it was?"

I didn't answer. I had just remembered. I had taken the handkerchief off to dig the hole, meaning to use it later to wipe off my fingerprints. And I had left it there. I didn't need to tell Mother. She saw it in my face.

"Of all the idiotic things!" she said. "With my monogram on it, too. What on earth are we to do!"

"One thing we're not going to do," I said shortly. "We're not going back to get it. If the police find it there tell them I make it a habit to blow my nose under a hemlock in the middle of the night. Also that I never use a handkerchief twice, like Queen Victoria and the blankets. Also that I have a complex about digging holes. Also—"

She stopped me with a gesture.

"You're hysterical," she said, which was about the truth. "I know you've had a bad time, but no use making it worse. Go to bed and let me think this over."

I don't think either of us slept that night. I was angry, as well as scared. I had a vague hope that the King man had killed himself when he fell, and after I had darkened the room I looked out. A late moon showed the garden clearly, but it was empty.

I must have dozed toward morning. Not much, for Mother sent for me as soon as she had had her early tea. Sarah brought the message, looking glum as usual.

"It's about the inquest," she said. "Mr. Lawrence says the police insist that you both go. He says as you found the body—"

"Larry found it," I said. "Get out and let me dress, Sarah. Mother can't go, of course."

However, it seemed that she had to go. I found her up in a

chair, looking fit to be tied. Sarah had followed me in, but she sent her out.

"We've got to do it, Judy," she said in a hollow voice. "I think Larry has lost his mind. And I've called that fool doctor. He says I'm all right. He's told the police so too."

Well, there we were. The tank in the bathroom might as well have whistled and rung a bell, so conscious of it were we both. And to make things worse, while Mother was dressing Alma came in with the morning mail. I think she had overheard some of Mother's protests, for she looked oddly at us both. Mother waved the mail away, but Alma didn't go. She stood there, watching us.

"I think I ought to tell you, Mrs. Shepard," she said. "There was something queer going on outside the house last night."

"There has been plenty queer going on," Mother said shortly. "Get my pearls, Sarah."

Alma didn't move.

"Two people were running," she said. "I saw them distinctly. One of them fell into the sunken garden. And one came into the house. I think you ought to know."

I take my hat off to Mother. She never blinked an eye.

"Don't be a nuisance, Alma," she said shortly. "If some of the servants choose to play cops and robbers in the middle of the night, it's their business. It's hard enough to get servants today."

Alma saw that she was beaten. She gave a small shrug and went out.

The inquest was not too bad. Luckily it was a private one, held in a room in the City-County Building. Except for a few reporters in the hall outside there was no crowd. Mother went in on Larry's arm, and as nobody notices me when she is around, I merely trailed behind like the tail of a kite. Don was there, as Larry's lawyer, looking not quite his usual debonair self. The real thrill was gone, so far as I was concerned. After all, as somebody had said, I was a big girl now.

Nevertheless, I watched him, and after a while I realized what was wrong. He was uneasy and I couldn't imagine why. He wasn't called, of course. In fact, I felt as things went on that the inquest was a pure formality. The police were not giving anything away.

It went smoothly enough at first. Isabel's body had been identified, part of the autopsy report was read—only a part, as we were to learn later—and then poor Larry, looking sick, had to tell about finding her.

"You did not touch the deceased?"

"I bent over and spoke to her. I may have touched her. I didn't move her, if that's what you mean."

"Following that, what did you do?"

"I ran back to my mother's house."

"Did you at any time see the weapon which was used?"

"I didn't look for it. I never thought about it."

"Then, when you went back to the other house, you did not carry the weapon with you?"

Larry lifted his handsome head.

"Certainly not. I never saw it."

I shot a look at Mother. Even in her black clothes that dyed hair of hers managed to look flamboyant, but she was gazing ahead of her, as if all this was merely inevitable but annoying. She was as calm as a May morning when Larry came back and they called her. Yes, she had gone at once to Larry's house. She told how she had found Isabel, and that she had touched her and realized she had been dead for some time. "No, there was no weapon by the body."

"Does that mean that you saw no weapon at all?"

"There are what you call weapons all over that house," said Mother. "How would I know which one killed her, if any of them did?"

"Do you know that a hunting knife belonging to your son is missing?"

"I believe his servants say so. It may have been gone for weeks. They're a careless lot."

I couldn't believe it when they let her go. There had been a few more questions, about the party, how the house and grounds were guarded, if Isabel had had any enemies, and if there had been to Mother's knowledge any incident in her past which might have led to her death. To this last Mother lifted her flaming head, much as Larry had done earlier.

"I would like to remind you that my daughter-in-law was a

Leland. I think that answers the question."

All in all she gave a magnificent performance. I didn't do so well. I expected that awful picture of me to be shown. I was looking for Mother's handkerchief to be waved at me in a sort of Chataugua salute, and all in all my knees almost gave way under me as I stood up. Here it comes, I thought, and went forward. For some reason however the coroner only asked me one or two questions. I had been with Mother when we found the deceased? Had I seen a weapon of any sort?"

"I saw no weapon whatever," I said truthfully.

"Did you know your brother's knife?"

"I gave it to him, years ago."

"You didn't remove it from his house?"

"Positively no."

That was about all. There were one or two questions about how Isabel was lying, had we moved her at all, and so on. But even I realized by that time that they didn't expect to learn anything from us that morning. Half a hundred policemen might be working on the case and probably were; but this was a polite farce. There was no mention of the chain found with the body, and Anna Griffin merely told of leaving the house to go up to Mother's "to see the party."

"You left the kitchen door unlocked?"

"Yes. The place was full of policemen. I thought she was safe."

She had found the door as she had left it, she said. Nothing had been disturbed. She had gone up to her room by a back staircase, and when Isabel's bell did not ring she had gone to bed.

But Mary, the parlormaid, was sure about Larry's knife. It had been there the day before the murder. It had a reindeer handle, and she had looked at it to see if the moths had got at it.

Rather to my surprise Patrick was called. I had not seen him. He was somewhere in the back of the room, and he came forward unwillingly. He testified to hearing Larry come back and to Alma's rushing back for brandy for him. Then they came to the waiter who had been put out.

"At what time was that?"

"Dinner was to be at half-past eight, but we were still serving cocktails at ten minutes to nine. I realized his condition at that time. He was intoxicated and dropped a tray. He was out of the house before nine."

"How was that done?"

"One of the men and myself took him to the service entrance. There was a police guard there. He helped him for a few yards. Then I believe he let him go."

"Did you know this man?"

"No, sir. He was an extra. We had employed a caterer, for extra tables, waiters, and so on. There was some trouble getting men, with things as they are. Mrs. Shepard's secretary borrowed a few butlers from families she knew, and also from different employment agencies."

But nothing really developed. One of the guards had seen the man leave by the main gate. He had let him go. Their orders, he said, were only to watch the people and cars coming in. He was uncertain at what time the man had gone.

"I wondered, because I didn't think the dinner was over," he said. "He was pretty tight. He was singing as he came down the drive. He hadn't any hat on. I said: 'What's the matter? Lost your hat?' He put his hand to his head and said by God he had. He seemed pretty cheerful."

But the light had been bad. Nobody could describe him except Patrick, who has needed glasses for years, and who had merely said he was tall and thin. I gathered that they were still checking on the men who had been at the house that night, but I was confident their interest was largely academic.

I hadn't expected Don to be called. But he was. The coroner held up the chain which had been under Isabel's body, and asked him about it. Evidently he had already told about it, but he looked uneasy.

"You recognize this chain, Mr. Scott?"

"I do. I gave it to Mrs. Shepard some years ago."

"Have you seen it since?"

"Not since—not since we broke our engagement."

"Have you any idea of the significance of this ornament on it?"

"Not the remotest."

"Did you see Mrs. Shepard the night of her death?"

"No. I have never been in her house, that night or any other."

"Have you any idea why it was found by her body?"

"I can't imagine. I had no idea she still had it."

I watched him. I hadn't been in love with him for years without knowing him, and I thought he was telling the truth. But not all of it. Back somewhere in that ambitious shrewd mind of his were things he had no intention of telling. But it did something to me. Not that I suspected him of killing Isabel. But it made me watch him. I think I felt then that he would protect himself and his ambitions at any cost. Anyhow I felt a little cold.

The verdict was what was expected, murder by person or persons unknown, and I helped Mother into her coat, picked her bag from the floor as usual, and followed her out into the hall. But that is as far as I got. A long arm reached out from the crowd of reporters and photographers in the hall and pushed me into a corner.

"You and I are due for a talk, Judy Shepard," said a voice. I looked up, and Tony King was grinning down at me.

VII

I stopped dead. The others had moved on. He was even taller than I had remembered, and he had a piece of white adhesive on his chin. I must have looked fairly shocked, for he reached out and caught me.

"Look," he said. "Can't we talk somewhere? I've got a lot to say."

"I hoped you'd broken your neck," I managed to gasp.

"Now is that friendly? After keeping my mouth shut just now? Anyhow, if it's any comfort to you, I broke a tooth."

He grinned again, and he had. Broken a tooth, I mean. It gave him a quizzical look, and I stopped shaking and pulled away.

"What is this? Blackmail?" I asked.

"What a nasty mind you have!" he said mockingly. "What's a dentist bill between friends? Does it mean nothing to you that I damn near broke my jaw last night? It still hurts me to talk."

"You must like to suffer," I said. "I suppose you gave that picture to the police."

"Not yet," he said calmly. "Now listen, Miss Judy. You look like a nice kid, and you're in a devil of a jam. How about a quiet bar somewhere and a little talk? Know the Bent Elbow?"

He sounded friendly, and heaven knew he held all of us in the hollow of his big hand. I nodded, and we started off. Mother and Larry had gone when we reached the street, and nobody noticed us. He had a small shabby car, and I climbed into it. He was smiling again when he took the wheel.

"I'll bet you didn't wear heels like that last night," he said. "Boy, how you can run!"

"Why on earth did you chase me?" I said sourly. "You had the picture, didn't you? You knew I had the knife. You could go to the police any time."

"The answer to that is I haven't. Not yet anyhow."

"Why not? You're working for them, aren't you?"

"Not necessarily," he said coolly. "I just happened to be around that night. I'm curious, that's all. A lot of things don't fit in the story. Maybe you are in it, maybe it's the jolly little mother, maybe it's big brother. Or maybe it's somebody else. I don't care much for the Leland crowd," he added conversationally. "Come the revolution I'm for hanging Andy to the nearest pole."

Somehow I felt better after that. Once he reached down and patted my hand.

"That camera of mine lies," he said. "You're a damned good-looking girl."

I loathe whisky, but I took some Scotch neat that morning, while he looked on approvingly. And then, in a corner booth with no one near, I simply told him the whole story. I even went back to the party, and Larry's hat being gone, and his finding the one which had been used to dip the fish out of the fountain. He stopped me there.

"What kind of a party was this?" he said. "Is that your usual home life?"

"Not really. It got out of hand."

"I should hope so," he said grimly. "Although the idea of your living in that kind of an environment makes me sick. Those parties of yours . . ."

"I like them," I said defiantly. "Anyhow, if they amuse Mother . . ."

"There's nothing amusing about murder. All right. Don't mind me. Go on."

I had to trust him. He knew too much already. So I told him about Larry's going home and then running back, sick and collapsed, and Mother's having her slippers off, and going in her stockings to find Isabel dead and the chain under her.

"What about this chain? Was Scott telling the truth

about it?"

"I imagine so. None of us had ever seen it."

"Fond of Scott, aren't you?" he said, eying me.

"I used to be. Why?"

"I saw you looking at him."

I suppose I colored, for he let it go. He listened carefully while I told him about Mother's finding the knife under the stair carpet and knowing it was Larry's, and I think he wanted to laugh when I told him about her putting it in her stocking, and then pretending to be faint so she could get home with it. But he was serious enough when I finished.

"Where is it now?" he asked.

"In the tank of the toilet in Mother's bathroom."

He grunted and looked disgusted.

"A house the size of yours, and that's all you could think of!" he said. "They'll find it, sure as shooting."

"Why? Wouldn't they have to have a warrant to look for it?"

"They won't work that way, my girl. Not in this case. You'll get a window washer in on Monday, and he'll do more than wash windows. Or a nice young man will take one of the maids to the movies tonight. For ways that are dark and tricks that are vain . . ."

"But they don't know we have it," I protested.

He leaned over the table.

"Don't underestimate them," he said. "They know your brother's knife is missing. They need only to look at your mother to know that she never fainted in her life. They let her get away with those half truths of hers this morning because they're not ready to jump.

"Look," he went on. "I was damned sure you people had that knife and would try to get rid of it. But that's not why I was there last night. I had a fool idea that whoever hid your brother's hat in that tree you were digging under might come back to get it and put it in a better place."

"Was that the tree?" I asked appalled.

"It was. And I was right, too. He did come. Only that flash of mine scared him off. I heard him. I didn't see him. He ran like hell."

I felt slightly dizzy, what with no food to speak of and the Scotch and trying to understand what was going on.

"Why on earth did he want Larry's hat?" I asked, feeling completely stupid.

"Look," he said, leaning forward. "Be reasonable, girl. Would your brother hide his hat in a tree? And don't forget this. Somebody is pretty anxious to pin this murder on him. The knife, left where the police would ordinarily be sure to find it—why was that done? But nobody but Balaam's ass would believe that Larry Shepard had any reason for hiding his own hat. What does it prove? Nothing."

"I see," I said slowly. "If someone else wore it, pretending to be Larry . . ."

He straightened and smiled.

"A gleam at last!" he said. "Two minds that click as one."

He finished his drink while I watched him. He puzzled me. I had a feeling that under his flippancy he was pretty serious; that he was trying to talk what he thought was my language. And he didn't look too well. Under what had once been a terrific sunburn, he lacked color.

"I think I ought to tell you," I said. "Mother's secretary heard you fall last night. And I'm sorry about the tooth."

He fingered the broken edge ruefully. Then he smiled.

"Forget it," he said. "There's something else on my mind. Has it occurred to you that whoever left the knife where your mother found it knows darned well she has it? Or you?"

"What does that mean?"

"That somebody beside the police might want it found. In that case—well, you might try locking a few doors at night." And seeing my face he went on: "It's like this, Miss Shepard. People will go a long way to cover up after a murder. It's the first killing that's the hardest. Nobody likes to kill. But after the first time the bars are down. You can't go to the chair—or hell—more than once. Just be careful. That's all."

If it hurt him to talk that day, he certainly suffered plenty. He wanted to know all about Isabel, her character, her life. "Because that's the real story, isn't it? Why was she killed?

Murder is an end, not a beginning. It's what goes before that counts."

But my recital of poor Isabel's short and simple annals disappointed him. She had gone to boarding school. She had made the usual debut in the Leland house, with her bouquets on a screen behind her and all over the big double parlors. She had gone to the usual dances, and had been neither more nor less popular than the other girls.

"What about Scott?" he asked.

"I think he was her one real love affair. Only he was nobody then. The Lelands wouldn't have it."

"So she married Lawrence. Big wedding, of course. Red carpets, white orchids and a dozen bridesmaids. I'd like to have seen you that day, Judy Shepard. You must have been something."

"I wasn't a bridesmaid. There weren't any. It was very quiet. She didn't even wear a veil."

He laughed.

"I'll bet Mother hated that," he said, and got up.

He insisted on taking me home. We rattled and banged along in his wreck of a car, but he didn't talk much. He seemed to be thinking. I wasn't very cheerful myself. All the talk about Isabel, as well as the inquest, had brought her back to me. Not the woman lying dead at the top of the stairs, but the living Isabel, sitting behind her tea table, coming up on Christmas Eve with her arms full of ribbon-tied bundles, tactfully giving Alma her beautiful clothes, and being lovely to Mother while she disapproved of so much she did.

That was when I remembered Mac's story about the man in the park, and told him. He whistled.

"Sounds like blackmail," he said. "Only as a rule blackmailers don't kill the golden goose. Any idea wo it was? Somebody out of her past?"

"She didn't have any past. I've just told you that."

"Everybody has a past."

He was still apparently thinking that over when we reached the house. I asked him to come in when we got there, but he refused. As I got out I saw him eying that hideous pile of ours with disapproval written all over him.

"Gives me the pip just to look at it," he said.

Then to my intense surprise he reached into his pocket and brought out something, carefully folded.

"With love, to Mother," he said, and drove away.

It was the monogrammed handkerchief I had left when he chased me.

VIII

When I went in it was clear that something had happened. Mother was standing at the foot of the stairs with stark desperation written all over her. She still wore her hat, and Alma beside her was making some sort of soothing noises. Sarah was on the balcony above, wiping her eyes, and Patrick and one of the footmen looked as if they were getting ready to duck behind chairs.

Mother shoved Alma away as I went in, and if Alma hadn't been a perfect lady she would probably have shoved back. She kept her temper, however.

"Don't maul me," Mother shouted. "Someone was in my room and took it."

"You wore it yourself this morning," Sarah wailed from the gallery. "I saw you. You had trouble getting your glove over it."

"What in the world's the trouble?" I asked. "What's lost?"

No one paid any attention to me. Alma seemed as puzzled as I was. She had evidently just come in. And then Mother turned a glittering eye on Patrick, who immediately began to shake.

"What's the matter with you?" she demanded. "I asked a perfectly simple question. Have you lost your voice? Who was in my part of the house this morning? And speak up so I can hear you."

I felt a cold shiver go down my spine. But there was something wrong with the picture. I couldn't imagine Mother's standing there with her hat crooked and shouting to all and sundry that someone had taken Larry's knife from the tank in her bathroom. And what on earth did Sarah mean that mother had worn it and had trouble getting her glove on over it?

Patrick however had recovered his voice. He clicked his false teeth into place and stated that a number of people had been all over the house. The upholsterer who was doing over one of Mother's boudoir chairs had delivered it and carried it up. There had been a man to read the meters, but he hadn't been out of the cellars. And Sarah broke in to say that she had been in Mother's bedroom all the time while the plumber had repaired the tank in her bathroom.

Mother sat down suddenly.

"What about my bathroom?" she said in a dreadful voice.

"It wouldn't work," Sarah piped hysterically from the gallery. "I couldn't let you come home and find it—"

"Never mind about that," Mother said hastily. "Why wouldn't it work?"

"The plumber said there was something disconnected. He was only there ten minutes. I never left the room. He hadn't a chance to take it. Anyhow you wore it out. I saw you."

Like Patrick I had found my voice by that time.

"Take what, Sarah?" I asked.

"The madam's star sapphire ring," she wailed. "He never took it. I'll swear to that."

"Did you know the plumber, Sarah?"

"No, Miss Judy. It was a new man. All the plumbers have gone to the war, although why an army needs plumbers when all they have is—"

She stopped there and burst into fresh tears. As for me, I could feel my legs wobbling. So Tony King had been right. Only it hadn't been a window washer. It had been a plumber. But the police hadn't sent him. We had sent for him ourselves. It didn't make sense, unless they had our telephone wires tapped.

"Who sent for him?" Mother asked.

"I did," said Alma stiffly. "I was on my way out when Sarah told me. It's Saturday, and it was hard to get anyone."

Mother got up. She looked utterly defeated. I remember Alma's asking what flowers we wanted sent to the Lelands, and mother not even hearing her. She went into the library and closed the door. All the life had gone out of her.

"It's gone, Judy," she said bleakly. "The knife. That plumber took it."

"What about your ring?"

"I had to find out who had been upstairs. Judy, if the police have it what on earth are we to do?"

All at once she was crying. She cried like a baby, with her poor face crinkled and her mascara running down her cheeks. I put my arms around her.

"We don't know that yet," I said. "Perhaps he just found it and gave it to one of the servants. After all, he might not know."

"With every newspaper in town howling about it!" she said. But the idea cheered her. She got up. She still looked pretty well shot to pieces, but her mind was working again.

"Go on upstairs and pretend to find my ring," she said. "I don't want Sarah to cut her throat. It's inside the radiator by my *chaise longue*. I'll try to think of something."

I went up. Sarah was on her knees turning back the edges of the carpet. I saved her throat by finding the ring, and later on we made a pretense of eating lunch. Alma was fairly cheerful, but Mother and I both knew we were about at the end of things. There was nothing to do about it, either. If the police had the knife, Larry was for it. And if either the plumber or one of the servants had it, we didn't dare to inquire.

None of us ate much lunch. Mother pushed away her plate warily.

"I suppose cooks have to get a percentage," she said. "But some day I am going to order tea and toast, and get tea and toast."

There was no word from Larry. We learned later that they had grilled him most of the afternoon. Had he any reason to believe that Isabel had—well, been friendly with any one else? Had he known she was meeting a man in the park? Had he known her long before they were married? Had he himself any idea why she had been killed?

Perhaps the thing that annoyed him most was the question of Isabel's will. Who inherited the money she had received from Eliza Leland's trust. It would normally have gone to her children, wouldn't it? Larry said coldly that money did not enter into it. He had adequate means of his own. He knew nothing about the trust fund, and as to a will, she had never mentioned one.

What really shocked him, however, was what followed all this. The Inspector leaned back in his chair and stared hard at him.

"Now about this weapon. It was almost certainly your own knife," he said. "Have you any reason to believe that some member of your family found it on the scene of the crime, and has since concealed it?"

"For God's sake, no," said poor Larry. "Why on earth would any one do such a thing?"

"There is such a thing as mother love, Mr. Shepard. If she thought she was protecting you—"

"Bosh!" said Larry roughly. "There was no weapon there when my mother and sister arrived. I'll swear to that. You heard my mother this morning at the inquest."

"I did," said the Inspector drily. "I'll read it to you." He picked up a paper from his desk and put on his glasses. "She said: 'No, there was no weapon by the body.' Then asked if she saw no weapon at all, she replied: 'There are what you call weapons all over the house. How would I know which one killed her? If any one of them did.' Is that your idea of a straightforward answer, Mr. Shepard?"

"Perhaps not," said Larry. "It's my mother's idea of my reply to any straightforward question, however."

He even smiled a little, and the subject was dropped for the time. They had, the Inspector said, gone over the entire list of the guests at the dinner. Comparatively few of them even knew Isabel, and none of them had left the house. They were now checking on the extra waiters and the orchestra. Then, without pausing for breath, he shot a question at Larry.

"And now, Mr. Shepard, why did you give the officer, Barnes, fifty dollars that night?"

Larry must have looked stunned.

"Fifty dollars!" he said. "For what?"

"That's what I want to know."

"I never gave him anything. I never saw him except in the

dark on the drive until you brought him back yesterday morning."

The Inspector picked up another paper.

"I'll read you this," he said. "It is his wife's statement, made here an hour or two ago.

"Jim came home Thursday night after he had put up his horse at the police stable. It was about midnight. He didn't act like himself. He said he had a headache and took some aspirin. Then he said he had a surprise for me. He reached in his pocket and took out fifty dollars, two twenties and a ten. He said: 'Go and buy yourself something pretty. That's the way the rich do things.' I couldn't believe it. Now and then he gets five or ten dollars for work like that when he's assigned to it, but never fifty.

"I was a little worried. I asked him if it was clean money. He looked funny but he said it was.

"He went to bed, but he didn't go to sleep. We were still both awake when the bell rang. He leaned out the window and someone said there was trouble at the Shepard place, and to come along. He acted queer about that, too. He told me not to mention the money. Then he dressed in a hurry and went out. There was a car waiting for him.

"He came back an hour or two later. He looked terribly worried. He said young Mrs. Shepard had been killed. Someone had stabbed her. But he did not know anything about it. Only he did not go back to bed. He stayed downstairs walking the floor. I did not understand it. Then before daylight I heard another car stop, and Jim went outside.

"I heard him go out to the car and it drove off. That is all I know. Only he has not been back since, and I am almost crazy."

Larry had listened, I gather, with his jaw dropped.

"What have you to say to that, Mr. Shepard?"

"What am I to say? You don't think I would do away with my only alibi, do you?"

"If Barnes *was* an alibi," said the Inspector drily. "Where were you that night, after we left your house?"

"At my mother's. In bed."

"Can you prove that?"

"Two of the men put me there. I wasn't in very good shape. What do you think I did?"

"I'm asking the questions. I want to know if later on toward morning you took a car out of your garage, or out of your mother's?"

"Certainly not. If you mean was I the person who picked up Barnes. Certainly not."

"Your garage is on a grade. It would be possible, wouldn't it, to get a car out without using the engine?"

But Larry had had all he could take. He blew up at that. After all he is not Mother's son for nothing. He told them quite a few things, mostly unpleasant, in what amounts to hysterics in a man. And he had just jammed on his hat and was leaving, willy-nilly, when the telephone rang. The Inspector shouted at him to wait. Then he picked up the receiver and listened. When he put it down he eyed him.

"They have found Barnes, Mr. Shepard," he said somberly. "He has been shot and killed."

IX

We knew nothing of all this that afternoon. Mother was shut in her room, waiting helplessly to be arrested, at the very least. But if the police had the knife they were not telling, and if the plumber still had it he had apparently not done anything about it.

Alma had gone back to the Lelands'. She said flowers were pouring in, and that Emily was completely helpless, poor creature. She borrowed my car again. She made plenty to keep one of her own, but as I may have said she never spent money if she could help it.

I had a bright idea after lunch, and called the plumbers who usually did our work. But of course it was Saturday afternoon. Nobody answered the telephone. Nobody rang us, either. It was a bright October day, and I knew the golf course at the country club would be crowded—at least by the people who had gas enough to get there. I wondered if Don Scott was there. After all he couldn't be really grieving for Isabel after all this time. Or could he? Wasn't there something about men never forgetting the women they had loved and couldn't get?

The hours sagged along, like slow motion. Alma came back from the Lelands at four o'clock with a headache and went to bed. There was no word from Larry, or from Tony King, and I didn't return Mother's handkerchief. It would have involved tellling her all the King man knew, and she was scared enough already.

Isabel's funeral was to be the next morning at ten o'clock.

We would have to go, of course. I looked up some black clothes and had Sarah take some flowers off a black hat. But by four I was having an acute attack of jitters. I went down to the library and tried to read. All I could think of was Larry's knife, wandering around somewhere, and Tony King's having the picture of me trying to bury it. He was holding out on it for a while, but when or if the knife was produced . . .

It was five o'clock when the totally unexpected thing happened. I was at a window when a taxi drove up and a woman got out. She was a small neat creature in a brown coat and a rather dreadful purple hat. There was something familiar about her, but I couldn't decide what. She had a small white parcel in her hand. She kept the taxi, and I heard her ask either for Mother or me. We were not receiving casual callers, of course, and anyhow she was the sort Patrick would definitely regard as a person and turn away.

He did just that. Perhaps she had not expected anything else. When she went down the steps, I had again the feeling that I had seen her somewhere. I went into the hall. Patrick was holding the parcel and inspecting it with interest.

"A person just called, Miss Judy," he said. "She said to give this to you or your mother."

I don't know why I didn't open it there, in front of him. I usually do. He loves parcels. I grinned at him and put it to my ear.

"No bomb, Patrick," I said. "It doesn't tick."

He looked abashed and turned away.

And that, if you can believe it, is the way the knife came back. I had let the woman go, I hadn't even noticed the taxi, and when in my room upstairs I opened the box and saw it, I simply couldn't believe it. To make things worse there was no writing on the paper and nothing whatever to indicate where the box had come from.

I stood there looking at it. Either it was incredible good luck, or it was definitely sinister. I hadn't an idea which. All I knew was that we had the damned thing again. It was lying in a nest of cotton, and if anything it looked more disreputable than ever. The hide on the handle was none the better for its long soaking in the tank, and some more of the hair had come off.

Then I remembered that it had killed Isabel, and I went into the bathroom and lost the lunch I hadn't eaten.

I didn't take it back to Mother. I locked it in my jewel case and then went across the hall. Mother was sitting up in bed with a tea tray beside her. For the first time in her life she looked like a wizened old woman. She could hardly hold the teacup, and when she looked at me all the life had gone out of her eyes.

"Any word from Larry?" she asked.

"Nothing. He's probably busy," I said, as cheerfully as I could. But she was not to be comforted.

"He's probably in a cell, Judy."

"Nonsense, Mother. They have nothing on him."

"What do you mean, nothing? They have the knife, haven't they?"

I took the teacup from her before she could spill it. Then I sat down on the edge of the bed.

"As a matter of fact, Mother, they haven't got the knife. They never have had it."

"What do you mean by that?" she said thickly.

"It's come back. It's in my room."

I told her the story. She isn't a particularly religious woman, although we have a pew at St. Mark's and she goes now and then. But when after she heard it she lay back without speaking and closed her eyes I knew she was saying a prayer. When she opened her eyes again, however, she was her old shrewd self.

"It's just what I thought," she said. "That plumber took it and his wife or somebody else brought it back. Probably they never read the papers. Where have you got it?"

"In my jewel case. But it's going to the police, Mother. There are to be no more tanks. We're just making things worse for Larry."

I think she would have agreed. After all she is nobody's fool, and as she said when Barnes was found he could validate Larry's alibi; that he had not gone to his house. But just then the telephone rang, and I answered it from beside her bed.

It was Tony King, speaking from a pay telephone, and his voice was grave.

"Listen, sister," he said. "There's a spot of trouble. Barnes has been found, out the Sunnyside Road. He's been shot."

"Oh, no!" I said beginning to shake. "I can't bear it. Do you mean he's dead?"

"Yes. Don't take it too hard. These things happen. It hasn't necessarily anything to do with the other affair."

"But the police think it has, don't they?"

He hesitated.

"Well, there's a chance. They may hold your brother for a bit. Only as a material witness, or something of the sort. Don't worry."

"Listen," I said. "Stop treating me like a child. Why are they holding Larry? They can't think he killed Barnes."

I heard Mother give a thin wail from the bed, but it was too late. She knew the worst by that time. And Tony King went on. It was possible that Barnes had known something about Isabel's death and had to be put out of the way. As for details, if I wanted them, the State Police had found the body some ten miles outside the city limits. There had been a brush fire, and one of the troopers had gone along a wood road to put it out. Barnes was lying there, among the leaves. He was dressed as he had been when we all saw him last. He had been shot through the head, and he had been dead over twenty-four hours. There was no sign of the gun which killed him.

And Tony added something else which practically sent me in to a tailspin.

"You might take a look at the cars in your garage," he said guardedly. "You may have some visitors before long. Somebody in a car took him to where he was found. I want a little time, if I can get it."

Mother was up and trying to get her nightgown over her head before I hung up. It stuck hopelessly, of course, and I jerked it back and shoved her toward her bed.

"What on earth do you think you can do?" I demanded. "Get back there and stay there."

"I'm going to my son," she said defiantly. "He needs me. He hasn't even a razor, or anything to sleep in. And bread and water to eat! As though he would kill a policeman he didn't even know. Or his own wife."

Which was Mother, of course, but which didn't help any. It

took some time to get her into bed again. She was threatening to go to Washington and see the President and the British Ambassador when I finally got out of the room. And of course, I was too late. When I got downstairs there were three men at the garage talking to Jim, our head chauffeur, and I didn't need to be told that they were detectives. I watched them go inside, and the lights go on—it was getting dark by that time—and after a few minutes one of them drove Larry's car out, another got into the car they had brought, and the third one started for the house.

That was when I panicked.

Panic is a queer thing. Either you think like blazes, or you don't think at all. I don't remember thinking. All I knew was that he would probably search the house, and that the knife was in my room. The rest was pure instinct, and pretty rotten instinct at that. I ran upstairs, put on a loose coat, dropped the knife in my pocket and started down again.

I was just too late. The doorbell was ringing, and one of the men was at the door opening it.

X

I did the only thing I could think of. I sat down on the edge of the fountain and slid the knife into the pool. I must have looked like an idiot, sitting there dabbling my hand among the water lilies, but perhaps that was the police idea of how people like us amused ourselves. Anyhow this one took it in his stride.

He came in and took off his hat.

"My name's Anderson," he said. "I would like to see Mrs. Shepard, or Miss Shepard."

"I'm Judy Shepard," I said, getting up. My voice sounded thin, but at least I could speak. "I'm sorry about Mother. She's in bed."

"Then I'd like to talk to you," he said, looking around him. "Is there any place . . ."

I didn't blame him. It was like trying to talk in Madison Square Garden. I took him into the library and closed the door. Then I sat down, because my knees were shaking. He produced a card and handed it to me, but I didn't even try to read it. He was polite enough, however.

"Miss Shepard," he said, sitting down rather close to me. "I wonder if by any chance you heard a car leaving your garage, the morning after your sister-in-law was killed. Early in the morning."

"No, I didn't. But the men sleep over the garage. They would know."

"You're sure of that? Your room faces toward the garage, doesn't it?"

They knew a lot about us, evidently. I began to feel indignant, which was at least better than wobbling.

"If you mean did my brother take a car out at that time you're crazy," I said hotly. "He was in bed, in a state of collapse. It took two men to get him up the stairs."

"I haven't said anything about your brother," he told me, and eyed me with sharp gray eyes. "I'm merely asking about your cars."

"Anyhow, who could get a car out that morning?" I said. "You had men all over the place. You even had a guard at the gate."

"There are two other gates."

"They were padlocked. The gardeners had orders to lock them that night. The Mayor—"

"I know all about that. Are there no other keys to them?"

Well, it was no use lying to him, with extra keys hanging inside the service door at the rear and tags on them in Alma's neat writing. I had to admit it, and he began to look quite amiable. He got up and took his hat.

"I'll take a look at them," he said, and went out.

I had a bad moment when he passed the fountain, but he merely gave it a glance and went on, with Patrick, who had appeared by that time, trailing behind him. He was not gone long, and when he came back he did not sit down again. He told me about Barnes, watching me like a cat as he did so; the car that had picked him up at his house, the finding of his body, the bullet wound in his head. If he wanted to break me up he certainly did so. And when he said they had taken Larry's car for examination, and that one of Larry's revolvers was missing from his house, I simply went berserk. I remember shouting, that there was a plot to involve us all; that Larry had never killed anyone, and that the whole damned police force ought to be put away as lunatics. He waited stoically through it. Then he opened the door, and Patrick was just outside.

"Get her some ammonia or something," he said. "And perhaps she'd better go to bed." He looked at me. "I'm sorry, Miss Shepard. Just remember this: It's pretty hard to send even a guilty man to the chair. If a man isn't guilty . . ."

He didn't finish. He put on his hat and went away, and I laid my head on Patrick's shoulder and cried. He put his old arm around me.

"Never mind, Miss Judy," he said. "Never mind. It will be all right."

I quieted after a while, but of course it was no use trying to get the knife, with the hall brightly lighted and somebody on duty there all the time. Neither murder nor sudden death could upset that routine. I went upstairs and washed my face in cold water. Also I put away my jewel case. It was six o'clock then, and it is odd to remember that it must have been about the same time when Andrew Leland walked into Inspector Welles' office at Headquarters. The finding of Barnes' body had been announced over the local radio, and he had evidently heard it. I can picture him sitting there in his big ugly house, red brick outside and red carpets and broacade hangings within. All the proper Lelandish arrangements made for Isabel's funeral the next day, the street to be blocked off from the curious crowd, the cards to be presented at the door and then because of the silence over everything, turning on the radio.

Anyhow he walked in, still neat, still stiff, and yet somehow pathetic. He walked over to the desk and stood there.

"I have come to demand my son-in-law's arrest for double murder," he said.

"I see," said the Inspector. "Won't you sit down?"

But he did not sit. He stood there, straight and terrible.

"He killed my daughter," he said. "And he killed your man so he couldn't tell that he had seen him on his way to do it."

"Have you any idea," said the Inspector quietly, "why he would have killed your daughter?"

He must have hesitated. He knew so much, and surmised so much more. There must have been a terrific struggle going on between his pride and his certainty that Larry had murdered Isabel. In the end his pride won.

"I do not pretend to know what goes on between husband and wife," he said. "He killed her. I know that. And if you let him escape the chair I will never believe in human justice again, or a God."

He went out after that, as stiffly as he had gone in.

Even Alma did not know of that visit. She came downstairs

to dinner, although she said her headache still bothered her. Neither of us had changed, and she was still in the heavy black she had worn to the Leland house.

But her rooms were in the same wing as mine, and she had seen the detectives.

"What did they want?" she asked. "One of them took a car away, didn't he?"

"Larry's car. Yes."

"But why?"

"Don't ask me," I said shortly. "They've found the policeman, Barnes. Somebody shot him."

She looked shocked.

"Shot him!" she said. "Why on earth would anybody do that?"

"It's perfectly simple," I said. "Larry killed Isabel. Barnes saw him, so he killed him too. Now all they have to do is to find blood in his car and he'll go to the chair."

She looked at me sharply.

"You'd better take a sedative," she said. "You're on the edge of a crack-up, Judy."

She followed me into the library. I wanted to be alone, but I saw she had something more to say, and she proceeded to say it.

"I think I'd better tell you something, Judy," she said. "I know you'll keep it to yourself. I'm pretty sure someone did take a car out of the garage the night Isabel was killed. Some time toward morning."

I must have looked startled, for she smiled.

"Don't worry, I'm not telling it," she said. "I couldn't sleep, and you know where my rooms are. It went toward the service gate. I didn't think much of it at the time. The place was crawling with cars. But later I remembered. Those gates were locked that night."

I was definitely frightened. I had never thought of Alma as a source of danger. Yet if she was questioned, she might be. There must have been times when she compared her lot with mine. And I hadn't even told her that I was trying at last to be a useful citizen. She would only have thought I was dramatizing myself. For the first time I wondered if she really liked any of us.

For a minute I had a wild impulse to bribe her, to offer her my mink coat, to try to buy her silence with anything I had. I think she knew it too. She stiffened.

"I've said I'm not telling, Judy," she said quietly. "Let it go at that."

Her headache was better after dinner. She suggested some gin rummy, and we played for half an hour or so. I lost three dollars—she could always beat me—and feeling that I had added a trifle to the silence fund went up to see Mother. We had dined early, and it was still only eight-thirty. Mother was over her hysteria. She was playing solitaire, as she always does when she is nervous. She was sitting up in bed with a board on her knees.

"I've put in a call for the Governor," she said. "Of course the wretch is out to dinner. You would think he had enough to do to run this State without going to parties."

"Like the Mayor?"

"I had a reason for asking the Mayor," she said coldly.

She deliberately cheated herself as usual, and when the thing came out she announced that she had won two hundred and eight dollars But she was still worried about Larry.

"You'd better go down tonight and pack a box for him," she said. "The poor boy hasn't even a clean handkerchief. And if those wretches use a rubber hose on him maybe you'd better take some iodine."

I assured her they would do nothing of the sort, and she relaxed somewhat. But I had to tell her about the knife, that it was in the pool, and why. She looked worried at first. Then she thought it over.

"Perhaps it's not such a bad hiding place after all," she said. "I read a story once, something about a letter. They merely turned it inside out or something, and left it where anybody could see it."

I laughed a little, and kissed her.

"Then you did read a book once," I said. "Well, chin up, old girl. We're not beaten yet."

Maybe it was the mention of a chin. Don't ask me. I know nothing about the human mind. But all at once I remembered why the woman who had brought back the knife that afternoon had seemed familiar. Her profile had been like the one in the snapshot I had found in the magazine in Isabel's room, chin and all. In that case . . .

I didn't stop to think it out. I didn't tell Mother. When I left her I went downstairs and got my coat from the powder room where Patrick had hung it that afternoon and started for Larry's house.

To my relief the police guard was gone. The place was dark, except for the service wing and a light upstairs, shaded for the dimout. I went in through the kitchen. Only Anna was there. She was listening to the radio, and her eyes were bright with excitement.

"They found that policeman, Miss Judy. Somebody killed him."

"Yes, I know, Anna. Is it all right if I go upstairs?"

"Why sure, miss, Mr. Scott's up there. He came to get some things for Mr. Shepard. He's not coming home tonight."

She was enjoying it, I thought furiously. It didn't matter to her that not far away Jim Barnes's wife and children were in trouble, or that Isabel was dead, or Larry might never come back. I left her there and went almost blindly up the stairs. A small bag of Larry's was standing packed in the hall, but there was no sign of Don. I suppose I had moved quietly. The carpets are very thick. For when I did locate him he was not in Larry's room. He was in Isabel's, bending over an open chest of drawers and fumbling in it.

He looked completely shattered when he saw me.

"Larry doesn't keep his things there," I said. "What's the idea, Don?"

I think he hated me just then. He shrugged his shoulders and gave me an imitation of a smile.

"You would turn up," he said. "Well, if you want the truth, I was looking for something. It isn't here, so—that's that." He fumbled for his cigarette case. "I suppose you know they're holding Larry?"

"Why on earth would they? They can't think he killed Barnes."

He didn't answer immediately. He lit a cigarette before he spoke.

"I'm afraid it's his car. I'm sorry, Judy, but they think Barnes was shot in it. Of course it's ridiculous but . . ."

I suppose I had expected it. I wasn't surprised. It was all part of the net closing around us. But I was angrier than I had ever been in my life.

"You believe it, don't you, Don?" I said bitterly. "You're standing by him, but you think he's a monster; that he's killed two people, the woman he loved and a man he didn't know. Then you come here snooping, to find something to prove him guilty."

It got under his skin.

"I wish you'd keep out of this," he said roughly. "There are angles you don't know. If I could only find out . . ."

I stood staring at him. He wasn't really angry. He was frightened, as he had been at the inquest. I took a step or two toward him.

"You didn't happen to have done it yourself, Don, did you? What are you doing here? What are you looking for?"

"Don't talk like a fool," he said. "Of course I didn't kill her. But somebody did. That policeman too. Good God, do you think I ran amok that night?"

"What about the man she was meeting in the park?" he went on more quietly. "Who was he? What sort of trouble was she in? Tell me that and I'll know why she is dead. I've got to know, Judy. If Larry did it he can go to the chair, and I'll be glad of it. It just happens that I don't think he did."

"You were still in love with her, weren't you, Don? What a frightful nuisance I must have been, running after you the way I did."

"Certainly not," he said manfully. "I'm fond of you, Judy. I always have been."

A few days before it would have been the death knell, of course. Now I managed to laugh. All at once I saw myself running in circles after the little tin god who was not god at all, but only tin. I laughed, and he looked embarrassed.

"Don't give it another thought," I said. "And now let's find what you were looking for."

It appeared that it was his old letters to Isabel. He said she might have kept them. She had kept the chain. I didn't believe him for a minute, but I stood by while he made a further perfunctory search. The room had been cleaned by that time. The bed had been made up, and when I remembered the magazine I could not see it. I found it, finally, with some others in Isabel's boudoir, but the snapshot was gone.

I called Anna. She remembered the picture. It had fallen out when she was helping to clean the room. She said she had put it on the mantel, but it was not there.

She stood eying us both curiously.

"It was just a snapshot," she said. "Maybe Mr. Shepard took it, or it blew out the window while the window washer was here."

So it was a window washer this time. Not a plumber. But then it never had been a plumber. I was fairly dizzy.

"What about it?" Don asked impatiently. "Why is it important?"

"Because I think I saw the woman in it today."

But I couldn't explain. I couldn't say that the woman had brought back the knife which had killed Isabel. Also I wasn't too sure of Don by that time. How did I know he didn't have it himself, in a pocket or in his wallet? When Anna had gone he confronted me.

"What about this woman?" he asked. "See here, Judy, if you're holding out anything, you'd better tell me. Where did you see her, and why do you want her picture?"

I told him half the truth, that she had called at the house, that we hadn't talked to her, but her face had been familiar, and that she resembled the woman in Isabel's picture. He made me describe her, which I did, palm tree and all. So far as I could see, however, it made no impression on him.

He left before I did. The last I saw of him he was carrying Larry's bag down the stairs, and soon after I heard his car starting up. He had left it out on Linden Avenue, which made me wonder rather.

I took another look for the snapshot after he had gone, with Anna helping me. I couldn't find it, and my heart was really not in the search. I dreaded going back and facing Mother. I dreaded the night, and still more the next day. The Sunday papers out, announcing that Larry was being held as a material witness, and Isabel to be buried somehow; the gaping crowds, a police line, masses of flowers, and nothing meaning anything to her any more.

When I went down the stairs I saw a small neat piece of carpet had been cut out from where Mother had sat. And one of Larry's automatics was missing from the gun room. The police were certainly building their case.

XI

When I left Larry's house, I stepped into complete blackness. Remembering Tony King's story of the man who had been in the grounds the night before I felt uneasy. But all I saw was an old-fashioned car driving out, which looked like the Lelands', and after it two of the maids, feeling their way down the drive, probably to a late movie. I had cut across the lawn so they did not see me. They were to be important later on, those two women, to figure largely in our solution. But I did not know it then.

When I got back to the house, I found Patrick looking unhappy, and Tony King sitting beside the fountain playing with the fish! My heart almost stopped. Apparently, however, he had not discovered the knife. He looked quite cheerful, with his hat on the floor beside him and a new haircut. He pulled his sleeve up further and made another swipe at the fish and brought up a wriggling fantail.

"Why don't you ever feed the creatures?" he said. "Throw them a little caviar now and then?" He grinned at Patrick and got up. "Any place with doors in this hovel of yours?"

"We can go back to the morning room."

"Even a special place to mourn, eh?"

But Patrick had stood all he could. He picked the hat from the floor and informed me that I had had several visitors. Also that if I would please inform him when I was going out . . .

"Who were here?" I said impatiently.

"The person who left the parcel this afternoon was back,"

he said. "She waited for some time. After she had gone there was a man who I believe was an officer in plain clothes. When he found you were out he asked for your mother, but she had gone to bed. And Mr. Leland has only just driven away. He waited for some time."

"Mr. Leland? For me?"

"He asked for Mrs. Shepard first. I told him she was resting and seeing nobody."

"What's all the excitement?" Tony King inquired as I closed the morning room door. "Sounds like the Pennsylvania Station. Has something new turned up here?"

"Nothing that I know of."

He gave me a cigarette and took one himself. I wanted to ask if he knew what they had found in Larry's car, but couldn't quite do it. And he was busy getting something out of his pocket.

"I'm not very keen about this," he said. "You look as though you've had about all you can take. But it's got to be done. It's the report of the autopsy on your sister-in-law. I'm afraid you'll have to look at it."

I drew back.

"Please," I said. "I don't want to. It's dreadful."

"I'm afraid you'll have to. There's a line or two in it you ought to see."

He had pulled out a handful of envelopes. Now he extracted a paper from among them, and handed it to me. I didn't want to take it, but there was something compelling about the way he held it out. It was a typed copy, on flimsy yellow paper, as if he had done it himself.

I turned on a lamp and read it.

I suppose it was the usual routine report. It gave Isabel's age as twenty-seven, and her weight. Then there was a report of findings: two incised wounds and the severance of some artery or other. But it was the final paragraphs which held me. They came under what was termed inspection, and it was cold-blooded enough to give me a chill.

The body, it said, was one of a white female, in apparently good health. All organs were normal. Examination revealed—and here I dropped the paper—that she had borne a child.

He was watching me.

"Didn't know about it, did you?"

"No, I don't believe it."

"I'm afraid it's true. I had to find out. She and your brother have no children, have they?"

"No."

"None born dead? Nothing of that sort?"

I shook my head. I was beyond speech. It looked to me as though Larry was finished. If they could prove he hadn't known she had ever borne a child and then had learned it . . .

He threw away his cigarette and pulled a chair close to me.

"Don't take it too hard," he said. "These things happen. In one way it might be dangerous. In another—well, put it this way. Suppose somebody knew this story, and was blackmailing her?"

"Why kill her?" I said bleakly. "She could have paid."

"Any idea who could have been the child's father?"

I shook my head.

"She wasn't that sort. She was engaged years ago to Donald Scott, but the Lelands wouldn't have it. He was nobody then. They made her break it off."

He whistled.

"Scott!" he said. "He'd go a long way to kill a scandal like that."

"He wouldn't kill her. Never. He was still in love with her."

He gave me his broken-toothed smile.

"Nice little motive for you, isn't it? The beautiful sister-in-law, the man who couldn't forget her, and the girl who couldn't forget him. Many a crime has been committed for less."

He got up, putting the report back in his pocket. He had succeeded in annoying me, which he probably thought was better than seeing me cry.

"What we have to do," he said cheerfully, "is to get the story behind this story. When we do, I'm taking all bets that Larry comes marching home."

I was surprised. "I thought you were working with the police," I said.

He looked shocked.

"My dear child, I'm on the side of law and order. Justice will prevail, and so on." He grinned. "Actually I'm working to get a poor little rich girl and her redheaded mother out of a jam."

"You aren't a police photographer?"

For some reason that seemed to amuse him. He chuckled.

"Poor little Judy!" he said. "What a sheltered life she leads! But I like sheltered women. They feed my superiority complex."

He left after that. Patrick gave him his hat, and he set it jauntily on his head.

"Take a little advice," he told me. "Go to bed and stay there. No use looking for trouble."

I felt rather lost when he had gone. As for going to bed and staying there, I couldn't of course. There was that miserable knife to be disposed of again, and I had no idea how to do it. With Larry under arrest I was certain the police would search both houses, and I was afraid to go outside again.

Nevertheless it had to be taken out of the pool, and at one o'clock in the morning I went downstairs in a bathrobe and slippers. I carried a flashlight and I went directly to the pool. The kitchen cat was on the brim, trying as usual to claw out a fish.

But the knife was gone.

I couldn't believe it at first. The pool is fairly large and I crawled around it on my hands and knees, with the fish rushing wildly about and the cat making sharp little dabs at them with her claws. What with the splash from the fountain and reaching under the water lilies, I was pretty wet when I finally gave up.

To my horror Sarah was on the gallery when I started up the stairs.

"What on earth were you doing, Miss Judy?" she said. "What were you looking for?"

"I thought I'd dropped my blue clip in the pool."

She didn't believe me. I could feel her stiffen in the dark. She did not persist, however. She said Mother had rung for her sleeping medicine, and she followed me into my room and made me change my pajamas before she left. Of course the blue clip was in plain sight on my dressing table. She pounced on it.

"Why, here it is, Miss Judy," she yelped. "I don't see how

you missed it."

But I had had enough.

"Oh, get the hell out of here, Sarah," I said, and crawled into bed.

Some time toward daylight I dozed off. I had had the bright idea that Mother had taken it herself. She was quite capable of it; slipping down while the servants were having supper and the hall was empty. But I didn't sleep long. I heard Sarah tap with Mother's morning tea, and after she had gone I went over to her bedroom.

Mother had taken off her chin strap and was looking fairly cheerful. She said she had decided to see our senator instead of the governor, and of course they couldn't hold Larry under any circumstances. After all we had always contributed to the Republican Party, and had I any black stockings for the funeral that day.

I broke in on her resentfully.

"If you took that thing it was a dirty trick, Mother," I said. "You could at least have told me."

She put down her cup and stared at me.

"Told you what?" she asked.

"About the knife."

She looked blank and my heart sank.

"What about it? What are you talking about, Judy?"

"Didn't you take it? Out of the pool?"

She looked as though I had struck her.

"Don't tell me it's gone again!" she gasped, and I caught her tray before it slipped off the bed. Her face was dead white. "I don't believe it. You didn't look properly."

"I looked all right," I said grimly. "I fished every inch of that damned pool. Me and the cat," I added. "Somebody's taken it."

She looked at me pitifully.

"Don't tell me it was somebody in the house. I couldn't bear it, Judy."

I was thinking hard.

"It doesn't have to be somebody in the house. There were four people down there last night, with Patrick rushing all over the house to locate me. Maybe it was in plain view of anybody who looked at the pool. The fish may have shoved it around, or moved the lily pads. I don't know, Mother. Somebody must have seen it. I—"

I stopped abruptly. I was remembering Tony King, his sleeve pushed up while he dipped a long arm into the pool; grinning and picking up a fish, and asking why we didn't throw them a little caviar now and then. He had it. He had had it all the time. Lighting my cigarette, giving me that horrible report to read, and all the time the knife which would send Larry to the chair in his pocket. Picking my brains, getting the name of the man Larry might have been jealous of, pretending to be sorry for me, and fitting together the little pieces of his puzzle until he had it all.

The dirty crook, I thought furiously. Smiling at me, showing his broken tooth, and all the time the knife in his pocket. I could have killed him out of sheer fury.

XII

We went to Isabel't funeral that morning. Mother was determined to do it, whether Andrew Leland suspected Larry or not.

"Why should we stay away?" she inquired tartly. "I was fond of her. If we don't go it will look queer, too; as though we suspected Larry ourselves."

It was pretty bad, the crowds on the street, the police and the awful funereal odor of flowers everywhere. But at least it was civilized. Nobody saw Isabel. She was somewhere upstairs. The family was there, too. Mother, shrouded in black, wept quietly all through the service. I tried not to bawl. And Larry, who came in rather late with a man who was obviously a guard, went back to some place in the rear. He looked like a man carved out of stone. Mother didn't see him, or I knew she would have followed him.

She didn't even notice what followed, when the service was over and people were filing quietly out. There was a space around us big enough to park a car. Nobody spoke to us except the undertaker, who asked if we were expected at the cemetery. I think Mother would have seen the whole thing through, but I had had enough.

"We are Mr. Shepard's mother and sister," I said. "I don't think we are expected anywhere."

He gave me a strange look and turned away.

I suppose that shows the state of my nerves. Mother hadn't even heard me.

The afternoon was dreadful. Mother had gone back to bed, with Sarah in attendance, Alma had not returned, and the house was deadly quiet. When I turned on the three o'clock local news the radio said that the police had located what they called the murder car in which Barnes had been taken to his death. They had found bloodstains in it, but were giving out no further information.

Soon after that I got my car and drove to the Barnes house. I couldn't bear to have her there alone, thinking Larry had killed her husband and that we didn't care what happened to her. It was a pretty little place, as neat as a pin, but I got no further than the front door. A strange woman opened it and looked at me.

"I'd like to see Mrs. Barnes," I said, rather breathlessly. "I'm so dreadfully sorry. If I can do anything . . ."

"What name, miss?"

"I'm Judy Shepard."

I never saw a face change so quickly. She gave me a hard look, from head to foot, before she spoke at all. Then she said:

"You'd better go back where you come from, Miss Shepard. We don't want you here."

She slammed the door in my face, and I felt as though she had hit me with it.

Alma was back when I went home. She was in the hall pulling off her black gloves, and she looked tired and strained.

"Thank God that's over," she said. "Although the Lelands were wonderful. They always are."

"I wonder what he wanted here last night?"

"I didn't know he was here," she said slowly. "Did he ask for me?"

"No. He wanted Mother or me."

It seemed to upset her. She stood there, straightening her gloves and thinking.

"He's been rather strange the last few days," she said. "Judy, what happened to the chain and the thing on it that they found? I suppose the police have it?"

"Yes. You knew Isabel better than I did, Alma. What in the world was that tassel arrangement on it?"

"I don't know. I never saw it."

She went up to her room, and I wandered into the library. The telephone was ringing, and I heard Tony King's voice.

"Hello," he said. "I hope you had a good sleep last night. You certainly needed it."

I almost choked with fury.

"Listen to me," I said. "I don't want to talk to you. I don't want ever to see you again. Go ahead with your dirty work. See if I care."

I slammed down the receiver. He was shouting into the telephone as I did so, but I didn't listen. When it rang again I simply took the receiver off the hook and left it off. After that I tried to think. It was no use, of course. When Patrick brought in the Sunday papers he replaced the telephone, but it did not ring again.

He was about to go when I called him back. He stood there blinking at me with the eyes which had needed spectacles for years, spectacles he refused to wear.

"About the detective who was here last night?" I said. "Did he say why he wanted Mother or me? When you couldn't find me?"

"No, miss."

"What was he doing when you came down?"

"I think he was watching the fish."

"And the woman? The one who had been here that afternoon?"

She too had stood by the pool while he looked for me again. But she had seemed uneasy, he thought. When he told her I wasn't around she had hurried out. As for Mr. Leland, he had walked up and down the hall, refusing to go anywhere else. He had been there alone for some time. Then suddenly when Patrick reported that he could not find me he had clapped on his hat and stalked out.

So it really came back to Tony King.

I remembered sitting down and trying to follow the knife in its wanderings. Mother's hiding it in the tank in her bathroom, the plumber's finding it and sending it back. For that was the only explanation I could think of, that he had realized its import and sent it to us. Then my hiding it, first in my jewel case and then in the pool, and its disappearance from there. Only—

why had the woman who had returned it come back again?

Out of sheer exhaustion I picked up the newspaper and glanced at it. There was no mention of Larry's car, but it said he was being held as a material witness. There was a full page of pictures of me, surrounded by flowers when I came out; of mother in a low dress and the high diamond collar she wears to hold her throat up; of the house, called "Suspected Millionaire's Castle"; and even one, evidently sneaked by a reporter, of the hall and fountain. The only thing missing was the tank in mother's bathroom, and by contrast was the Barnes house, set in the center of the page and entitled "Home Of Murdered Policeman."

All in all I wondered why the decent people of the town didn't march out and burn us down. I tore it out and put it in the fire, but by that time I was in what amounted to a frenzy. I tried to read again. I saw that Barnes was to be buried the next day, with full Police Department honors: the Commissioner and his deputies, an honor guard of patrolmen and the department band. But there was another item which caught my eye and held it in frozen horror.

A woman had jumped off one of the downtown bridges late the night before. Another woman who happened to be near her had tried to catch her, but had failed. She had not fallen into the water, however. A barge was passing below, and she fell into it. She was critically injured, but was conscious when found. She had refused to give her name.

She was about forty years of age, and she had been neatly dressed in a brown coat and a small purple hat!

I had to know. I called Police Headquarters and asked for Inspector Welles, but he was out, and when I asked for Tony King nobody seemed to know anything about him. The officer at the switchboard had apparently never heard of him.

It was impossible to settle down. At five o'clock I got my car again and drove to the hospital, only to be rebuffed. So far as the girl on duty in the office was concerned, there was no woman there who had worn a purple hat and jumped off a bridge. I was still standing, unwilling to leave, when Inspector Welles came down in the elevator. I turned my back quickly, but he saw me.

He looked surprised and came over.

"I was just inquiring for a sick friend," I babbled. "They won't let me see her. I do think it's disgraceful, the money we give these places and—"

The girl behind the grill looked up.

"She was asking for the woman in Forty-Two," she said.

There was a queer little silence. The elevator came down again and Tony King got out. He looked even more surprised than the Inspector had.

"Hello," he said. "What are you doing here?"

Well, there I was, with all three of them staring at me. You would have thought I had pushed the woman off the bridge myself. I couldn't even speak. It was the Inspector who broke the silence.

"Suppose we go into the reception room," he said. "See that we aren't disturbed, Miss Clark."

When we were inside he closed the door and confronted me.

"Just what is your interest in this woman, Miss Shepard?" he inquired grimly.

"I saw the description of her in the paper. A woman dressed like that came to the house yesterday. She asked for Mother or me, but we weren't at home to anybody."

"How did you know how she was dressed?"

"I saw her get out of the taxi. I suppose it was silly. There must be a thousand women around with clothes like that. I just thought . . ."

He made me sit down. I suppose I looked excited. He even offered me a cigarette, although he continued to watch me. As for Tony King, he had wandered to a window and stood there looking out. What his back said was that this was up to me. He was through. If I wanted to go on making a fool of myself . . .

"Now let's get at this," said the Inspector. "Why did she call on you? Did she leave any message?"

I suppose I hesitated. I could see Patrick holding the white parcel containing the knife and eying it curiously. He would tell them if I didn't. But I couldn't say it was the knife.

"She left a small parcel," I said. "Perhaps Mother has it. I haven't asked her. She's not well. Besides, dozens of packages come to the house."

I thought I had done rather well, but Tony King had turned and was looking at me, and the Inspector plainly didn't believe me.

"So you read the paper, and saw that a woman in a brown coat and a purple hat had been hurt, and rushed here to see her. Is that it?"

"I didn't rush. I simply came."

Behind the Inspector Tony King was shaking his head. I stopped, and the Inspector hitched his chair closer.

"Are you sure that's quite correct, Miss Shepard?" he said. "Suppose I suggest that it was exactly the reverse of what you say; that this woman came to your house, but instead of leaving this parcel it was given to her? What would you say to that?"

"It isn't true," I said wildly. "You have to believe me. Nobody gave her anything."

His voice changed. He didn't raise it. It simply became harsh and cold.

"What do you know about this woman," he said. "Who was she? What was she doing there? And what are you doing here, trying to see her?"

It wasn't any use. I saw that. I never even offered a protest when he got up and asked if I had brought my car. When I said I had, he told Tony to drive me in to town. And even Tony King had little to say on the way. He had abandoned his cheerful grin entirely. He looked older and very tired.

"What was the reason for that outburst of yours this morning?" he asked.

"You ought to know."

He frowned over that.

"I?" he said. "What had I done?"

"Gone fishing in the pool last night. Don't deny it. I saw it myself."

He raised his eyebrows.

"I see," he said thoughtfully, "and what did I find? It wouldn't by any chance have been a knife?"

"I thought you were helping us, and all the time you've been working against us."

To my surprise he took a hand off the wheel and patted

my knee.

"I am helping you, little Judy," he said. "At least I'm trying to, but you make it so damned hard I'm thinking of giving it up."

That was all until we got to the Inspector's office. There was a man in the outer room waiting, and at a gesture from the Inspector he followed us in. He was a taxi driver, and he carried his cap in his hand. He stood in front of the desk while the Inspector questioned him.

"You're Johnson?"

"Yes, sir."

"You've seen her?"

The taxi driver nodded.

"It's the same woman. I'd know her anywhere. I saw her hat too. She's the one."

"You waited for her?"

"Yes, sir. The man at the door let her in. She wasn't there very long. Only a couple of minutes."

"Where did you take her after that?"

"I left her at Fifth Street, downtown. I think she went into the park."

He was sent out and told to wait. The Inspector picked up some papers and glanced over them. Then he took off his glasses.

"I brought you here, Miss Shepard," he said, "because I think it's time you talked. You are not helping your brother by your silence. What about this woman? Did you know her? What was her name? Where did she live?"

"I've told you. I never saw her before. I didn't speak to her that day. I'd told the butler to say I was out. The only thing—"

"Yes?"

"Well," I said desperately. "I told you I saw her when she was leaving. I thought—well, after Isabel's death I found a snapshot in the magazine she had been reading that night. There was a woman in it, standing by a palm tree. She looked like her."

"Where is this snapshot now?"

"I don't know. I've looked for it. It's gone."

"That was all it was? A woman and a tree?"

"There were some children in it. I didn't notice them particularly."

He looked at Tony King, who merely lit a cigarette.

"What did I tell you?" he said. "Curiouser and curiouser, isn't it?"

The Inspector didn't think that was funny. He sat still, apparently undecided about something. Finally he threw the something at me.

"What about this knife of your brother's? Was it you or your mother who smuggled it out of the house that night?"

I didn't answer. I couldn't.

"All right," he said, "let that go. How did the woman who tried to kill herself last night get hold of it? Did you give it to her?"

"Do you mean she had it?" I said wildly. "Then she did get it, after all!"

"She had it," the Inspector said. "She had it when she fell. It was in her bag. She is dead now, so she can't tell her story. But I think you can." He lifted something and held it out to me. "You might look at this."

I did. It was a greatly enlarged picture of me looking like a skinned rabbit and digging frantically at the hole under the hemlock. There was no question either of what I was digging with. It was a knife. Larry's knife.

XIII

I knew then that it was over; all our struggle, the lies I had told for Larry's sake, the fight we had put up to save him. When Tony King sauntered over to look at it, I was speechless.

"Not bad, is it?" he said complacently. "Not that it flatters you any. But I told you I took pretty good pictures. Some day you'll have to let me— Here, sit down!"

I did sit down. I also, when I got control of my vocal cords again, told him what I thought of him, that under pretense of helping me he had thrown me to the wolves. I'm afraid I made it stronger than that, for I remember his saying that it was no language for a lady, and a young one at that. I must have got under his skin, for he put a not too gentle hand on my shoulder.

"Listen," he said. "You're a pampered brat, but for some strange reason I don't want to see you locked up, or your mother either. The beds are bad. Now come clean, or it's going to be bad for both of you."

That was how I came at last to tell the story of the knife. It was dark by that time. Someone turned on the lights. A uniformed stenographer came in and sat at a table. A couple of detectives stood by. Tony King chain-smoked. And because there was nothing else for me to do I told it all, from Mother's finding the knife under the stair carpet to my scratching her leg to account for the blood on her stocking; from my trying to bury it to Tony King's discovering me, from my hiding it again in the bathroom tank to the plumber's getting it out and taking it away; and from the woman's bringing it back to my dropping it in the fish pool, and its disappearance from there.

I stopped there except to add that the dead woman had come back to see me again the night before, and that she must have seen it and taken it.

The Inspector sat back in his chair when I finished.

"Has it occurred to you," he said drily, "that if you had told this story sooner you might have saved at least one life? Maybe more."

"How could I? I didn't know she had it."

"That's what you say," he stated unpleasantly. "How did she know it was in the pool, Miss Shepard? Granting that it was in the pool. And I will add something else. One of our men has been killed. That makes three deaths, all apparently connected. We don't like our men being killed."

There was a sort of movement in the room, like a wave of anger. I could feel it. The men there were hostile, almost menacing. I think Tony King saw it, for he got up.

"If that's all, Inspector," he said, "I'll take her along."

So at least they were not holding me. I relaxed somewhat, and I managed to sign the statement. But once outside the building Tony stopped and looked at his wrist watch.

"Time to eat," he said. "How about a hamburger? Ever try one?"

I hadn't enough spirit left even to resent that. I nodded, and before long I was finding I was hungry. I ate four hamburgers and drank incredible amounts of coffee. I realized I had hardly eaten for three days. He watched me, looking kinder than he had before.

"You've been carrying quite a load, haven't you?" he said. "You'll feel better, now it's off your chest. How about a little apology? Since I didn't take the knife."

"I feel like a heel," I told him. "I'm sorry. But I told the truth. She got the knife herself. I never gave it to her."

He yawned and stretched.

"I know it," he said. "You weren't there to do it. You were in your brother's house with Scott." He yawned again, then he grinned. "I hope to God you stay in bed tonight. I need some sleep."

"You don't mean . . . ?"

"Sure I mean it. How about the man who came looking for your brother's hat? How about the knife? I couldn't have you getting any more ideas about doing away with it in the dark of the moon. I've been practically living on your front lawn. Don't worry. I can sleep tonight. The knife's gone. Get someone else to find it."

"Find it?" I said. "I thought the Inspector had it."

"That's just his little way. As a matter of fact, somebody got to the hospital ahead of us and took it."

He told me what had happened. At nine o'clock that morning a man—description, tall and thin, rather shabby—said he had seen the article in the paper and asked to see the woman. She was unconscious, but he had identified her as his wife, and had looked so faint that the nurse had gone to get him some aromatic ammonia. He had given the name of Johnson and an address which turned out later to be nonexistent. He had stayed an hour or two. Then he had gone, promising to come back. He had not done so.

Beyond the usual inquiry and report the police had not been interested in the woman. Certainly no one had connected her with the case. But according to hospital routine the contents of her pocketbook had been listed at the office on arrival, before it was taken to her room. Among them was a hunting knife wrapped in a clean handkerchief. It was not until an alert young receptionist came on duty that afternoon that anyone took particular note of the knife. She thought it was odd. She went up to ask the nurse about it, and the knife was gone. She reported it at the office, but nothing was done about it.

Then the nurse, interested by that time, came down to say that she had found a slip of paper in an inner pocket of the woman's bag. It was folded very small, and on it were the words "Strathmore House, Linden Avenue bus." The receptionist had read the papers. She knew of the search for the knife that had killed Isabel, and so she notified the police.

"We got there too late," Tony said gloomily. "The woman had just died. And the man hasn't turned up. But we got a full description of the knife from the night clerk who listed it. He even said the handle was damp, as if it had been in water. Now what's the connection between this woman and Isabel Shepard's death? There has to be one."

"I don't know," I said helplessly. "If I could find that picture—"

"The snapshot?" he asked. "Did you really make a search for it?"

So I told him about finding Don Scott in Isabel's room and about hunting everywhere for the picture.

"It had been left on the mantel?" he asked.

"So Anna said."

"Then, if Scott saw it there and took it, why did he want it? And what else was he looking for when you found him?"

"He said he was afraid she had kept some of his letters."

"Nice boy, your old pal," he observed. "Getting out from under, wasn't he? What's scandalous about love letters seven or eight years old?"

He paid the check and leaned back scowling and silent for some time. Then he got up abruptly.

"Why the hell didn't you tell me this before?" he said. "Come on. We're going to the Lelands'. I want to speak to Andrew."

He refused to explain, although I protested. After all Isabel had been buried only that morning, and the family had a right to their decent grief.

But to my surprise we were admitted to the house, and we found Andrew in his dismal library, sitting alone. He had apparently not even been reading. There was the dank smell of funeral flowers still in the room, and only one lamp was lighted. He had aged perceptibly. He looked stricken, and even Tony King saw it. He apologized.

"I'm sorry to disturb you, Mr. Leland," he said. "But certain things have come up. You ought to know them. My name is King. You know Miss Shepard."

He asked us to sit down. He didn't like me, he never had; but he was civil enough. It was to Tony King, however, that he spoke.

"What things? I'm afraid I don't understand."

"Your daughter's death. The murder of a policeman. And the suicide of a woman who jumped off a bridge last night."

"I have no knowledge of any except the first two, Mr. King."

"Are you certain of that? Suppose I describe this woman? She was small. She had an aquiline nose and rather a receding chin. She was probably forty, maybe less. Does that mean anything to you?"

"Nothing at all," Mr. Leland said coldly. "I know of no such woman. If this concerns my daughter's death I still have not changed my opinion. She was killed by her husband."

But Tony King was relentless. He bent forward, his face set and intent.

"Why would Larry Shepard kill his wife, Mr. Leland? Because he learned she had borne a child before he married her?"

The effect was more than shocking. Andrew Leland suddenly crumpled, as if without his pride he was nothing; just a little elderly man who had fought a long battle and lost it.

"For God's sake, don't tell her mother," he said, with stiff lips. "It would kill her."

"It may not be necessary," Tony said, more gently. "Is the child alive?"

"So far as I know, yes."

"You haven't seen it?"

"I never saw it," he said fiercely. "But I wish to make this statement: the boy was legitimate; my daughter had married the father and divorced him."

"The father was Donald Scott?"

He nodded. The room was going around me in circles, but they paid no attention to me. The hardness was gone from Tony's face. He drew a long breath.

"I'm sorry to bring this up," he said. "I know it is painful. Do you know where the boy is now?"

"He was adopted by a family in the West. I suppose he is still there. At least I still—"

"You are still paying them for keeping him?"

"I send them a little every month," he said carefully. "What has all this to do with my daughter's death?"

"Just this. Unless your daughter left a will to the contrary, the boy is her heir."

He looked startled. Then he merely shrugged his shoulders.

"He was born under another name. The people who adopted him don't know who he is. I have never sent them checks. The money was sent indirectly."

"Nevertheless by law he is her heir in this state," Tony persisted. "You are a lawyer. You know that, Mr. Leland. And those people may know it too. Suppose they have discovered or always knew the child's identity. They have adopted him. They are his legal guardians and he will have a considerable fortune on the mother's death. That's as good a motive as I know for murder."

"How could they have known it? Even the father didn't know he had a child. I took Isabel away as soon as she told me."

He went on. It had been a most unsuitable marriage. He had traced them and found them, and Isabel had come home willingly enough. It had been an impulse, which she regretted. There had been a bad time with Scott, but in the end he let her get a divorce in Reno. They managed to keep it a secret. The boy was born later in a hospital in California.

Tony King listened attentively.

"What do you know about the people who adopted the boy?" he asked. "Surely you had them investigated."

"The doctor guaranteed them. I saw the woman myself. She—" he drew a long breath—"she impressed me very favorably. A quiet self-respecting sort. I never saw the husband."

"And the name?"

"It was Armstrong, John P. Armstrong."

Tony got up.

"I think we will find it was Mrs. Armstrong who jumped off a bridge here last night. If you'll give me the address in California, I can find out tonight. She had a knife in her bag. You probably know what knife I mean."

XIV

I don't remember how we got out of the house. I know we left Mr. Leland still sunk in his chair, and that I felt I had outraged every bit of decency left in me. We had torn away his pride, laid bare the secret he had fought so long to keep, and exposed poor Isabel't tragic story. I must have shown how I felt, for Tony took one look at me and shoved me away from the wheel of my car.

"Pretty grim story," he said. "It hurts, doesn't it? I sort of gather you've been crazy about Scott for a long time."

I stared ahead. Had I ever really cared for Don? Or had I simply held on to an adolescent dream?

"That's over," I said honestly. "I suppose really it was because there was nobody else."

"No candidates?" He raised his eyebrows.

"That's not what I said. But Don never killed Isabel. Why should he?"

"Maybe not. But he's in this up to his neck."

At Police Headquarters he got out and gave me the wheel. "I'll discuss the matter of candidates with you later," he said. "In the meantime, for God's sake relax. Big brother may be out before you know it. And another thing." He jerked his hat down over one eye. "Go home and stay there. I may like you—and Mother, of course—but I also like my little bed. I'd like at least one night in it."

Well, he was right in one thing. Larry was released that same evening. But Tony King did not get that night in bed. Nor did the rest of us.

I shall never forget Mother's face when Larry came in. She put her arms around him and held on to him, without speaking. He leaned over and kissed the top of that dreadful henna-ed hair of hers, his eyes tender.

"Poor old girl," he said. "It's going to be all right, my dear. "It's going to be all right."

She let go of him suddenly.

"What do you mean, going to be? They've let you go, haven't they?"

"They still don't know who did it, Mother."

"They know you didn't," she said valiantly.

She wouldn't let him go, not even back to his house for the bath and extra suit he wanted. She made him sit by the bed, holding tight to his hand, and she rang for someone to go down to bring him what he needed. However, most of the men were having their Sunday out, and in the end it was Alma who volunteered to go. Larry protested, but it was no use. She went to get a coat, and I stayed to hear his story.

What with ordering a tray supper for him, and finally tellling my own story of the woman in the hospital and the knife, the next hour passed without our noticing it. The knife bewildered Larry. I had to begin with Mother's finding it under the stair carpet and go on from there. He asked again about the plumber.

"How did he know it was there?"

"All he had to do was look," Mother said. "After all, the papers were full of it."

"So he took it away, gave it to this woman who returned it, and she gets it out of the fountain and jumps into the river. Why?"

When Patrick came in for the tray, Larry asked him to send Sarah down. Her gloomy face lightened when she saw him, although all she said was that she was glad to see him back. It's a queer thing but in a family of women like ours it's the man who gets all the adoration. But when he asked Sarah about the tank, she blushed with embarrassment.

"There was something broken in it," she said. "It—it wouldn't flush."

"How long had it been that way?"

"It was all right in the morning. Nellie, who does the bathrooms, told me about it."

"And who called the plumber?"

"I think it was Miss Alma. She usually does."

Sarah, like Patrick, hadn't noticed the plumber much. She had stayed in Mother's bedroom while he was there. She thought she had never seen him before, but these days, with workmen a good deal more scarce than diamonds, we took what we could get and were glad to get them. He was a tall man, about forty or more, but he hadn't taken off his cap. No, he hadn't mentioned finding the knife. He was there only about ten minutes.

After Sarah had gone, we began to wonder why Alma had not come back. Then one of the women servants knocked at the door.

I opened it. She was leaning against it, and she almost fell into the room. She was dressed in her street clothes, her hat awry and her face chalk white.

"It's Miss Alma," she gasped. "She's lying in the driveway with a knife in her back."

That was how Larry's knife came back for the last time.

We couldn't believe it. Why would anybody kill Alma? She was a part of the family, and Mother at least had loved her. We could not believe it even when we reached the drive and somebody turned on the lights. But it was true. She was lying face down, with the things she had brought for Larry scattered all around her.

We had a dreadful time with Mother at first, while the police were on the way. She wouldn't leave, and at last I sent for a fur coat for her, and made her put it on. Then the police arrived, and it was the same thing as Isabel's death all over again: the same squad car, the same homicide outfit roaring up later, and the same reporters, some still trying to get over the fence after the gates were closed. Larry looked fairly haunted. The servants were huddled around the front door. Flash bulbs went off as photographs were taken, a car was driven up and its headlights turned on the body.

There was hardly time to realize what had happened. The drive was jammed with men with flashlights, men with cameras, men with pencils writing busily on yellow paper, men inside using the telephone and men trying to keep other men out. Once I thought of Tony King, but he disappeared in the crowd.

The night was cold, and it seemed to me that they left Alma lying there for hours.

We stayed until the body had been taken away, and Inspector Welles and Larry went into the house. I didn't like the look on the Inspector's face. I knew no alibi Mother and I could give Larry was worth anything. For once there had been no servants to check who had left the house, and there was something diabolic about the whole thing; that Larry had been released, to have another murder within an hour or so of his homecoming.

Not that I was worrying about alibis just then. I was worrying about Mother. She had followed Larry and the Inspector into the library, and she had looked so stricken that I went into the dining room to get her some brandy.

I was pouring it when there was a tap at the window. It startled me so I nearly dropped the decanter. When I looked, I saw it was Tony. I raised the window and he crawled in.

"Quick," he said. "Can you get me to her rooms without anybody's seeing me?"

"Whose rooms?" I said stupidly.

"The Spencer woman's. I want to get there before the mob gets in. Where are they?"

"Look," I said, "do you know why she was killed? If you do, tell me. I think I'm slowly going crazy."

"There's usually a reason," he said. "Do I go up or don't I?"

He went up, of course. There was a small staircase leading almost directly to Alma's rooms, and nobody saw us. The lights were off, and he drew the shades before he turned on the lamps in her bedroom and he looked around. The room was as neat as Alma herself had been.

"Lived pretty comfortably, didn't she?" he said.

"The sitting room was her office," I told him. "She had plenty to do."

"Liked her, did you? Nice woman and all that? How about your brother? Fond of her?"

"I don't think he really noticed whether she was around or not. Certainly he didn't kill her. He hadn't left Mother's room since he got home. And I was with him, too."

I told him all I knew, about Larry's needing another suit and Alma's insisting on getting it. But he hardly listened. He was going over the room, opening the closets, looking in the dresser drawers. It was her office, however, to which he paid the most careful attention. It was as orderly as the rest of the place: her typewriter covered on the table by a window, a row of steel files in a corner, and the big desk in the center of the room practically bare.

There was a fresh blotter on it, and something had been blotted on it not long before. He took her hand mirror and tried to read it. The only word that stood out clearly was "worrying." He tore out the blotter and rolling it up put it under his arm.

"Something bothering her," he said. "Any idea what it was."

"Not the slightest."

"If she wrote it where is it?"

He began going over the room again, moving quietly for so big a man, but there was no sign of what she had written. I stood it as long as I could.

"Do you have to do all this?" I said, when he started for the files. "I don't think I can bear much more."

He turned and looked at me. Then he came over quickly and put both hands on my shoulders.

"Look, Judy," he said. "There's been another murder, and we have to get after it fast. I don't like your being here. It's no place for you." He leaned down unexpectedly and kissed me. "Somebody ought to come along pretty soon and marry you, to get you away."

And tired and half-sick as I was, I tried to smile up at him.

"Is that a proposal?"

"God, no," he said, looking shocked. "Whatever put that in your head?"

He went back to the search, and I wandered out to the hall. Behind me I could hear drawers opening and shutting, and the metallic squeak of the files as he drew them out and pushed them back. He was still busy when I heard Mother's voice below. I went to the gallery and looked down. There was no sign of Larry, and Mother was raging at the Inspector.

"I assure you," she was saying, "that if necessary I shall carry this case to the Supreme Court. To say that my son—"

And the Inspector, exasperated but keeping his temper.

"My dear Mrs. Shepard, I have not said that your son did this thing. I am not placing him under arrest. I would like to talk to him where we are not disturbed. That's all."

"Talk to him? You've done nothing else for the last three days."

He looked down at her, small as she was, defiant, and blazing with fury. Evidently he decided she could take it.

"Suppose I ask you what I have already asked him," he said. "Why did you or your son give the mounted officer Barnes fifty dollars the night of your party for the Mayor?"

Mother fairly squealed.

"Fifty dollars! Don't be ridiculous. I didn't give him anything. And Larry hadn't any money at all that night. He had forgotten to go to the bank. I gave him ten dollars myself that afternoon."

Some detectives came in just then and he sent them up to Alma's rooms. I warned Tony in time to escape, but although he looked rather smug he told me nothing. He got out as he had come in. Astride the window sill he said he would probably be at Headquarters all night, and when he saw me again we could discuss my future. After which he simply disappeared, and as no shouts followed I gathered that no one had seen him.

I felt rather blank after he had gone. Larry and the Inspector had driven off, and Mother had gone to her room and locked the door.

I took the drink I had poured for Mother. It put some starch in my knees, and I went out into the hall. One of the uniformed men was standing by the fountain. He had a cup of coffee and a roll in his hand, and he was dropping crumbs for the fish.

"They don't know it's night," he said disconsolately. "Same as me. I've forgotten what a good bed looks like."

I don't know why looking at the fish made me think of Donald Scott, unless it was because one pop-eyed little black Japanese one was fighting the others off and getting all the crumbs. Anyhow I did.

Tony King had said Don was in something or other up to the neck. I wondered if Alma had known about the child. She had an uncanny way of learning things. Suppose she was blackmailing him? She might have. She liked money, and no man would want it known that after a week or so of marriage his wife had divorced him. But it wasn't Don who had taken the knife from the hospital that morning. It had been a thin shabby-looking man.

I was getting excited by that time, what with the brandy and sheer nervous exhaustion. The policeman had tired of feeding the fish. He wandered off and stood looking out at the men still working in the grounds. And once again I heard Don's voice, asking me about the tassel on the chain they had found under Isabel's body.

I was sure I knew about that now. Isabel had given up her baby, but not entirely. She had slipped the chain around its neck, and on the chain she had hung one of the tassels from her bed jacket. It had to be that way. She had even marked a cross on it with ink. She might have hoped to claim the boy some day. She might only have been protecting herself against having another child substituted for her own. But that was what she had done.

I went up to bed finally, so tired that I was staggering. Mother's light was out, and I didn't go in. Down the hall the police had locked and sealed Alma's rooms for further examination. My bedside clock said three when I went in, and I sat down on the bed, too exhausted even to undress.

That was the state I was in when I saw the note on my dressing table. It was in Alma's neat handwriting, and she had evidently left it before she had started down for Larry's clothes. "Dear Judy," it said, "my conscience is worrying me about the car I saw the other night. Can you come in later and discuss it?"

I sat there, turning it over in my hands. So Alma had intended trying a spot of blackmail on me after all. And the police had the blotter, with that message on it.

XV

I sat up in bed for hours, smoking endless cigarettes. At four in the morning I picked up the telephone and called Tony King. He was there, but the operator said he was using the long-distance phone. I tried at intervals for an hour. Then at last I gave up and went unexpectedly to sleep.

I wakened at nine, dressed in a hurry and drank a cup of coffee. The maid who brought my tray said Larry had not come home, and that Mother had dressed and gone downtown without even calling Sarah. I knew something had happened, but no one knew what it was. I was still in a state of helpless anxiety when I got my car and drove to Headquarters.

Mother was sitting in the waiting room outside the Inspector's office. She was in what Sarah would have called a state, her hat crooked and unmatched shoes on her feet.

"Why, Mother!" I said. "What on earth—"

"I've come to take Larry home," she said. "I don't budge from this spot until those"—here she used a most impolite word—"until those ——s let him go."

The weary-looking officer at the desk looked up.

"I've told you, madam. He is not in there."

"I don't believe it."

She got up suddenly and opened the door to the inner office. There was no sign of Larry, but Donald Scott was there; a Don I had never seen, his face unshaven, his eyes sunken in his head. He didn't apparently notice that we were there.

"That's the truth, so help me God," he was saying. "I

couldn't help her, but I never killed her. Or Alma Spencer either."

His voice broke, and Mother hastily closed the door.

"They're crazy," she said. "They're all crazy. As if he would murder the mother of his own child."

I suppose my jaw dropped, for she told me impatiently to close my mouth. But she had apparently abandoned her idea of rescuing Larry. She trotted down the stairs, her two odd shoes making clacking noises and her hat more crooked than ever. When I caught up with her, she was talking to herself. I took her arm and stopped her.

"Don't babble," I said. "How long have you known about Isabel's baby?"

"Since before Larry married her, of course."

I got the story from her on the way home. She let me take her in my car, sending her own away. As she had no confidence whatever in me as a driver I think this shows her state of mind. She was lucid enough, however.

She sat beside me in the car, that wild red hair of hers blowing in all directions, and told me the story.

You have to hand it to the Lelands of this world after all. When Larry wanted to marry Isabel, Andrew Leland had come to Strathmore House; come stiffly, I gathered, in morning coat and striped trousers, but with two small spots of color on his cheeks. He had lost no time, either. He had not even sat down. He had stood—still stiffly—in front of the fireplace and said:

"I understand your boy wants to marry my girl."

"And why not?" said Mother.

"That's what I came to talk about."

He told her the whole story. Isabel was determined not to tell Larry. She had threatened to kill herself if the affair came out. On the other hand, in fairness to everybody . . . I suppose Mother surprised him then.

"Listen to me, Andrew Leland," she said. "It's you who are ashamed of Isabel. I'm not." And she had added maliciously: "There are some advantages of coming from below the tracks even a generation or two ago. Keep your mouth shut and let them alone."

It was settled between them finally. I believe he even

condescended to take a glass of sherry before he left. But he would not let Isabel have a church wedding, or even a veil. The veil, he said gravely, was symbolic, and Isabel was no longer a virgin. Which was why, it appeared, I had cried all night when I learned that Larry was going to be married, and there were to be no bridesmaids. It's a queer conventional world the Lelands and their kind make for themselves, and others.

I got Mother home safely and persuaded her to go to bed. And that is the way things stood with us at ten o'clock on Monday morning. Isabel had been killed on Thursday night and Barnes early on Friday morning. Alma had been stabbed Sunday night. Donald Scott was probably still being interrogated, and we heard nothing whatever from Larry.

Sarah disappeared at noon that day. The police had unlocked Alma's rooms, and I had been helping her go through Alma's things. We had no idea what to do with them. She had a stepbrother somewhere, but I could not find his name or address anywhere.

We were still working when one of the men came to say Sarah was wanted on the telephone, and she went and didn't come back. I waited a half hour. Then I tried to find her, but all I learned was that she had put on her hat and coat and simply walked out. In thirty years with Mother she had never done such a thing, and Mother was furious.

"She must have lost her mind," she snapped. "Not a word to me! What does the old fool mean by such a thing?"

She was still in a bad temper when just after lunch—and still no Sarah—a message came from Headquarters. It was quite polite. Would Mother and I come to Inspector Welles' office at three o'clock? I said with equal politeness that we would, and hung up, feeling that it had sounded like an invitation to tea. But I didn't trust them, nor did Mother when I told her. But she agreed to go. She apparently intended to make up for her morning appearance, for warm as it was she put on her mink coat and all her pearls, and she walked into the Inspector's office like a combination of the Queen of Sheba and a woman who has just had a severe chill.

There were a number of people in the office. Andrew Leland got up when we entered. So did Don. And Larry came over and kissed Mother. Tony King nodded from the telephone. He looked as though he had been up all night again, but he smiled at me.

I could not take my eyes from the Inspector's desk. There was a queer collection on it: the shabby felt hat, Larry's new opera one, none the better for its hours in the tree, a woman's worn pocketbook, a slug from a gun and some magnified photographs of it, the platinum chain and tassel found under Isabel's body when she was killed, and the blotter Tony had taken away from Alma's desk.

The knife was there too, its reindeer handle looking more moth-eaten than ever. I looked away quickly, and Mother went pale under her make-up.

There was a silence in the room. Tony put down the receiver and looked at the Inspector.

"Check," he said.

The Inspector nodded. He looked grave. He picked up the chain and looked at it, but it was a minute or two before he spoke.

"I have asked you all to come here," he said slowly, "because you are all vitally concerned. This has been a curious case, in that one or two of the people most concerned in it have hardly appeared at all. It also involves baring certain hitherto concealed facts. I regret that this is necessary, but as you all know them . . ."

He put down the chain.

"From the first," he said, "we had only one or two clues. We had this chain, we had a man's old felt hat, and we had the curious episode of Barnes, one of our own force, denying that he had seen the woman Anna Griffin who claimed to have spoken to him.

"I am going to read you the statement made by Barnes's wife as to that night."

He picked up a paper and put on his glasses.

"Jim came home Thursday night after he had put up his horse at the police stable. It was about midnight. He did not act like himself. He said he had a headache and took some aspirin. Then he said he had a surprise for me. He reached in his pocket and took out fifty dollars, two twenties and a ten. 'Go and buy yourself something pretty. That's the way the rich do things.' I couldn't believe it. Now and then he gets five or ten dollars for work like that when he's assigned to it, but never fifty.

"I was a little worried. I asked him if it was clean money. He looked funny but he said it was.

"He went to bed, but I don't think he slept much. I wakened up when the bell rang. He leaned out the window and someone said there was trouble at the Shepard place, and to come along. He acted queer about that, too. He told me not to mention the money. Then he dressed in a hurry and went out. There was a car waiting for him.

"He came back an hour or two later. He looked terribly worried. He said young Mrs. Shepard had been killed. Someone had stabbed her. But he did not know anything about it. Only he did not go back to bed. He stayed downstairs walking the floor. I did not understand it. Then before daylight I heard another car stop, and Jim went outside.

"I heard him go out to the car and it drove off. That is all I know. Only he has not been back since, and I am almost crazy."

He put down the paper.

"Now there are several curious things about that story," he said. "Barnes gets fifty dollars for an ordinary routine job. That's a lot of money for a police officer. But we know Barnes. He wouldn't have been easy to bribe. If he had, and a murder was committed . . .

"Let that go. He had a headache and he asked for aspirin, and later after we had questioned him and he went home he was called out to a car and taken away. That, coupled with his confusion when we sent for him that night and his denial that the maid Anna Griffin had spoken to him, pointed to several things. Either he had not seen the Griffin woman, or he was lying for some reason of his own.

"I think we know now that he was lying, and why. When he was found he had been shot. But there was also a bruise on his head. It had been there long enough before his death to be swollen and discolored.

"That—in spite of a statement I shall read to the contrary—pointed to one thing. Barnes had been attacked and knocked unconscious before or during Mrs. Shepard's murder. He wouldn't admit it. No police officer likes to admit a thing like that. And he never had another chance to admit it. He was kidnaped a few hours later, probably at the point of a gun. Kidnaped and shot.

"We don't like things of that sort happening to our men."

He paused. There was not a stir in the room. Tony King was listening intently. Larry looked uncomfortable. Don seemed puzzled, and Andrew Leland had not moved.

"Now we have to remember the circumstances at the Shepard place that night," the Inspector went on. "Nobody could get in who didn't show a card, both at the gate and at the door. The rear service gates were padlocked and watched. Even the house doors, with Barnes guarding the main entrance. Then why was Barnes knocked out? We felt it was because someone had to get either in or out of the house—or both—without being seen."

He gave a thin smile.

"That is why we held Mr. Shepard," he said. "He has however a completely clean slate."

I think Mother drew her first full breath in days, and he looked at her.

"We had some excuse, of course," he said. "The issue was confused by Mrs. Shepard, who found the knife and hid it. I am sure she meant well, but—"

"You found it," Mother said grimly. "You sent that plumber, didn't you?"

"I'm sorry to say we didn't find it, Mrs. Shepard. That is part of what I am going to tell. I may say before I begin that fine work on the part of Captain King has helped us greatly; he deserves great credit, especially as he is still recovering from a wound received in Africa."

I suppose I jumped. I know I looked furiously at Tony. He didn't give me a glance, however. He merely started ruffling through some papers in front of him, and it was the Inspector who smiled at me.

"It was Captain King," he went on blandly, "who first drew our attention to the statement in the autopsy that Mrs. Shepard had borne a child. He learned that Mr. Shepard was not—had not been—a father, and he found a significance in the chain which we had missed. He was also aware of certain movements of the knife which for reasons of his own he kept to himself for some time.

"This case, as most of you now know, began with the elopment and marriage of Isabel Leland to Donald Scott. For reasons I need not go into, the marriage was ended by a secret divorce within a short time. It was not until after the divorce that Isabel Scott realized that she was to have a child.

"She did not tell her mother. She went to her father, and he took her to California. The boy was born in a hospital there, and ten days later was handed over to a childless couple. The baby's mother resented this. She wanted the child, but her father opposed the idea. What she did was to put this small chain around the baby's neck, and to make with ink an ornament from something she was wearing—possibly a bedjacket—so that in the future she might at least identify him.

"Her own identity had been carefully shielded. She was there under another name. But the unexpected happened. Someone in the hospital, a patient recovering from an appendicitis operation, had seen her door open and had recognized her. Isabel Scott, as she was at that time, did not know this; but it was not hard for the patient to learn why she was there—or that the whole affair was being kept secret.

"What was learned also was that the doctor on the case was looking for a respectable family to take the child. Such a family was brought forward. The name was Armstrong and two or three years later, with the consent of Mr. Leland and the mother, who had since married Lawrence Shepard, adoption papers were taken out. The boy took the name Armstrong, that of his foster parents, but he remained his mother's legal heir, and there was a considerable fortune involved.

"All this time the Armstrongs remained in the West, with Mr. Leland still paying a monthly sum for the child. Then something happened. Mrs. Shepard's second marriage had produced no children. She began to want her son. She talked to her husband about adopting a boy, and at the same time she heard from the Armstrongs. They were willing to give up the child, but for a large cash payment—fifty thousand dollars. With her estate in trust and her father completely opposed to any such action, she was pretty desperate. She had never told Donald Scott that he was a father. Now she thought of him. He had risen fast. He had made considerable money. She wrote him the facts, and she enclosed a snapshot of the Armstrong woman taken in California, with the boy one of a group of children.

"But he called her up and told her he couldn't help—not to that extent anyhow. He had lived well. He hadn't saved a great deal. He sent the photograph back, asking her to destroy it.

"Then the Armstrongs came East with the boy, whose first name is Scott, by the way. Mrs. Shepard had some meetings with Armstrong in the park. Her chauffeur has identified him. She also saw her son at least once. He is an attractive child and she became more anxious than ever.

"However, the Armstrongs still held out for their fifty thousand. They even threatened to raise the ante. She explained her situation to them; she had only her income, no capital, but the boy Scott would have her entire estate on her death. That was her mistake. A terrible one, for now she was more valuable dead than alive."

I looked at Mother. Her poor chin was quivering. She could understand that pitiful story of Isabel's, wanting her son, begging for him, seeing him and loving him, and then never getting him. Larry got out his handkerchief and blew his nose.

The Inspector went on.

"I must say here that Mrs. Armstrong was not a party to much that happened. She was willing to give up the boy if it meant a better life for him. Otherwise she refused to co-operate."

He looked at Andrew Leland, sitting with his head bowed.

"I'm sorry, Mr. Leland. I shall have to go into some details here. If you care to leave . . . ?"

"Go ahead," Andrew said quietly.

"In a sense," the Inspector resumed, "Mrs. Shepard's death goes back to the hat here. It belongs to Armstrong, who was the drunken waiter who was ejected before the dinner that night. He has identified it himself.

"His drunkenness was an act. He was sober enough when he left. Perhaps I'd better read you his testimony. I shall read it as it was given. You will notice that he has refused to answer certain questions."

He took up several sheets of paper fastened by a clip and put on his glasses again. "It is in the form of question and answer, but I think it is clear." He began to read:

Question: What did you do when you were put out of the house?

Answer: I was only playing drunk. One of the policemen at the back door took me a few yards. Then he let me go.

Q. And after that?

A. Well, I was in the evening clothes I had rented, and I had somebody's top hat from the men's room. I went to the officer on the horse and told him I'd give him fifty dollars to let me ride his horse around the place for a while. I suppose he thought I was a guest, and tight at that. He considered it a minute. Then he got off his horse. He said fifty dollars was worth a ride in any man's money. I didn't get on the horse. Not then anyhow. I hit him on the head with a rock I'd picked up. Not too hard. Just enough to put him to sleep.

Q. What did you do with him?

A. I dragged him away from the drive. It was pretty dark. I put on his cap and coat. Then I heard the woman coming—Anna Griffin is her name, I think. So I got on the horse and when she spoke I answered.

Q. Why was it necessary to knock out Barnes?

A. Well, the place was full of cops, and we had business that night.

Q. What sort of business? To kill Mrs. Shepard?

A. I told you we never killed her.

Q. Then why did you attack Barnes?

The Inspector looked up.

"I shall skip the next few questions and answers. We felt he was lying. He mumbled something about Mrs. Shepard's being prepared to pay over the money that night, in exchange for an agreement to let her adopt the boy. But there was no money in the house when she was found. Barnes was a danger, of course, if murder was contemplated. Armstrong, however, has persisted that murder was never part of the plan." Then he read:

> *Q.* You say "we." Do you mean yourself and your wife?
> *A.* My wife wasn't in it. Leave her out. She wasn't near the place that night.
> *Q.* Then you did it yourself. You knocked Barnes out and then killed Mrs. Shepard.
> *A.* I never put a foot inside the house. That's the truth, before God.

He put down the paper.

"He collapsed at that point," he said quietly. "We got the rest of his testimony later. I think I should explain our own situation, as it was until the death of Alma Spencer last night.

"You must remember that at this time none of us had ever heard of the Armstrongs. The autopsy had told us Mrs. Shepard had borne a child. King learned that she had not had a child by her present husband. He remembered the chauffeur's story of her meeting a man in the park. And when Mrs. Armstrong was murdered by being thrown from a bridge, her bag was thrown with her. It contained not only Mr. Shepard's knife; there was also a small piece of paper in it with the words 'Strathmore House. Linden Avenue bus.' That connected her definitely with the case."

"I thought she committed suicide," I said, in a thin voice. "Do you mean her husband killed her?"

"No," he said gravely. "He did not kill her, Miss Shepard."

XVI

There was a rather prolonged silence after that. The King man lit a cigarette and smiled at me. His broken tooth had not been repaired.

The Inspector picked up the knife from his desk.

"There has been a determined effort all along to pin his wife's death on Mr. Shepard," he said. "This knife was left where we would be sure to find it, under the stair carpet. When Jim Barnes was killed, it was with Mr. Shepard's automatic, and in his automobile. Even the opera hat, which Armstrong got rid of after he had used it to deceive Barnes, belonged to Mr. Shepard.

"But to get back to the knife, which has wandered all through these tragedies. Yesterday here in this office Miss Judith Shepard told how her mother had taken it and where it had been hidden. She told us something else, however. She said that the tank in Mrs. Shepard's bathroom had gone out of order while they were at the inquest, and that a policeman, pretending to be a plumber, had taken the knife away.

"Now we use indirect methods of that sort now and then, but we had sent no plumber to Strathmore House. It looked like another effort to produce the knife and thus close our case against Lawrence Shepard. Here's what Armstrong says." He read:

Question: Did you get the knife from Mrs. Shepard's bathroom?

Answer: Yes.

Q. How did you know it was there?

No answer.

Q. Why did your wife take it back?

A. She wasn't standing for putting the blame on Mr. Shepard. She talked and talked, so I gave it to her. She left it at Strathmore House.

Q. How did she get it back after that? She had it in her bag when she fell. You know that, don't you?

A. (After a pause) I don't know how she got it again. I took the boy for a walk that night. When I came back, she was gone. I never saw her again until I found her in the hospital.

He took off his glasses and looked at me.

"Where had you put it, Miss Shepard?" he said. "Have you any idea how it got back to Mrs. Armstrong's bag?"

I shook my head.

"I don't see how she found it," I said. "She came back to see me that night, but I was out. She may have seen it, of course. She was in the hall alone for some time."

"You had hidden it in the hall?"

"It was in the fish pool," I said, and felt myself flushing.

He nodded without speaking, and picked up his papers again.

"However Mrs. Armstrong got it," he said, "she had it in her bag Saturday night when she was killed. The bag was found in the barge when she fell. It went to the hospital with her, and the knife was still in the bag when Armstrong, after waiting for her all night, read what had happened in the morning paper.

"I don't think he knew she had the knife. He probably opened the bag and found it there. He was in bad shape, anyhow. He either grew faint or pretended to. Certainly he got it while the nurse was out of the room getting some aromatic ammonia for him. Now let's get back to our own side of the case.

"By that time, as late as yesterday morning, we knew only certain things. We knew through Mr. Leland that Mrs. Shepard had borne a legitimate child, which had been adopted in Los Angeles by a family named Armstrong. We knew Donald

Scott was the father of the child. And we knew that a woman who had refused to give her name in the hospital had died, apparently a suicide. There was nothing to connect her with the case, or to indicate that she had not tried to kill herself.

"At the same time Mr. Leland was convinced that Lawrence Shepard had killed his wife in a fit of jealousy after he had discovered her past. The murder of Barnes was still unsolved, and the identity of the woman wo had jumped off the bridge was still unknown to us.

"Then we got a break at last. A clerk at the hospital reported finding a slip with the words 'Strathmore House, Linden Avenue bus' in the woman's bag, and also discovered that the knife, which was on the list of its contents, had disappeared.

"We set out to locate Armstrong. He was using another name, but it was fairly easy, with the woman missing and a six-year-old boy around. We finally located them at a boarding-house in a respectable part of town, but Armstrong himself was missing. He never went back to the hospital."

He stopped and drew a long breath.

"Last night Alma Spencer was stabbed," he said. "That made four murders. It looked pretty bad. We didn't locate Armstrong immediately, but we decided this morning to bring Mr. Scott here for questioning." He looked at Don. "I'm sorry, Mr. Scott. I'll have to go into this."

Don said nothing, and he went on.

"We kept him here for some time. He admitted his marriage. He admitted that Isabel Shepard had appealed to him for money to help get their child back. But he denied everything else. And by that time we had picked up Armstrong himself. He was attempting to leave town."

He looked at Mother.

"He had been identified as the plumber who repaired your bathroom. He knew the knife was there. Now that was a curious thing. Who knew it was in the tank in Mrs. Shepard's bathroom? For someone did know, either an occupant of the house or someone who had free access to it. We had interrogated the servants at various times, without result.

"However, to go back to Armstrong. This is what developed

at his second interrogation. I need not say, of course, that the felt hat left at Strathmore House was his." He read again.

Question: What do you know about Alma Spencer's death?

Answer: Nothing.

Q. Where were you last night?

A. Just walking around the streets. My wife had been murdered. What do you think I'd do? Go to a movie?

Q. You say your wife was murdered. What do you mean by that?

A. She was. She'd never kill herself. She was crazy about the boy.

Q. Who would kill her?

No answer.

Q. Why do you think she was killed?

No answer.

Q. All right. How do you think it happened?

A. She wasn't very big. Anybody could have lifted her over that railing and thrown the bag after her. The knife was in it. Or maybe she climbed up to throw the bag into the river, and somebody gave her a shove.

Q. Who would do a thing like that?

No answer.

Q. How did she get the knife again?

A. I'm not talking.

Q. Why did you kill Barnes?

A. I never killed him. I didn't know he was going to be killed.

Q. But you helped to dispose of the body?

No answer.

Q. Who did kill him, Armstrong? You'd better begin to talk.

A. I've nothing to say. I didn't shoot him. I don't own a gun.

Q. You were fond of your wife, weren't you?

A. She was the best ever.

Q. Did she stab Isabel Shepard?

A. Who? My wife? Good God, no.

The Inspector looked up. "He broke down at that point," he said. "It was some time before he was ready to talk again. And as I say we already had an idea of the truth through Captain King. I'll ask the captain to tell you about that."

Tony looked surprised. He threw away his cigarette and walked over to the desk.

"Well," he said rather shyly for him. "I suppose you might say that my interest in this case started when I heard how Mr. Lawrence Shepard and his wife were married. There was no big wedding. There was no veil, no orchids, no white satin bride's dress. I simply tucked it away in my mind and forgot it. Later on I remembered it and what it might mean; a second marriage, not a first.

"I felt all along that a woman was the murderer, the way Mrs. Shepard was dressed when she was found—or wasn't dressed. Only two or three women were apparently involved, except for the servants, so I had to consider Mrs. Shepard and her daughter. But the Mayor was certain Mrs. Shepard had been with him until he left. That left the daughter, Judith."

He glanced at me and looked away. I suppose my face must have been something.

"Somebody had done away with the knife, and it looked as though Mrs. Shepard had taken it from under the stair carpet. She sat there almost all night, and I had a bit of the carpet examined. I needn't go into that. The knife had been left there.

"Then, Friday night, I found Judith Shepard trying to bury the knife. I got a flashlight picture of her. But she's a good runner. She escaped with the knife."

Larry half rose from his chair.

"Are you trying to say that my sister had anything to do with my wife's death?" he demanded.

Tony shook his head.

"She and your mother trying to protect you, Mr. Shepard," he said. "They had a fool idea that it would send you to the chair. It might have, at that."

He paused and looked in Mother's direction. Mother was

practically purple.

"However, I had to let Judith Shepard out. There was no motive, and I checked with the men she ate and danced with that night. She apparently hadn't left the house.

"There was still no motive up to Saturday afternoon, when I saw Mr. Leland. The autopsy had revealed Isabel Shepard had borne a child, and Mr. Leland said the child was legitimate. That might have been a motive. She had inherited a trust fund and the boy was her legal hair, adopted or not. At least we began to work from there.

"The Los Angeles police reported that the family who had adopted the child had left the city a month ago. We began looking for them. But one thing puzzled us. According to Mr. Leland they had not known the identity of the mother.

"I got the name of the hospital where the child had been born. It was an institution for women only. It was possible that someone, either a patient or an attendant, had seen Mrs. Shepard—Mrs. Scott—there. I learned the date of the birth, and had the lists checked.

"I got it a few minutes ago." He looked at the Inspector. "Take it away, sir," he said. "Your turn."

He sat down, looking rather smug, and lit a cigarette. Nobody had moved. The Inspector cleared his throat and picked up his papers again. Then he glanced at Mother.

"I'm sorry, Mrs. Shepard," he said. "This may be a shock to you. As Captain King has said, the list of the people in the hospital came through only a short time ago. We knew the facts before, but we recognized one of the names." He put on his glasses. "I shall skip part of the second interrogation of John Armstrong. He was in bad shape, and much was purely evasion." He began to read.

Question: Why did you kill Alma Spencer?

Answer: Who says I killed her?

Q. I do. You took the knife from your wife's bag at the hospital and stabbed her with it. Don't deny it. We know it.

"There was a long silence here," said the Inspector, looking up. "He seemed to be thinking things over."

Question: Why did you kill her?

Answer: All right, I did. I did it because she killed my wife.

Q. What do you mean by that?

A. She threw or pushed her off the bridge. She knew too much.

Q. What did you wife know?

A. She knew that Alma had stabbed Mrs. Shepard and shot the policeman. She was afraid he would remember me. But I swear to God I didn't know she was going to kill anybody that night.

Q. How did the Spencer woman become involved in all this?

A. She knew about the boy. She'd been in the hospital as a patient when he was born. She fixed it for us to adopt him.

Q. You knew her at that time?

A. Knew her! I'll say I did. She was my stepsister.

XVII

Tony King drove me home after it was over. He stopped the car once and took me into a bar for some brandy. I guess I needed it. But he didn't talk and I couldn't. You can't live for years with a woman and then learn without shock that she has killed three people. I was still confused, too. I had seen the Armstrong man only once. That was when he dropped the tray of cocktails the night of the party; a thin mild-looking man giving a good imitation of having had too much to drink, but not vicious. Never vicious.

"What will they do to him?" I asked in a small voice.

"Probably only manslaughter. She killed his wife, remember. He'll get a parole eventually."

"I don't seem to understand it all yet, Tony," I said. "What about the knife? It kept moving all over the place."

"Listen, dimwit," he said. "What about Alma Spencer? You can bet she was moving all over the place, too. She'd left it for the police to find. Mother spoiled that, so Alma looks about and finds it in the tank. She's too smart to take it. She sends for her stepbrother to come as a plumber, and he nabs it. All clear."

I nodded.

"But things don't work out so well. Stepsister-in-law isn't having any. She brings it back, all nicely tied up in paper. And what do you do? You have the bright idea of burying it again. Only somebody catches you out. You drop it in the pool, and Alma sees you from that Romeo and Juliet balcony of yours and fishes it out.

"She's getting pretty nervous, however. She doesn't want the damned thing. That night she plays Juliet again and sees stepsister-in-law has come back. That looks like trouble, but you're not there. Stepsister-in-law leaves and Alma meets her outside the house. She says: 'Come along. You did a silly thing to bring it back, but let's take a bus to the river and drop it in.' Only she dumped stepsister-in-law in with it."

"You think it's funny, don't you?" I said resentfully. "It isn't, you know. I saw them that night. I thought it was two of the maids."

He dropped his light touch immediately.

"No," he said soberly. "No, it isn't funny, Judy. Only this is no place for you to have the screaming meemies, and that's what you were headed for."

He told me a little more on the way home; that Alma had called her stepbrother toward morning after Isabel's death and asked him to meet her near the Barnes house. She said they would have to talk to Barnes. The stepbrother didn't want to go. He said Barnes had the fifty dollars, and he wasn't likely to talk. Especially he wasn't going to admit he'd been knocked out on duty by a man half his size. But she insisted, and he met her.

She had Larry's car. She told Barnes he was wanted back at the scene of the murder, and that she had been sent to get him. He said Barnes was scared. He didn't recognize Armstrong, in the back of the car. But the last thing Armstrong expected was to have her shoot him in the head before they reached our gates. Armstrong was frantic, but he says she was still cool. They drove on out a few miles, and he helped her to carry Barnes to where he was found. They tried to clean the car, too. There was a creek near-by. But they didn't make much of a job of it.

"And you suspected me," I said when he had finished.

"Well, think about it," he said. "What did I know about you? What do I know about any of you economic royalists? I'm only a soldier. When I found you were only a pampered child of the rich, who could run like blazes, I changed my mind."

"That was another dirty trick," I said violently. "You hadn't any business in civilian clothes, posing as a photographer. I don't think it's even allowed. And if you think I'm impressed by all this play-acting . . ."

He grinned at me, broken tooth and all.

"What was I to do? Go around in a uniform chasing down clues? I'd have been a pretty sight, wouldn't I? Not that I'm not a pretty sight in it. You ought to see me. I'm something."

"It might help," I admitted.

He laughed out loud.

"I'll show you some day," he boasted. "Incidentally, I didn't try to fool you. Welles is my uncle. I'm staying with him until I go back."

"Back? To the war?"

"What do you think?"

And with that and the shock of the last few days and what not, I simply burst into tears and put my head on his shoulder. As I had on Don's once, and on old Patrick's. Only this didn't go down as well. He gave a yelp and jerked away.

"Hey!" he said. "Keep off, will you? I've had a dirty Nazi's bullet in there. It's no pillow."

Which of course didn't help any. I sat there with the tears rolling down my face, thinking about Alma and his going back to war and what on earth had happened to Sarah and how soon I could get a war job until he finally stopped the car.

"Look here, haven't you got a handkerchief?" he said. "And stop wailing. You'd make a hell of a soldier's wife."

"Who said anything about my being a soldier's wife?" I said indignantly.

"It was just an idea. Forget it," he said, and let it go at that. I could have slapped him.

He wouldn't come in when we got home. He looked at the house and said it gave him the pip, as usual. And I was angry enough at last to tell him the truth.

"Why don't you read the papers now and then?" I inquired stiffly. "Mother offered this place to the Government as a convalescent home for soldiers six months ago. They're taking it over next month."

He actually looked embarrassed, but he was still flippant.

"My apologies," he said. "Give her a great big kiss from me, won't you?"

"And I'm getting a war job," I went on. "And Larry's going

into the Navy. We're not such a bad lot after all, are we?"

"You break my heart," he said, and showed that broken tooth of his again. "First you get it and then you break it. Well, that's life."

He drove off, leaving me standing there.

I stopped inside the front door. Mother was there, and Sarah; and chasing the fish around in the pool was a six-year-old boy. He was wet, the floor was sopping, and in the background Patrick was beaming and holding a mop.

Mother hardly noticed me. "The police sent for Sarah to look after him," she said. "Isn't he a pet?"

Well, he was, but as he chose that moment to fall in the pool, to be hauled out dripping, I hadn't much chance at him. I knew he was a godsend to Mother, however. Already Alma was water over the dam, so to speak.

They bathed him and put him to bed, finally, quarreling bitterly over how many covers he needed and how high to raise the window. And that night after dinner Captain King arrived.

He was terrific. There were all sorts of insignia on his uniform, including a decoration the President had pinned on him, and Patrick looked stunned as he admitted him. The last time he had seen him he had been playing with the fish in the pool, in a suit that looked as though it had been slept in.

I blinked.

"Couldn't you have done it a little at a time?" I said. "Say the trousers first, and so on? It's rather overwhelming."

"That's the idea," he observed complacently. "Overwhelm them. That's my motto."

But he was sober enough when he sat down. He looked around the library, and not through the open door to the hall, with its tapestries, its marble and fountain, and the gallery above.

"I hope the poor devils who come here to get well can take it," he said. "It's a grand idea and I'm for it. But has it ever occurred to you what the effect is on the people employed in a place like yours? It does something to people. It does something to me. And it did something to Alma Spencer. You've got to remember that, Judy."

"Are you asking me to feel sorry for her?"

"Not exactly. But consider this: It was all right at first. She saw a chance to get some support for her stepbrother and his wife, and when she learned the baby was open for adoption she had the Armstrongs apply. But I'm guessing that she wasn't thinking of murder then. It took her a long time to come to that. Fifty thousand, divided between herself and the Armstrongs, looked like a fortune to her.

"Then—probably from Isabel herself—she learned that her fortune was in trust. Two million dollars, to go to the boy if she had no other children. And a long time before he would come of age to claim it. If Isabel died, of course.

"So she brought the Armstrongs East, and Isabel saw the boy and wanted him desperately. Alma hadn't counted on that.

"She had to work fast. Suppose Isabel told her husband and he agreed to put up the money? What was fifty thousand compared to the control of two million until the child came of age? Remember, Alma liked money. She craved it. She'd seen it spent like water here for years. Maybe she wasn't quite sane.

"She chose the night of the party, but the party almost defeated her. She had to get out of the house, and the doors were guarded. At the last minute she got her stepbrother here as a waiter.

"She told him what to do, to play drunk and knock out Barnes. He says he didn't want to do it. He was afraid. But even then he still believed she was only to collect the fifty thousand.

"Anyhow, with Barnes unconscious and out of sight, the rest was easy. Nobody could say she had left the party at all. She took down the chain and tassel which Isabel had insisted on as the final identification of her son, and she picked up your brother's knife. She gave the chain to Isabel, and then—well, you know the rest. I imagine something scared her just then—perhaps Anna Griffin coming back—for she forgot the chain. If she hadn't . . ."

I felt sick again. And he seemed to be blaming us as if we had driven her to it.

"We were good to her, Tony," I protested.

"I'm sure you were, after your fashion. Like your brother Larry, who didn't know she was around."

I was on the sofa, and I remember leaning back and closing

my eyes.

"You still don't think much of us, do you?" I said.

He got up and came over to sit beside me, but I wasn't leaning my head on his shoulder. I knew better.

"Let's forget it," he said. "What about this war job you're taking?"

"It's just an idea," I said meekly.

"Any other better ideas?"

"I wouldn't mind a good strong man helping to support me. I could work while he was away, couldn't I?"

"What about after the war? If he's just a common ordinary sort of guy—maybe he couldn't even get a job."

"I could support him, couldn't I?"

"The hell you could," he said, and took me in his arms. Almost immediately he let go of me, groaned, and rubbed his shoulder. "Goddamn Hitler," he said and kissed me.

He insisted on seeing Mother before he left. We went upstairs, to find her in her nightgown and bare feet, padding out of Isabel's boy's room. She didn't mind her condition—as I have said, she sees nothing shameful in good honest flesh—but she gave Tony a good long look.

"Good heavens," she said. "Don't tell me it's you!"

"Just my working clothes," he explained. "I thought I'd better tell you, Mrs. Shepard. Judy here has just made me an offer of marriage. At first I was inclined to refuse, but on thinking it over—"

You have to hand it to Mother. There she stood, looking like nothing on earth, her hair in curlers and her chin strap hanging around her neck. And did she care? She did not. She looked at Tony and gave him a heavenly smile.

"I hope you accept her," she said. "I never could handle her myself. You look as though you might."

"I'll handle her all right," he said grimly, and kissed her.

That's the romantic way in which I was given away in marriage. . . .

The Man Who Hid His Breakfast

The inspector stood at the door of the bedroom. The woman's body had gone, but the bed remained as she had left it. It was almost smooth, as though she had made little or no struggle. And there was no disorder in the room, save where the fingerprint men had left their smudge of powder. On the floor lay a discarded flash lamp, and Brent stooped and picking it up put it in his pocket. He was a tidy man.

His sergeant was standing in the hall when he went out. He closed the door behind him.

"Better stick around, Joe," he told him. "I'll be coming back. Nobody to go in, of course."

He went slowly down the stairs, aware that Joe's eyes were following him with something like pity. For this was his last case before he was retired, and it looked like a stinker. A man ought to be able to get out quietly, to end his long service with dignity. But this murder was front-page stuff. The big substantial house, the social standing of the family, insured that it would be plastered all over the front pages of the newspapers. Already reporters were crowding the pavement outside. Soon he would have to call them in and tell them something. He didn't know what.

The house was quiet. The precinct men had gone. So had the Homicide Squad, except for Joe. In the lower hall he called his wife over the phone. Her familiar voice soothed him, as usual. But her tone was sharp.

"Now see here, Tom Brent," she said, "have you had any breakfast?"

"Just about to get it, Emma," he told her pacifically.

"Well, see that you do. How are your feet?"

"Fine," he said. "Just fine. Don't worry about me."

It was a lie, of course. He had a bunion on each big toe, and they burned furiously. What he wanted was to sit down somewhere and take his weight off them. But Emma kept on.

"I think I'll go out and look over that place today, Tom," she said. "The paper said four acres. It sounds pretty good, doesn't it?"

He supposed that Joe, in the hall above, was listening. He'd know what it was about, too. Emma had set her heart on a chicken farm when he retired, but he hated chickens.

"Don't be in too much of a hurry," he said. "We'll talk it over tonight. Just now I'm busy. I'll call you later."

He hung up and stood listening. Queer, how still a house was after tragedy. Even the street was quiet except for the voice of the patrolman trying to keep the crowd moving.

"Move on," he was saying over and over. "There's nothing to see. Move on, please."

Brent knew that the girl and the young man were waiting for him in the library, but he did not go in immediately. Instead he wandered back to the dining room, with its mammoth Georgian silver tea service on the sideboard and a wide window overlooking a scrap of city yard. Standing there he saw a dog, a Scottie, apparently burying a bone. And he watched him for a minute or two. He liked dogs. One of his dreams when he retired was to have a kennel and raise them. But for some reason Emma was hell-bent for a chicken farm.

When at last he went into the library the girl had stopped crying. She sat, red-eyed and practically collapsed, in the corner of a sofa, and a man in his late twenties beside her had his arm around her. He got up as Brent entered.

"Can't you put this off for a while, Inspector?" he asked. "She's quieter now, but she needs rest. I've sent for some coffee for her."

Brent eyed the young man. His name was Townsend, and the girl called him Ken. He was a likable-looking fellow, but Brent knew that looks meant nothing in a case like this. Angel faces sometimes committed murder. But his voice was friendly.

"I'll be as easy as I can, son. Better sit down. You a friend of Miss Ingalls?"

"We're engaged to be married."

"I see. Mother approved of it, did she?"

The girl gave him a quick, almost desperate look. She was still in a negligee over a nightgown as she had been earlier. She must have been rather lovely, he thought, before long weeping had swollen her face and reddened her eyes. His own girl would have been about her age, had she lived. It was young Townsend who spoke, however.

"No use lying, Joy," he said. "He'll find it out sooner or later. No, she didn't approve of it, sir. She didn't approve of anything that would take Joy away from her. There are women like that. They hold on like grim death—"

He stopped abruptly, as though the word had been a mistake. The girl however did not seem to notice.

"She was sick," she protested. "You know that, Ken. She had a bad heart. She needed me."

Ken had recovered his poise.

"I'd like a post-mortem to prove that," he said grimly. "It's a queer heart that only acts up when you take an evening out with me." He glanced at Brent defiantly. "I suppose you'll suspect me after that."

"Not necessarily." Brent lit a cigarette and eased his feet in his shoes. "But I'd lke to know more about last night. You were here, you said, until one o'clock."

"I was. We came in about twelve, and I stayed awhile. What's more, I let myself out. Joy's room is back of her mother's, and I waited to see if the old—if her mother called her. When she didn't I left. There's a Yale lock on the front door. I tried it from the outside to see if it was all right."

"And it was?"

"It was. Locked tight."

"And after that?"

"I went home, believe it or not. I live in a walk-up apartment. Nobody saw me. I slept until seven o'clock, and I slept alone."

"Sure making things hard for yourself, aren't you?" Brent smiled faintly.

For the first time the girl showed some spirit.

"What are you trying to do, Ken?" she said. "What's all that got to with it? You went out. I heard you close the door."

Brent looked at her. Was she afraid that young Townsend had done it? Certainly she had risen quickly to his defense. But the boy—he was that to the older man—gave her a quick look and went on.

"You'll learn it all anyway, Inspector," he said. "What's more, I had the hell of a row with Mrs. Ingalls yesterday afternoon, because I wanted to take Joy out last night. I don't remember what I said, but it was plenty. That Filipino in the kitchen heard it. Just ask him."

The girl sagged again. Evidently this was what she had been afraid of. She sat back, looking at her finger tips from which Brent saw with annoyance that the ink had been poorly removed by the men who took her prints. But it was his method to put his suspects at ease when he queried them. He lit a cigarette and smiled at her.

"You remind me of a hen pheasant," he said easily. "Ever see her try to lead somebody off from her chicks? She don't fool anybody, but she sure gets 'E' for effort."

Townsend grinned. He reached over and patted her.

"Thanks, darling," he said. "Only don't try to fool the Inspector. He knows his onions. You didn't hear me close the door. Yours was shut before I left."

Brent put down his cigarette. He was all policeman now. He fixed steady eyes on the girl and reached into his pocket and pulled out a long sheer silk stocking. "This belong to you?" he inquired.

She stared at it, looking sick.

"Was that—was that what did it?"

"Yes. Is it yours?"

"I don't know," she said feverishly. "They're all alike. Don't make me look at it," she added, her voice faint. "I don't want to see it. Put it away."

Brent rolled up the stocking, but he still held it in his hand. He kept his eyes on the girl.

"It's still kind of damp," he said. "That mean anything to you?"

It did. He saw that. There was incredulity in her face—and terror.

"No, of course not," she said. "Why should it? And don't stare at me like that. I didn't do it. I didn't. My own mother!"

Brent put the stocking back in his pocket and got up. He was not satisfied, but it was hard to connect those two good-looking youngsters with murder. Nevertheless he tried.

"I think it belongs to you," he said. "I think that last night before you went to bed you washed your stockings. My wife does the same thing, so I know about it. And you hung them in your bathroom to dry. There's only one there now. The other is here in my pocket."

The girl looked stricken. Young Townsend reached over and put an arm around her. "Easy does it, darling," he said. But Brent's face had hardened.

"I've been in your bathroom, Miss Ingalls," he said. "To get to it somebody would have to go through your bedroom. How soundly do you sleep? You had to listen for your mother, didn't you? If she called you?"

"No. She had a bell. She didn't ring for me at all last night. And I was tired."

"What about the dog? Didn't he bark?"

"I didn't hear him. I put him out when I was ready for bed. He sleeps at the head of the back stairs, and the door was closed."

"But someone knew those stockings were there. Someone who knew his way about the house."

"Meaning me, I suppose," young Townsend said. "Well, that lets me out. I've never been upstairs in my life. By Mrs. Ingalls' orders the newel post in the hall was my limit. And if you think Joy did it you're crazy."

"Who knew those stockings were there? The Filipino?"

"He never comes upstairs to our part of the house," Joy said. "And he's been with us for years. Anyone could have seen those stockings. It was hot last night. My door was open, and I keep a light in the bathroom all night in case mother rings for me. Rang for me," she added, and went if possible paler than before.

Brent felt vaguely dissatisfied. The girl had the best motive so far, but she had all the answers too. According to her anyone who could get into the house could have done it. The dog was shut off, the stockings in full view from the upper hall. But an outsider would have to get into the house, and apparently all doors and windows had been found locked that morning. He got up. The smell of coffee from below reminded him he had had no breakfast.

"I guess that'll do for now," he said. "There's a police sergeant upstairs, but he won't bother you. Just keep out of your mother's room. That's all."

He went out to the front door. A dozen reporters and cameramen were there, and beyond them the usual curious onlookers. To escape the crowd he let the newsmen into the hall. He knew most of them and liked them. Also they knew it was probably his last case. They did not push him. They stood and waited.

"It's like this, boys," he said. "Mrs. Ingalls was strangled somewhere about three this morning. That's what the medical examiner thinks, anyhow. If it was attempted burglary something scared the killer off. Nothing was taken. She was an invalid. Apparently she didn't put up much of a fight. Nothing more so far."

They grumbled a bit. They knew most of that already, so they fired innumerable questions at him. How had the intruder got in? Who was in the house at the time? Were there any prints? How was she strangled? At the last one he put a hand uneasily in his pocket, but no part of the stocking showed. And he had removed the one left in the bathroom. He knew their sharp eyes would discover it. In the end he let them go upstairs, on condition nothing was touched or moved.

"Keep an eye on them, Joe," he called up the stairs. "Only the one room. No place else up there, and give them half an hour. That's enough."

One of the men did not go up at once, however. He was an older man, and he watched the others out of sight. Then he turned to Brent.

"Bad luck, Inspector," he said. "The Commissioner has

been on your neck for a long time. Unless you get a break on this it means trouble."

Brent nodded.

"I've got to get one," he said. "Just now I've given you about all I have. It isn't much."

The reporter hesitated. Then:

"I'd hate like hell to see you reduced before you retire," he said. "He'd like nothing better. You've been too good. That's his trouble. And the press likes you. It hates his guts. And he knows it. Would mean a cut in your pension, too. If I can do anything . . ."

"Thanks. I'll call on you if I need to, Clarke. I—I appreciate your interest. You know that."

He felt depressed as he watched Clarke go up the stairs. It was true and he knew it. Ever since the new commissioner took office he had resented him. It was notorious at headquarters. Probably it was because there had been talk that Brent would get the job. After all he had been almost forty years in the service, and the newspapers had been for him. But it was a political plum, and so he lost out.

He grunted and turning to the back of the house went down to the basement kitchen. He did not expect to get any information there, however. He had already interrogated the Filipino cook, now busy over the range, and he was the only servant who slept in. The other, a woman, came by the day, and had not yet appeared. And the Filipino, after the impassive quality of his race, had been of no use whatever. His room was on the third floor back. He had heard no noise, except once about three o'clock when he had heard the dog scratching at the door on the landing. And he had been the one to notify the police after he heard the girl screaming at seven that morning and had investigated.

Brent sat down on a kitchen chair and rested his feet.

"I'll have some of that coffee," he said. "It smells good. I missed my breakfast."

"Is ready, sir."

The man brought a cup and filled it. He put sugar and cream beside it, and went back to the stove.

"Tell me something, Miguel," Brent said. "You heard Miss

Ingalls screaming and found her in her mother's room. Had she moved the body? Or touched it?"

"I think no. No time. She say she touch a hand, and it is cold. She scream for me and I go up. She act faint, so I put her in a chair and run to telephone."

"Could you see what had killed Mrs. Ingalls?"

"Not then, sir. All covered up. After the police came I see. It was a stocking of Mrs. Ingalls."

Brent finished his coffee and felt somewhat better. The Scotty barked at the door to the yard, and Miguel let him in. He dropped what he was carrying and proceeded to rub his whiskers on the floor. But the linoleum did not help him. He came to Brent trustfully and scraped against his trouser leg. Brent leaned over and scratched his ears.

"Anything to oblige a friend!" he said. "What's that he brought in, Miguel?"

"Just a cork. He bury, then he dig up. Is a nuisance, that dog."

He picked up the cork and threw it in the garbage pail. After that he washed his hands and went back to the tray he was preparing. Brent watched him. There seemed no reason to suspect him. He was probably losing a good job at high wages.

"How come you're the only help in the house?" he inquired. "It's a big one."

"No other servants to be had. I been here a long time. Now I get extra pay so I stay."

"That makes sense," Brent said casually. "What kind of woman was Mrs. Ingalls? Easy to work for?"

"Not good, not bad." The man gave a faint smile. "You think I kill her, maybe? Why I go to the chair for her?"

It was logical, of course, provided the Oriental had not gone berserk in the night. Those fellows did that sometimes. But it was hard to imagine Miguel, in his clean white coat, going berserk at any time. When the Filipino started upstairs with the tray he followed. As he left, the little dog was digging frantically in the garbage pail.

The pair in the library were much as he had left them. Apparently Joe had got rid of the press, for the house was quiet again. Brent stood at a window while the girl drank some black coffee. Then he turned.

"Let's go back over this, Miss Ingalls," he said. "How about yesterday? What happened before Townsend had the fuss with your mother? How did she seem?"

Joy put down her cup. There was a little color in her face now.

"She seemed better," she said. "She came down to tea when my cousin Harry Ingalls brought his new wife to see her. They're on their honeymoon. Ken was here. He saw them."

"And after that your mother and Mr. Townsend had some words?"

"Yes. He didn't like Maud. She's the wife, and—"

"Maud," said young Townsend succintly, "is a cheap Chicago tart. He had no business bringing her here."

"And that led to the fuss?"

"Well, not exactly. He wanted to take me out last night, and she objected. That was really it."

"And I didn't like Harry," said young Townsend. "He's been hanging on her for years. Even lived here for a while. They came here for money yesterday, and they sure as hell got it. When I came in he was putting a check in his wallet."

"It's no good to them, now that Mrs. Ingalls is dead. They couldn't cash it last night."

"No. It's the only satisfaction I've got out of the whole murderous business."

So that canceled Harry and Maud, Brent thought stoically as he got into his car and headed downtown. And it sounded innocuous enough. Two people came in for tea, or highballs, or what have you. They had just been married, and they got a check for a wedding present. Maybe the bride was a wrong one, but how account for a man's tastes?

Nevertheless, because it was the only lead he had, he decided to visit the honeymoon couple. Joy had said they were staying at the Davis House, and he headed in that direction. He knew it looked like an inside job, and that everything pointed to the girl. But he felt more than reluctant to turn her over to the wolves at headquarters. Especially to the Commissioner. Everything else aside, it was a bad time to do it. Everyone in the organization knew he was working on his annual report to the

Mayor, which always left him in a villainous humor.

He did not want to see him himself. He could visualize him behind his big desk, red-faced and scowling, if he appeared there. He would sit glaring at him.

"Don't be a fool, Brent. This is your last case and it better be good. The girl did it, and you know it. Or else she let the Townsend fellow into the house and he did it. In either case, she's guilty as hell."

Yes, it would be like that, he thought, steering his way through traffic. And what could he say? That the girl was young and tragic, that she reminded him of the daughter he had lost? That it took a strong hand to strangle so quickly that the body and bed were barely disturbed. The Commissioner wouldn't even listen. He could almost hear his raucous voice.

"Get her down here, Brent. If you don't, I'll take the case away from you. I'm no fool about a pretty face. She had all the motives, the money and the fellow she wanted to marry. And don't think she couldn't do it. These modern girls are strong. They play tennis and golf. By God, my own daughter can throw a baseball harder than I can."

He would know about the stocking, too. Brent put his hand in his pocket. It was still there, and still damp. It had been a smart move, using that stocking, if the girl was innocent. Maybe it had only been added later after the woman was dead. He'd have to ask the medical examiner about that.

He did not stop for breakfast, although he felt empty and his feet hurt like blazes. He drove directly to the Davis House, which proved to be a third-class commercial hotel, with Harry Ingalls and wife registered as on the third floor. He went up without being announced and looked for their number. The long hall was shabbily carpeted and empty, except that at the end a trained nurse in uniform was smoking a surreptitious cigarette at a window. Outside the Ingalls door he paused. There was acrimonious talking going on inside the room, but he could not hear what it was about.

The voices ceased when he rapped, and a sharp woman's voice spoke through the door.

"We're not ready yet, porter. I told you half an hour."

He rapped again and the door was flung open. A small redheaded girl with hard eyes confronted him and stared at him.

"Who the hell are you?" she demanded.

"I'd like to talk to Mr. Ingalls," he said. "I'm afraid I have bad news for him."

"You're telling me!" she retorted. "With a check in my bag that's no damned good! Come in if you like. He knows about his aunt. This cheap dump supplies radios."

The room was a mess. Half-packed bags lay on the unmade twin beds, and the girl herself looked as though she had merely crawled out of bed, thrown on a negligee and let it go at that. Even so, with the remains of yesterday's make-up still on her face, she had a pert sort of prettiness. She had a backless evening dress without sleeves over her arm. She flung it on a chair and eyed him.

"All right," she said. "We know it. So what?"

Brent did not reply. He was looking at Harry Ingalls, a tall scrawny man with a weak chin, just now covered with lather as if the news had come while he was shaving. He was pale, and he looked shocked. He did not get up from his chair. And the girl spoke for him.

"He's kinda shot," said the girl. "His own aunt! And that check was to get us out of this hole and home again. I've been to the cashier downstairs, but they know she's dead. They won't cash it."

"Bad news all around, isn't it, Mr. Ingalls?" Brent inquired. "I suppose you were fond of your aunt?"

"Doted on her," said the girl. "Like a mother to him, she was."

"Why don't you let him speak for himself," Brent inquired mildly. "All right, Mr. Ingalls. You saw your aunt yesterday?"

Ingalls moved. He lit a cigarette, but his hands were shaking.

"Sorry," he said. "I've had a blow. She was all right yesterday. Never saw her better. Who are you, anyhow? Should I know you?"

"I'm a police officer," Brent told him. "I'll have to ask you both a few questions. As the last people to see her—"

"Not the last," interposed the redhead. "That stuck-up daughter of hers. She was there last night too when it happened, wasn't she?"

"She was, but as a matter of fact daughters don't often murder their mothers," Brent said, still mildly.

"Oh, don't they? You'd be surprised!"

"Shut up, Maud." Harry Ingalls had pulled himself together. He got up, he wiped the lather off his chin, cleared a chair and asked Brent to sit down.

"I'll be glad to help you," he said. "I was fond of her. She'd always been good to me. Don't mind if I take a drink, do you? I'm not feeling too good. Maybe you'll have a snort yourself."

Brent declined, and Harry Ingalls poured himself a substantial whisky out of a half-empty bottle. With the glass in his hand he gave the Inspector a long look.

"What are you?" he said. "Captain, Lieutenant? I don't know much about the police."

Brent took out the folder with his badge pinned to it and showed it to him. Ingalls whistled.

"High brass, eh?" he said. "Well, sorry if I acted upset, Inspector. I just got the news."

"Very understandable," Brent told him. "As I said, this is only a matter of routine. But I'd like to know your movements last night. That's my job, you know."

"Last night?" Ingalls stared at the ceiling. "Well, I had that check in my pocket, so we blew ourselves to a large evening; dinner in the Rose Room at the Belmont and a show afterwards. I expect I've got the ticket stubs somewhere."

"And after that?"

"Home here and to bed. After all, when a man's on his honeymoon . . ."

He grinned, but Brent eyed him steadily.

"Know what time you got in?" he inquired.

"About half-past eleven, wasn't it, Maud?"

Maud lit a cigarette before she answered, indifferently.

"I ain't got a watch, but it was early. I wanted to go somewhere and dance, but Harry said he was tired."

It sounded all right, but Brent was taking nothing for granted. He was still watching Harry.

"I suppose the night clerk saw you come in?"

"Maybe, maybe not. The way this place is run . . . Say, what is this, anyhow? Can't a fellow take his bride out for an evening without being suspected for murder?"

"I didn't say you were suspected of murder," Brent said smoothly. "But just to be sure I'd better have those ticket stubs."

Harry looked startled. Then he smiled. "Sure," he said. "We were there all right. Look in my dinner coat, honey."

Maud found the stubs and brought them. After that she poured herself a drink and sat down on one of the beds. Brent put the stubs in his wallet, although he had no reason to question them. In fact, these people puzzled him. And Maud was looking entirely confident.

"If you're after an alibi," she said, "we were here all night. And we can prove it. Just ask the night nurse next door. When I took in our breakfast this morning she was just going off duty."

Brent eyed the room again. Both beds had been slept in. There was nothing to disprove their story, and he felt fairly sure the night nurse in question would corroborate it. Rather unwillingly he got up.

"I guess that's all then. But I advise you not to go to the house yet. Miss Ingalls is pretty much upset. And I'll have to ask you to stay in town for a day or two. Sorry to keep you."

"Not too long," Maud said. "Without that money we're busted."

But Brent sensed relief in her voice. He stopped in the doorway, his hand on the knob.

"How long have you been here?" he asked.

"Three days, and that's plenty," the girl said sourly. "Now we're stuck in this hole, unless they throw us out."

She slammed the door behind him, but he did not leave immediately. The nurse was no longer in the hall, and after a moment he tapped at the door of the next room. When she opened it he beckoned her outside. She looked suspicious, but she came.

"Look," she said. "I'm busy. What's it all about?"

"Not you, sister," he told her. "I just want the name and address of the night nurse on your case. The one who was here last night. Do you know it?"

"Sure I do. But she'll be asleep. Don't you go waking her.

And while you're at it I wish you'd shut up those people next door. Report it at the desk, or something. My patient's going crazy. Fighting like mad, and the radio going at the same time."

"Know what they were fighting about?" he inquired.

"I couldn't hear much. I think she wanted to leave, and he didn't. That's all I got."

She gave him the night nurse's address, on the promise to let her get some sleep first, and he went rather unhappily down to the lobby. Here, however he had no luck at all. The night clerk was off duty, and he had recently moved. Nobody knew where he lived.

Back in his car again he pondered his next move. So far the Harry Ingallses had accounted for their time shrewdly unless the night nurse could prove that one or both of them had gone out again after they came home. He could send one of his men to see her, of course, but he preferred to do it himself. She might be important. Or again she might not. It seemed a slim thread to hang a case on.

But he had the usual policeman's aversion to a perfect alibi, and already he knew that the Ingallses had not been entirely truthful with him. They were planning to leave when the radio told them of the murder. That did not argue that they had no money. Then why the beef? Unless the check . . .

He thought that over. Suppose they expected to get a considerable sum by Mrs. Ingalls' will? That would take time and the inability to cash the check would be a part of their defense. Why kill a woman when she meant badly needed cash in hand to you?

There was just a chance the night nurse would break their alibi, and rather reluctantly he turned his car downtown. The girl could have had only an hour or two of sleep. But murder could not wait. Twenty minutes later he drew up in front of a small walk-up apartment. He climbed to the fourth floor, and after repeated knocking was confronted by a sleepy and highly irritated young woman in a negligee over a nightdress. He did not tell her his business. He merely showed her his badge and asked if she had seen anyone from the room next door while she was on duty at the hotel the night before. She was slightly mollified and certainly curious.

"If you mean the redhead, I saw her this morning. What about her?"

"That's all you saw? Nobody left or came into the room during the night?"

"Not a soul. And believe you me, I was there. You don't know my patient."

Brent was a modest man. He looked uncomfortable.

"But see here," he said. "You must have needed to—well, to powder your nose, or something. You were on duty eight hours, weren't you?"

"Sure," she told him. "The day nurse is on from eight in the morning until four P.M. The family takes over until midnight."

"The family?" he said. "Know where I could locate them?"

"All over town. Uncles, aunts, cousins, sons and daughters. It's not a family. It's a population."

It looked hopeless. If Harry and Maud came back before twelve o'clock . . .

"So you never left your post for eight hours?" he said, avoiding her eyes. But she only laughed at his discomfiture.

"So I did. I'm human. I powder my nose every now and then. But before I leave that door for any purpose I have to ring for a bellboy and put him there. My patient's a nervous case She won't let me lock her in before I go, and she won't be left with the door unfastened. So I get a bellboy and he gets a dollar. If it's over two dollars a night she raises the roof."

Brent retired, somewhat flushed and certainly discomfited. So far as he could see the case was going to pieces under his feet. Undoubtedly the bellboy would be off duty for the day. Only the Belmont was left. He expected nothing from it and he was not disappointed. Evidently Maud had made an impression on the head waiter, who in shirt sleeves was overseeing the preparations for lunch in the main dining room.

"Redhead in a black dress," he said, "and a tall lanky fellow with no chin? Sure, I remember them. They had table twenty-nine. Girl was a looker, all right. Man didn't eat much but drank a lot. First cocktails, then champagne. Carried it pretty well, though."

So that part of the alibi was all right, although Maud and

Harry Ingalls spending their last cent for champagne was curious. Still some people lived that way, he thought, from hand to mouth although he and Emma, saving every cent for years for the chicken farm, would find it difficult to understand. Chickens! he thought, and tried to put them out of his mind.

He looked at his watch. He had had no breakfast. And this was as good a place as any to get it. The grill would be open, and it was not expensive. First, however, he called Joe at the Ingalls' house. The sergeant himself answered the phone.

"How's everything?" Brent inquired.

Joe lowered his voice.

"Bad for a while. Girl had a hysterical fit. She's over it now. All right to let her put on some clothes?"

"So long as she keeps out of that room."

"I got both doors locked," Joe said laconically.

"Anybody try to get in?"

"Only the dog. He's scratched at the door once or twice. The Filipino's kind of hanging around, keeping an eye on the girl. And the fellow's gone. Townsend. Went about half an hour ago."

"That all?"

"Well," Joe said with obvious reluctance. "The Commissioner's been on the phone. He didn't sound too good. I told him I'd have you call him soon as I heard from you."

"Then you haven't heard from me," Brent said and hung up.

He went down to the grill and ordered a substantial breakfast. He never had worked well on an empty stomach, and he needed food before he called the Commissioner. So far he had got exactly nowhere. He was hot, too, and his feet were still bothering him. He reached down to unlace his shoes, and found the left side of his trousers sticking to his hand. He bent over and examined the spot. He could see nothing, but he could feel it, a long smear that felt like molasses.

It puzzled him. It was a fresh suit; Emma had sponged and pressed it the day before. Where and how had he got it? He was still wondering about it when he felt a hand on his shoulder.

"Hello," said a voice. "Thought you were counting eggs somewhere in the country."

It was Carver, the hotel detective. Brent glanced up at him.

"That's next week," he said drily. "Still stooging for divorce cases?"

These courtesies exchanged, Carver grinned and sat down.

"Understand you're on the Ingalls murder," he said. "What was it? Robbery?"

"Nothing taken. Might have been scared off, of course."

The waiter brought Brent's breakfast at that moment, and Carver glanced at it and grinned.

"Ham and eggs and rolls," he said. "Funny. What would you say about a man who ordered that same breakfast up in his room and then hid it in the tank of the toilet in his bathroom. Sounds crazy, doesn't it?"

"Probably is crazy," Brent said indifferently. "Still there? Better keep an eye on him if he is."

"Gone. Checked out right after. Left fifty cents on the tray for the waiter, too. Can you beat it?"

Brent however was not interested. He ate hastily, knowing he would have to call headquarters when he finished. Carver talked on but he hardly heard him. It was almost twelve when he looked at his watch, paid his check and got up.

"Better follow that fellow up," he said. "He might be dangerous."

He left Carver there and went to a telephone booth. As he had expected the Commissioner's voice was a blast in his ear.

"Where the devil have you been?" he roared. "This place is busy with reporters. What do you mean, hiding out when all hell's breaking loose around here?"

"I've been working. After all I haven't had much time."

"You've had time to call me. Now see here, Brent, I want that girl down here for questioning, and I want her soon. I want the man too. Townsend. He's in it up to his neck."

"It may take a little time," Brent said, thinking fast and ignoring what Joe had told him. "She'll have to get some clothes on. And she's in poor shape, too. Give me a couple of hours."

"Make it an hour if you can," said the Commissioner, and banged down the receiver.

Brent hung up slowly. There was an implied threat in what had been said. Do it and do it fast or else, was what it meant. He was to take the girl down, to be mentally drawn and quartered, to be screamed about in the press, and to have the stigma of the interrogation to follow her the rest of her life. Or he would be demoted, even broken.

He thought of the future, of his pension cut, of Emma's chickens, his own plan for a kennel. He even had a plan for one in his desk, the runways were to be painted green outside and whitewashed inside. Then he walked slowly out to his car and down to the Ingalls house.

The patrolman was still there on the pavement, trying to marshal the crowd.

"Keep moving," he was saying monotonously. "Nothing to see. Keep moving."

Brent nodded to him and went inside. Joe was at the top of the stairs, and he went up to him.

"Anything new?" he inquired.

"The laboratory reported. No prints in the room except the woman's and the daughter's. The doc says plain strangulation. That's all so far."

"Where's the girl?"

"Downstairs. Townsend hasn't come back."

He found Joy in the library. She had put on a black dress and touched up her lips. And in spite of reddened eyes she looked very pretty. Very pretty and very innocent, Brent thought. She even tried to smile when she saw him.

"Ken went to get a lawyer," she said. "He seems to think I need one. That's silly, isn't it?"

"Well, it won't do any harm," Brent said guardedly. "Fact is Commissioner wants to talk to you. Might be as well to have somebody around to look after you."

She looked appalled.

"The Commissioner! Then they think I did it!"

"Not necessarily," Brent said stoutly. "Just a few questions. That's all. Better get your hat, or whatever you girls wear these days. I'll take you down."

He watched her as she went out. Maybe she played golf and tennis. Maybe she could throw a baseball hard and fast. But to think of her killing her mother was as impossible as to see her in a chair at headquarters, surrounded by hard-faced men firing question after question at her. He lit a cigarette and wandered unhappily back to the dining room window. The Scottie was again in the yard, but he was not digging. He was sniffing at the hole from which he had retrieved the cork. All at once Brent remembered the little dog wiping his nose on his trouser leg, and he went down the back stairs and into the kitchen. The Filipino gave him an unpleasant look.

"How long we have police hanging around here?" he demanded.

"Not long, I hope," Brent told him. "Where's that cork he carried in?"

"He take it out again."

Brent went out into the yard. The Scottie was still sniffing around the hole, and Brent bent down and dug his fingers into it. The dog grumbled and nosed at him angrily.

"It's all right, old boy," Brent told him. "I got business here."

For already he had found the *cache* from which the cork had come. It was a small bottle, and whatever had been in it had leaked out. Brent sniffed at it, and then put a finger inside. He stared at his hand and whistled. Then he carried the bottle into the kitchen.

"Ever see this before?" he asked.

The Filipino looked at it and shook his head.

"No see," he said laconically. "Not mine."

Brent dropped it in his pocket and went rapidly up the stairs. Joe was sitting in a hall chair, half asleep, and the girl was moving about in her room. He roused the man with a touch.

"When she comes out tell her I've gone, but I'll be back in a few minutes," he whispered. "Where's the key to the room?"

Joe gave it to him, and he slipped quietly through the door, closing it behind him. The room was as he had left it. The bed still bore the imprint of the dead woman's body, but careful examination revealed nothing else. Brent straightened and surveyed the room itself. It was elaborate, with its taffeta hangings, its handsome toilet set on the dressing table, and the *chaise longue* with a half dozen lace-trimmed pillows.

Except for traces of print powder apparently nothing had been disturbed. It was the room of a woman accustomed to comfort, even luxury. And almost certainly *Social Register*. No wonder the Commissioner was having a fit, he thought drily.

But he did not give up easily. He heard the girl go down the stairs, and Joe tell her he was out. Then very cautiously he got down on his knees and examined the floor. It looked hopeless. The heavy pile of the carpet had been disturbed by many feet, and his eyes were not as good as they had been.

He had accumulated quite a bit of dust and he was sweating profusely when at last he drew a small magnifying glass from his pocket and went over the floor inch by inch. It was slow work. He had left his flashlight in the car, and the light was not too good. Nevertheless he found one or two almost infinitesimal objects and put them carefully into an envelope in his pocket. He was looking more cheerful when he went out into the hall.

"Girl's gone down," Joe said. "Do I get lunch, or don't I?"

"Try working on the Filipino," Brent told him heartlessly. "Perhaps he'll feed you. Just sit tight for a while, Joe. Maybe it won't be long before this thing's sewed up."

Joe glanced at him.

"I sure hope so. It's likely to be your last case. Only I hope it's not the girl. She's a nice kid."

Brent went down the stairs. His feet did not hurt him any more, or at least he did not notice them. There was almost a spring in his walk. From the voices in the library he judged that young Townsend had returned, but he did not go there at once. Instead, and breathing hard, he made for the telephone; called Carver at the Belmont.

That gentleman seemed annoyed when he heard his voice.

"Look, Brent," he said. "I was at my lunch. What's eating you anyhow?"

"It's about the fellow who hid his breakfast this morning," Brent said. "Got any idea who he was?"

"Sure I have. Name's Somers. Comes from Cincinnati. As if I care!"

"You said he wore a goatee, didn't you?"

"I did. I was curious about the guy. Gray hair, moustache and a goatee, according to the chambermaid. What makes, Brent?"

"Don't know yet. When did he leave?"

"I told you that. Between eight and nine this morning. Only here one night."

"How about his room? Has it been cleaned yet?"

"God knows," Carver said. "With these conventions and service what it is . . ."

"Well, see here, Carver. Do something for me, will you? Go up yourself and lock it. I don't want it touched."

"Ha! Getting interested, are you? What's happened? Commissioner take you off the other case?"

"He's going to, in about an hour."

"Like that, is it? I'm sorry, Brent. Well, what if the room's already done. Still interested?"

"Lock it anyhow. I'll be there as soon as I can make it."

Back in the library he faced an enraged young man, with his fists clenched and his face flushed with fury. Joy Ingalls, wearing a hat and coat and looking more frightened than ever, had evidently been trying to calm him. Townsend whirled when he heard him.

"You're not getting away with this," he shouted. "She's not going downtown to be interrogated. She's not going anywhere. And if you try to pull a fast one I'll forget your age and give you something you won't forget in a hurry."

Brent winced not at the prospect of a beating, but at this reference to his age. Perhaps a little of his exuberance died. His voice however remained mild.

"How about taking her to lunch at the Belmont?" he said. "Find a quiet corner, so people won't notice her, and give her a drink. I expect she needs it."

Townsend looked astonished.

"The Belmont? But I thought—"

"Never mind what you thought. Do what I tell you. I'll drop you there if you like. Any back way out of this house? There's a crowd and a patrolman out front."

"There's an alley," Joy said. "We can go out through the yard."

Townsend was still not convinced, however.

"If this is a trick," he said, "what I said before goes. And then some."

"No trick, son," Brent said blandly. "I'll meet you down the street at the corner. And it's the Belmont. Nowhere else."

He called up the stairs to Joe.

"We're going out. I'm taking Miss Ingalls downtown," he said. "Through the yard. There's a crowd in front." And he added rather wryly, "If there are any messages just hold them. I'll be back."

"They'll murder her at headquarters," Joe said somberly. "Before they're through with her she'll think she did it in her sleep."

Brent grinned, and going back to his little party led the way down the stairs to the kitchen. There he confronted an outraged Oriental with a large carving knife in his hand.

"You take her to jail?" he demanded.

"Don't be a fool, Miguel," Brent told him. "They're going out to lunch. Only I don't want it known. If anybody asks where they are you haven't seen them. That clear?"

Even then he might not have got away with it except for Joy. She put a hand on his arm and smiled at the Filipino.

"That's right, Miguel," she said. "The Inspector's our friend." She turned trusting eyes on Brent. "That's true, isn't it?"

He nodded. It was true. It was as true as hell. He felt like a man on a wire over Niagara Falls with all he had to help him an infinitesimal scrap in his pocket and a vague hope he could get across. But he managed to smile.

"Out with you," he told them. "I'll pick you up in a minute or so."

He watched them go. The Scotty tried to follow them, and they had to send him back. He waited while the little animal trotted resentfully to the house. Then he turned to the Filipino.

"If you're the lad I think you are," he said, "you'll give that dog the best meal he ever had." But he added, "Or choke him to death. He may have cost me my job."

The crowd on the street had largely dispersed. He sent the precinct man away and got into his car. He had a picture in his mind of the Commissioner waiting behind his desk instead of eating his usual hearty lunch at the club. He felt a trifle sick at the thought, but he had gone all out now. Either his hunch was right or it was dead wrong. If it was wrong . . .

He picked up two dazed young people at the corner and drove them rapidly toward the Belmont. Behind him they were quiet, as though they were still bewildered. Young Townsend spoke to him once, however.

"I'd like to know what's changed your mind, sir," he said to Brent's back. "If you don't mind saying."

Brent negotiated a corner before he answered. Then: "It's like this, son," he said. "I've been in the service a long time, and you get to know people that way. You learn to listen when they talk, and you learn to know what they can do and what they can't. I nearly slipped up this morning because I didn't listen when I should have."

"That's the hell of an answer," said Ken, and relapsed into silence.

He left them in the lobby of the hotel and went to Carver's office. Carver was smoking an after-lunch cigar and he eyed Brent curiously.

"Room's the way he left it. Want me to take you up?"

"It's not necessary. All I need is the key."

Carver gave it to him, but he was still inquisitive.

"I've been up. There's nothing there, Brent."

"Maybe. Maybe not," Brent said. "If you want to be useful, get a descripton of Mr. Somers. How he acted. If the waiter saw him. What luggage he had. Anything you can pick up."

"I told you a lot of that before."

"Sorry. I had other things to think about just then."

"I noticed." Carver grinned. "Your feet, wasn't it?"

Brent left that unanswered, and went upstairs. The room when he entered it had obviously not been touched. Only in the bathroom two large soggy rolls and a substantial slice of ham had been removed from the tank and placed on top of the porcelain washstand. Brent examined them and left them where they were. But he gave the washstand itself a good going over before he abandoned it.

The room itself offered nothing at first. The ashtrays had not been used, but a burnt match on a window sill indicated that Mr. Somers had just possibly emptied them out the window. Brent opened it and looked out. The hotel doorman was standing just beneath. And he permitted himself a wry smile. He wondered what would have happened had Somers attempted to dump his breakfast the same way.

He went over the bedroom carefully. The bureau showed no use whatever. If the late occupant had emptied his pockets before he went to bed, or even placed a pair of brushes on it, there was no sign of it on its virginal cover. But Brent wasted no time on it. He went to the bed and stood looking down at it. It was unused, as though some one had lain in it, but the creases were rather shallow. Mr. Somers had not slept hard, or long. Then he struck gold. He moved a pillow and there it was. It was his case. All he had to do now was to prove it.

He knew how and why Mrs. Ingalls had been murdered. He was fairly sure who had done it, and he was confident that if his evidence held up the girl would not be arrested. But he grunted as he prepared to leave. It was up to the Commissioner now, and to his co-operation. Or was it? Perhaps he could go a step farther first.

He called Carver on the house telephone and instructed him that the room was to be left as it was. Then, locking the door behind him, he went down to the elevator and stopped at the desk.

"Will you see if you have a card for an F. C. Somers, from Cincinnati?" he asked the clerk. "Think he checked out this morning."

The clerk grinned.

"Fellow who dumped his breakfast in the can?" he said. "What do you want to know? He left this morning about eight, traveling light on a cup of coffee."

"When did he get here?"

"Last night, about nine-thirty. Carver's been looking up his card, so I know. Some asylum looking for him?"

"Remember what he looked like? He must have paid his bill."

The clerk looked bored.

"Look, Inspector," he said, "we had two conventions here. One of them came in last night. One left this morning. How in blazes could either the cashier or I remember that fellow. His card says he paid for one night in advance, so he probably had no luggage. That's all I know."

Nor was the waiter who had taken up the breakfast any help. Mr. Somers apparently had been in the shower when he got there. The hall door was open, so he merely left the tray. He hadn't noticed anything later when he went back for it. The money for the check was on it. And a half-dollar tip. Somers had gone. But the waiter had seen one thing. There had been a small black overnight bag on the bed.

"And that's all?" Brent inquired. "There was no other luggage?"

"That's all I seen, mister."

He gave the man a dollar and went to the dining room. Ken and Joy were still at the table. They had found an inconspicuous one in a corner, and were quite openly holding hands.

"Just a question or two and I'll let you go," he said. "Either of you been to any masquerade parties lately? Where you had to dress up, and so on." The speech was to them both, but it was Townsend he watched. And it was he who replied.

"Not since college," he said. "And that wasn't a party. It was a play. What's the idea, Inspector?"

"How long ago was that?"

"Seven or eight years ago. There's been a war since, I seem to remember."

Joy, when queried, had never been to anything of the sort. Brent had an idea that parties of any sort had played a small part in her life. He smiled at her and got up.

"Just thought I'd inquire," he said. "You may be asked that later on. It's all right. Don't worry." He got stiffly to his feet. Damn a man's knees. First his feet go, then his knees. Maybe Emma was right, and he ought to go to church oftener. Keep them exercised. He glanced down at the young couple.

"Just stick around," he told them. "If the waiter gets upset wait on the mezzanine. I'll be back. I may be a little while."

Ken had risen when he did.

"Does this mean . . . ?" But Brent shook his head.

"Listen," he said, "I don't know what the hell it means. Not for sure. But I've got an angle and I'm following it up."

He glanced at his watch after he left them. His two hours

were up and he hoped to God someone had brought the Commissioner his lunch. Or at least coffee and a doughnut. He could not hope for anything more.

He needed a wash and a brush-up, but there was no time for either. As he got into his car he felt the stubble on his face, and that his collar was soaked with perspiration, and as he felt the familiar wheel under his hands he realized that he would not have it very long. He felt a real affection for it. There was a bullet hole in one of the doors, where he had almost lost his life a year or so ago, and the glass had been replaced more than once. He would miss it, he thought. It had been a part of him for several years.

He grunted, and before he drove off he unlocked the glove compartment and took out his police positive. He examined it and put it back again. He did not like carrying a gun, and this time he did not think he would need it. Still it was best to be sure it was around.

After that he drove to the theatrical district, and to a certain part of it. The traffic was heavy there, however, and after a time he parked the car by a fire hydrant and saved time by making his rounds on foot.

However, his feet were agonizing and he had visited a half dozen places before he found what he was looking for. He took out the bottle he had found in the garden and showed it to the man in charge. The label was gone, but the druggist recognized it at once.

"Sure," he said. "Handled it for years. Not much doing this time of year though. Not the season."

"Sold any the last day or two?"

"Sold one yesterday, as a matter of fact," he acknowledged. "Just remembered. Girl bought it. Kinda funny, too. Most of our customers for it are men."

He could not describe the girl, however. It had been raining, and she had sort of waterproof hood effect over her head.

"Think she had a fellow with her," he said. "He didn't come in, though. Just hung around outside. Maybe it was for him."

Unfortunately he had not noticed the man, except that he was tall, and Brent could get no more out of it. His evidence, he realized, could fit Joy Ingalls and even young

Townsend. And as a result he was depressed as he went back to his car. There was a young traffic man standing beside it, near one of the back fenders, with a pad in his hand.

"Just in case you don't know much about our fair city," he said acidly, "this hydrant is intended for the sole use of the neighborhood dogs and incidentally the fire department."

"Smart, aren't you?" Brent said. "Well, brother, if you want to stay in that uniform you'd better look at the bumper of this car. You'll find a little shield on it which says P.D. And it doesn't mean pretty damn funny either."

He left the traffic man looking about to faint and drove away. He was tired to the point of exhaustion, his time was up long ago. And he had a strong conviction that even coffee and doughnuts—if he had got them—would not take the place with the Commissioner of his usual substantial meal.

Certainly it was no time to see him. He drove around uncertainly, thinking of Emma and what he would tell her. One thing he was sure, she wouldn't get her chickens, although why any one wanted to keep them puzzled him. You couldn't talk to a hen, or take her for a walk. Or even watch her bury a bottle. Which last brought him back to his problem again. Somehow, the night before, Harry Ingalls had got out of the Davis House and strangled his aunt. He knew it, but he could not prove it. And he had lost time. If he had only paid any real attention to Carver that morning it would have helped, but he had been busy with his feet and the smear on his trouser leg.

"Gray-haired guy," Carver had said. "Wore a goatee, too. Only a fellow with a weak chin wears a thing like that."

Fool that he was, it was not until he had found the bottle of spirit gum that he had remembered and knew what it might mean; that some one, preferably Harry Ingalls, had built up a beard to cover something, probably a receding chin, put on a gray wig and almost certainly got away with murder.

His mind went back to the untidy room at the Davis House. They couldn't have burned the stuff there. It would have smelled to high heaven. But he was confident it had been Harry at the Belmont. Harry whose bits of glued beard had come off in the hotel bed as it had on his aunt's carpet. Harry, who afraid of losing his disguise, had carried the bottle of spirit gum in his pocket and lost it. And Harry who, completely unnerved by what he had done, had been unable to eat his breakfast and in a fit of desperation had put it in the tank.

He must have been in a bad way to do the idiotic thing he had done. But at least it had given him time to dispose of the bag and its contents, and to take his shattered nerves back to Maud who had no nerves whatever. Where had he made the shift, he wondered. There were thousands of places, men's rooms anywhere, comfort stations, even a back alley. But perhaps he had kept the bag. In that case . . .

He did not go to the Davis House at once. He stopped at the Belmont to go to the mezzanine and discover Joy sitting alone and Townsend pacing the floor impatiently. He sat down beside the girl to notice that she was quietly crying. He reached over and took her hand.

"I'm sorry, my dear," he told her. "These things happen, and after all death comes to all of us, sooner or later."

"Not like that," she said brokenly. "And Ken thinks I did it. Not intentionally, but that's what he thinks. Ask him if you don't believe me."

He glanced at Ken. That young gentleman was carefully avoiding him. He stood at the edge of the balcony gazing at the crowd below, and his tall body looked sagged, as though the youthful exuberance had gone out of it.

"What do you mean, not intentionally?" he asked.

"He asked me if I ever walked in my sleep," she said. "I used to, when I was a child. I told him that, and he's been queer and sort of upset ever since. You see, the house being locked and all that—"

"I'll talk to him," Brent told her. "I don't think you did, and I'm the one who matters."

He got the name of the family lawyer from her before he walked over to Townsend and touched him on the shoulder.

"You young fool," he said. "What's the idea of scaring the girl into a fit? She didn't do it, in her sleep or any other way."

The younger man brightened.

"Oh, God," he said. "Am I glad to hear that! I've been going slowly crazy. She's such a gentle little thing, but the way her mother treated her . . ."

"Forget it," Brent told him briefly. "Go over there and get down on your knees and apologize. And stick around a little longer. I want to know where you are."

Down on the main floor, however, he had a shock. The reporter, Clarke, was standing there, staring up at the gallery. He grinned when he saw Brent.

"I don't get it," he said. "That's no place to hide the girl. I suppose you know there's an alarm out for her. And headquarters is a madhouse. The Commissioner—"

"Listen, Clarke," Brent said. "Give me an hour or two, won't you? She's staying there, so you won't miss anything."

"So you're onto something," Clarke said shrewdly. "Well, so long as I'm in on it I can walk. What have you been doing with yourself? Rolling in the gutter?"

But Brent was in a hurry. He started off, then turned.

"If you're a friend of mine," he said, "you'll see that some one sends the Commissioner his lunch. It might help some."

Clarke grinned again.

"Last time I saw him he was hurling doughnuts out the window," he said. "All right. I'm all for you. But you'd better make it snappy. He's watching the clock."

Brent caught a glimpse of himself in a mirror before he left the hotel. He was dirty and unshaven, and his trousers were a disgrace. Moreover he found himself limping, as though he had picked up a blister somewhere. He had no time to worry about his appearance, however. He might know who had killed Mrs. Ingalls, but he knew he still had no case. It had been skillfully and carefully planned, and carried out.

He even had a motive; when during a brief visit to the Ingallses' lawyer he prodded that unwilling gentleman to the admission that Harry profited by the will to the extent of fifty thousand dollars. But without the bag or its contents he was lost. Under ordinary circumstances he could have alerted a hundred men or more to the search. The circumstances however were not ordinary, as he discovered when he called his office at headquarters from a booth in the hotel. To his surprise it was Joe who answered the phone.

"What are you doing there?" Brent inquired sharply.

"You're asking me?" Joe said. "They've pulled me in and it looks as though I'm in for it, letting that girl escape. Where the hell are you hiding her, anyhow? The whole force is after her."

"Who pulled you in, Joe?"

"Maguire's got the case now. He did it."

So that was it. He was not only off the case. He would probably be broken, and retired as a lieutenant. It was the hell of a slap at a man who had only been doing the best he knew how. Brent hung up and stood still, mopping his dirty face with a dirtier handkerchief. He was not through however. With an air of dogged determination he got into his car and drove to the Davis House.

There, however, bad luck pursued him. A hard-faced clerk told him the Ingallses were out—probably paying a funeral call on Joy—and refused to let him examine their rooms.

"Got a search warrant?" he demanded.

"No. I can get one, of course."

He produced his badge, and the clerk looked up from it coldly.

"Radio says you're off the case," he said. "Guess that settles it, mister."

After some argument, however, he got permission to speak to the nurse on the sixth floor, but he felt slightly sick and not a little dizzy as he left the elevator. Here, though, he had a bit of good fortune. The day nurse was once more standing at the window, smoking and looking out. She jumped when he touched her on the shoulder, and turning gave him a black look.

"What's the idea, scaring me to death? Oh, it's you again. Police, aren't you?"

"Yes, I wanted to see the people next door. But they seem to be out."

"Yes, thank heaven. That radio of theirs has been going all day. What did they do? Kill the old woman?"

"I'm checking up on them. May be something, may be nothing. I don't suppose you saw either of them this morning when you came on duty?"

"I saw him about nine o'clock. He'd been out for a paper."

"Didn't carry a small bag, did he?"

"A bag? No. Just the paper. Why?"

The picture was complete now. Harry Ingalls had not gone out for a paper. He was coming home, to Maud and fifty thousand dollars. And he had not brought anything back with him to incriminate him. Somewhere between the Belmont and this hotel he had got rid of his disguise.

Well, this was it. He had to have help and have it fast. There was no use telephoning. He had to tell his story and hope to God the Commissioner would listen to it. He left her staring after him, and went down to the car. He drove crazily to headquarters and took the elevator upstairs. The operator eyed him queerly, and he was aware, not only that the news was all over the building, but that he himself looked as though he had been rolling in the gutter. There was no time even to wash, however. He pulled up tired shoulders and entered the Commissioner's office. That gentleman immediately let out a yelp that could be heard for a considerable distance, and then out of sheer fury was silent. Brent was rocking on his feet, but his voice was steady.

"I'm reporting on the Ingalls case," he said.

"*You're* reporting! You damn fool, you've been off that case for the last two hours. I told you I'd break you, and I will. Never before," roared the Commissioner recovering his voice, "have I had one of my top men behave in this manner on a job like this. What in God's name were you doing? Sleeping? And where's that girl? Where have you hidden her?"

"She's not hidden. She's on the mezzanine of the Belmont Hotel. She didn't do it, Commissioner. I know who did, only now I need help and need it right off."

"You don't need a thing, unless it's a bath."

"If you'll just listen—"

"I'll listen to Maguire. It's his case."

For the first time Brent saw a man standing by a window. When he turned he saw that it was the district attorney.

"Why not let him tell his story?" he said, eying Brent. "Maybe he's got something."

"I've got it all," Brent told him, "if I can find a black bag somewhere between the Belmont and the Davis House. It's got some false hair in it, a gray wig, and some loose hair, to build up a beard. Or it may be empty, but the bag itself will help."

He steadied himself against the desk. "That bag will solve the case, Commissioner," he said doggedly. "We need it. We've got to have it. And soon. It may be in a locker room at the railroad station, or checked there. It may be in a trash or garbage can, or in some areaway or alley. All I know is that it's somewhere between the Belmont Hotel and the Davis House. And I'd like some prints of a room at the Belmont. It's locked. Man's name was Somers, registered from Cincinnati."

Then, because his feet would not hold him any longer—or indeed his body—he sat down abruptly.

The Commissioner inspected him. After all, he had been in the service for almost forty years. And he did not look as though he had been asleep. He looked more like a man at the end of his string and desperate.

"All right, let's have it," he said. "And it better be good."

He told his story to both men, producing the hairs from the murdered woman's carpet and from the room at the Belmont Hotel, the fact that Harry Ingalls had often stayed in the house and so must have had a key to it, that he inherited under the will, and last of all the bottle the dog buried in the garden.

"It was a nice plan," he said. "Ingalls and his wife ate at the Belmont and went to the theater. She stayed there, but he didn't. He went somewhere, put on the wig, built up the hair on his face with the spirit gun out of that bottle. And registered at the Belmont as Somers. He probably wiped out his prints in the room there, but it won't hurt to try for them."

The district attorney looked puzzled.

"What put you on to him?" he asked.

Brent put his head back. The chair felt wonderful.

"Well, it was two things," he said tiredly. "The dog burying the bottle was one. People don't generally have spirit gum around, and Harry Ingalls must have had it in his pocket when he went there last night. He couldn't take a chance on a struggle and that goatee of his coming loose. It probably rolled under the bed, and the dog found it there. Anyhow it was his. I located the place where he bought it."

"And the other thing?"

He smiled faintly. "Well, that's funny too," he said. "It was because Ingalls was too scared to eat his breakfast this morning at the Belmont. He was afraid to leave it, so he hid it in the toilet tank in his bathroom. I happened on that by accident," he added modestly.

"That's the hell of a place to hide a breakfast!" said the district attorney.

"Well, maybe you never tried it," Brent said. "But you can't flush two large rolls and a slice of ham down a toilet, and you can't very well throw them out the window. That's where Harry Ingalls outsmarted himself. He didn't want the waiter to know he was too scared to eat, so he hid them in the tank." He yawned. "The wife's in it too. She bought the gum. He waited outside."

He glanced at the Commissioner. Why, the old buzzard was actually looking excited. He braced himself and went on.

"Ingalls was still Somers when he checked out of the Belmont this morning. All the luggage he had was the bag. He got rid of the hair and the bag somewhere, bought a morning paper and went back to the Davis House, as if he'd just gone out."

But that was as far as he went. He leaned back and closed his eyes. He was very tired, and his feet hurt like hell. He unfastened one shoe and slid it loosely off his heel. That was better. And after all he had done his work. The rest was up to the other men. Let them go around dumping garbage pails. He was through with that. As from a great distance he heard the Commissioner yelling into the inter-com, and uniformed men hurrying in and out of the room.

"I'm sorry about Maguire, Brent," the Commissioner said, in the comparative silence which followed. "But look at it from here. I hadn't heard from you, and—"

He stopped abruptly. Brent was sound asleep. His reply was merely a snore, and suddenly the Commissioner smiled. He looked quite human when he smiled.

So he's going out in a blaze of glory after all, he thought. Him and his wife's chickens! It's a pity these fellows have to quit when they're still as good as that.

But of course he did not know about the dogs, preferably Scotties, on which Brent had decided before he slept; or the two young people in a taxi, holding hands and looking into each other's eyes. In this last instance only the driver knew, and it meant nothing to him. Nor did the fact that the wig had been already found in a trash can and the bag in a locker at the railroad station, or even that Harry Ingalls was on his way in due time to the chair, with Maud as an accomplice.

"Them police ain't so smart," he said to his wife that night over the midnight edition of a morning paper. "Got the fellow right off. He must have bungled the job."

Brent himself did not read any papers that night. He sat at home with his feet in a basin of hot water while Emma fed him and fussed over him. She did not mention the chicken farm. Nor did he. There would be plenty of time for that. All the time in the world, he thought uneasily. But as he rested he felt better.

"The Commissioner's not so bad," he said. "He was pretty decent, as a matter of fact."

"Why not?" said Emma. "You'd done a fine piece of work for him, and he'll get all the credit for it."

"I liked the girl, Emma. She reminded me of ours. I guess that's why I knew she was innocent."

She bent over and rather awkwardly kissed him.

"What's over is over, Tom," she said stoutly. "How are your feet?"

He lifted one and inspected it.

"Fine," he said. "Looks like the blister's going down."

She looked at him. He was no thing of beauty. He was a tired elderly man who needed a shave and a bath, but he was hers, and she loved him.

"That dog helped you a lot," she said. "Maybe it means something, Tom. If you still want the kennel you'd better have it. I guess barking is no worse than cackling, although I never knew a dog that could lay an egg."

It was surrender, and he knew it. He reached up and patted her hand, while his mind saw the runways he meant to build. Green outside and whitewashed inside. He got a towel absently and dried his feet.

"Better take a bath and get to bed," he said. "I'm still on the job for a while, you know."

The Secret

I

Hilda Adams was indignant. She snapped her bag shut and got up.

"So that's that," she said. "I'm not young enough or strong enough to go abroad, but I can work my head off here. Maybe if I'd had a new permanent and a facial I'd have got by."

The man behind the desk smiled at her.

"I'm sorry," he said. "It looks as though this war is about over. Anyhow your heart—"

"What's the matter with my heart?"

"It skips a beat now and then. Nothing serious. You'll probably live to a ripe old age. But—"

"It skipped a beat because I was making up my mind to commit a murder," she said coldly.

She put a hand on the desk. It was alarmingly near an inkwell, and the medical man looked slightly uneasy.

"Now look, Miss Adams," he said. "I didn't make these rules. We need nurses over there, all we can get. But suppose you had to fly at twenty thousand feet?"

"I'd like it." However she had moved her hand, and he was relieved. "All right," she said. "Maybe I did want to be useful, Doctor Forbes. And maybe I wanted some excitement too. At my age there isn't a great deal. Well, I know when I'm licked."

She did not say good-bye. She walked out, and Forbes looked after her thoughtfully. She was a small neat woman, with short graying hair and childlike blue eyes. Her black suit and white blouse showed a sturdy body, and he scowled as he pressed a button on his desk.

"Get me Inspector Fuller," he said to the girl who came in. "Here's the number."

He shoved a piece of paper across the desk and sat back. Damn it all, they could have used the Adams woman abroad. She was capable. No nerves, he thought, and she was a motherly sort of woman, too old to upset the boys and not too old to take care of them. But the Board had ruled against her.

When the telephone rang he took it up sharply.

"Fuller here," said a voice. "How about it, doctor?"

"I wish you fellows would keep out of my hair," he said, disregarding the fact that he had little or none. "We had to turn her down, if that's what you want to know."

"Why? What reason?"

"She's no chicken," the doctor said sourly. "She has a heart too."

Fuller's voice was startled.

"Good God! What's wrong with her heart?"

"Nothing that will kill her. Skips a beat now and then. She says it was because she was feeling like murdering some one. Maybe we can review the case. I'd be damned glad to use her over here anyhow."

There was more than a hint of alarm in Fuller's voice.

"Now look," he said, "lay off that for a week or so, won't you? I may need her."

"She says there isn't much excitement in her life at her age," the doctor said drily. "I had an idea that wasn't exactly true. However . . ."

Fuller was apparently stunned into silence. He grunted.

"Besides, as I've said, whether the war's over or not we still need nurses, Inspector."

"Crime's never over," Fuller said, recovering somewhat. "And she's one of my best operatives." His voice was almost pleading. "Don't let that face of hers fool you, Forbes. She sees more with those blue eyes of hers than you'd believe. I plant her in a house, and what comes up would make your hair curl. This idea of hers has had me running in circles."

Dr. Forbes was unmoved.

"I wouldn't count too much on her," he said. "She looked

pretty sore when she left here. Said there wasn't much excitement in life at her age."

Fuller laughed.

"I wonder what she calls excitement," he said. "The last case she was on she warned the guilty woman to kill herself or she would go to the chair."

"And did she?"

"Did she what? Oh, the woman! Yes, of course. Put a bullet in her brain. Well, thanks a lot, Forbes. I don't mind her nursing soldiers, but I didn't want her to be where we couldn't get her when we need her."

"Better send her a box of flowers," Forbes suggested. "She's not feeling very happy just now. Nor am I," he added and slapped down the receiver.

Hilda went back to her tidy apartment that afternoon, to her small sitting room with its bright chintzes, where above a Boston fern a canary hopped about in its cage and piped a welcome. And to her austere bedroom where in a locked suitcase she kept the small bone-handled automatic which was as much a part of her nursing equipment as her hypodermic, forceps, bandage scissors, thermometer, and so on.

She took off her neat black hat and ran her hand over her short hair. Then, which was unusual for her, she lit a cigarette and stood by the sitting room window, staring out. All she saw was a series of flat roofs and chimneys, but she was not really looking at them. Her mind was back in the office she had just left. They should have taken her. She knew all about her heart, which had taken a lot of beating and could still take a lot more. Even if she wasn't young she was strong. She could work circles around most of the younger women she knew.

The canary beside her chirped again, and absently she got some lettuce from her small icebox and gave it to him. It wasn't good for him, she thought, but after all why not get some enjoyment out of life? It was dull enough as it was. She had lost a month trying to get to the war. Any part of the war. Now with things as they were she would have to register for a case again. She was needed. They were all needed.

She was too disgusted to go out for dinner. She fried an egg on the two-burner electric stove in her kitchenette and made coffee in a percolator. Then, having put up a card table and covered it with a white cloth, she sat down to her supper.

She was still there playing with the food when the flowers came. The landlady brought them up, avid with curiosity.

"Somebody sure thinks a lot of you," she said. "That box is as big as a coffin."

But Hilda was staring at it suspiciously.

"Thanks," she said. "I guess I know who they're from. And if I had a chance I'd throw them in his face."

"Well, really!" The landlady looked shocked. "I must say, if some one sent me a box like that I'd be pleased, to say the least."

"That depends on why they're sent," Hilda said coldly, and closed the door with firmness. She didn't look at the flowers. She merely took the lid off, glanced at the card—which said "To Miss Pinkerton, with admiration and regards"—and, ignoring the remainder of her meal, went to the telephone and dialed a number.

"Give me Inspector Fuller," she said, and waited, her face a frozen mask.

When she heard his voice she was so shaken with fury that her hands trembled. Her voice was steady, however, steady and very very cold.

"Why the flowers?" she inquired briefly.

"Now listen, Hilda—"

"Why the flowers? How did you know I'd been turned down?"

"Well, you see, I happened to know Forbes. So when he told me what had happened today—"

"Don't lie to me. It was a put-up job and you know it. I'm to stay at home and do your dirty work. That's it, isn't it?"

"Look, Hilda, don't you suppose I want to be in this thing, too. I've pulled all the wires I can and here I am. The country's got to go on, you know. Anyhow, what with your heart and the fact that we're neither of us as young as—"

He realized then that she had hung up, and sat gazing rather forlornly at the receiver.

Hilda did not finish her supper. It was her custom when off duty to take a brief walk in the evening, and in many ways she was a creature of habit. In the winter she walked a certain number of blocks. When the weather was warm enough she walked to the park and sat there on a bench with her knitting. Now, taking the box of flowers under one arm and her knitting bag on the other, she stalked downstairs. She left the flowers outside the landlady's sitting room, and with a grim face started for the park.

She did not even look up when a man sat down on the bench beside her. She knitted bleakly and determinedly until she heard him laugh.

"What a face!" he said. "And I'll bet you're skipping stitches, Hilda."

She said nothing, and Fuller realized it was serious. But then it was always serious. Hilda did not like working for the police.

"Heard a curious story today," he said. "I call it the mystery of the black dot."

She looked up then. "Do I have to listen?" she inquired coldly. "I like it here, but I can go home."

"It's nothing to do with you, or me," he said. "Just a nice little spy story. A black dot on a letter to certain prisoners of war in Germany. The letters weren't meant to reach the prisoners, and didn't. They were picked up and the dot magnified from the size of a pinhead to a complete message. Neat, wasn't it?"

He watched her. At least she had stopped knitting, but she made no comment. Not for the first time he thought that, except for her hair and her small mature body, she looked almost girlish. It was her skin, he considered, and the clear blue of her eyes. But her face had not relaxed.

"I might as well tell you now," she said. "I'm not working for you any more. I'm too old, and I have a bad heart. I'm going to the country and raise chickens. I've always wanted to."

"Oh, my God! Is that what they've done to you?" he said unhappily. "Now listen, Hilda. I put no pressure on that situation. I said if they wanted you they'd have to take you. But I said I could use you if they couldn't. And I can. Right now."

"I want no more murder," she said flatly.

"Would it interest you to try to stop one? After all, life is life, here or at the front, Hilda. There's a situation building up that's got me worried. At least let me talk about it. Sometimes it helps me."

"I can't stop your talking," she said briefly, and picked up her knitting again.

He lit a cigarette and stared out over the park. The October sun had set. The nurses had long ago taken their small charges home to early supper and bed, and now the children playing about had come from the tenement districts. For this little hour the park was theirs. His eyes softened as he looked at them.

"Life's a damned queer thing," he said. "Look at those kids. They haven't much, but they like what they have. There are other children who have everything and don't like anything." He cleared his throat. "I'm thinking about a girl. She's perfectly rational, so far as I know. She's nice to look at, she has money and clothes, she has a young officer who wants to marry her. And I think she intends to kill her mother."

Hilda looked startled.

"What has the mother done?"

"That's the devil of it. Nobody knows. There's an aunt, and she's about frantic. She thinks it's a fixed idea, abnormal. I'm not so sure."

In spite of her anger Hilda was interested.

"There are such things as psychiatrists."

"She's smart. We've tried it. No soap. She wouldn't talk."

"How do you know she has this idea?"

"She's tried it already. Twice."

He stopped at that. Hilda turned exasperated eyes on him.

"Is this like the sailor who promised to tell the little boy how he'd lost his leg, if he wouldn't ask any more questions?"

"Well, how did he lose it?"

"He said it was bit off," Hilda said calmly, and Fuller laughed.

"All right," he said. "The first time she shot at her. The idea is that she was walking in her sleep. Went to the door of her mother's room and let go twice. Only she missed. That was about two months ago."

"People do walk in their sleep."

"They don't fire a gun twice. The first shot would waken

them. And they don't run cars into trees in their sleep. She did that too, with her mother in the car. This time it was to be an accident."

"The psychiatrists claim there are no accidents, don't they?"

"I wouldn't know," Fuller said, restraining a feeling of triumph. "What I get out of it is that she's tried twice and weakened each time. I've seen where the car hit. Ten feet further on it would have gone into a ravine. The tree saved them."

She was silent for some time. Darkness was falling, and the children were wandering back to whatever dingy spots they called home. Overhead the lights of a plane flashed on and off. Its muffled beat mingled with the sounds of traffic, of buses and cars and trucks, to make the subdued roar of the city at night.

"I don't like it," Hilda said, after a pause. "I don't know anything about abnormal psychology, and I loathe neurotic girls."

"She isn't neurotic," Fuller said positively. "She's in trouble of some sort."

"And murder's the way out?"

"There's one motive the crime writers never touch on, Hilda. That's desperation."

"What has driven the girl to that?"

"I wish to God I knew," he said heavily. "Anyhow the aunt fell downstairs today and cracked some ribs. Apparently it's okay. She wasn't pushed. But they need a nurse there. You might think about it."

"I've told you I'm taking no more cases for you."

He had to leave it at that. They walked slowly back to her small apartment, but Fuller did not go in. He said a few rather awkward words about her disappointment, to which she replied with frozen silence. But as he was leaving she spoke abruptly.

"That girl," she said. "Does *she* say these things are accidents?"

"She doesn't say anything. I gather it's the mother who does the explaining, sleepwalking and faulty steering gear."

"Anybody hurt in the car?"

"The girl hurt her arm. That's all. The aunt's been to see me. Says they took an X-ray at the hospital. No break. She behaved nicely, apparently. Thanked everybody but wasn't talking much. I've seen the surgeon who examined it. He says she didn't look crazy. She looked—well, defeated was his word. Otherwise she seemed like a nice child."

"She doesn't sound like it," Hilda said drily. But she made no further comment, and he left her at her door and went on. All things considered, he thought, he had done rather well. Hilda would think it over, and after that either she would call him or something would happen and he would call her. She might not like crime work, but her bump of curiosity was very large.

II

He went back to his comfortable bachelor apartment and telephoned his office. There was no message however, and he mixed himself a mild drink and sat down in an ancient leather chair to think.

It was the aunt, Alice Rowland, who had consulted him. As he had told Hilda, he had known her slightly, a frail middle-aged woman, and she had told him the story, first with an attempt to conceal the identity of the girl involved and finally laying all her cards on the table.

She was, as he knew, unmarried and until the war she had lived alone in the large Rowland house on Center Avenue. Her brother Charles was a colonel in the Army. He had been stationed in Honolulu, and his wife and daughter had been with him there. He had got them out after the Japanese attacked, but had remained himself. Now he was somewhere in the Pacific, and his familiy was living with the aunt.

The first two to three years had been all right, she said. At the beginning Nina—the sister-in-law—had been suffering from shock, and the daughter had been overanxious. She was only sixteen then, but she might have been the mother rather than the child.

"It worried me at the time," Miss Rowland said. "I laid it to what had happened, but she wouldn't talk about the attack, or even about the islands. Nina did. She loved Honolulu. But Tony, the daughter, would get up and leave the room if it was even mentioned."

"She gave no reason, I suppose?"

"No, and she got over it in time. She became entirely normal. She went to boarding school and made friends there. She was very popular, I believe. When she graduated she came back, and a year ago I had an informal tea and gave her as much of a debut as I could in wartime. She's been home ever since. Nina's rather delicate, but we all got along splendidly. Or did. Then about two months ago Tony—her name is really Antoinette, after my mother—Tony began to change."

"Just how? What did you notice?"

Alice Rowland looked distressed.

"It's hard to put into words," she said. "She was sick for a day or two, but she got over that. I thought it was because something had happened and she broke her engagement. Maybe that was part of it, but it was the other change in her."

"What sort of change?"

"Well, she began to watch her mother. Nina's always been in bed a good bit—she likes being coddled—and Tony's room is across the hall. Then she practically stopped going out and she kept her door open all the time. Whenever I went in to see her mother she went in too. I got the idea she didn't want me to see her. Not alone anyhow. And she never let her go out of the house if she could help it. I began to wonder . . ."

She hesitated, coloring faintly.

"You see," she explained, "my sister-in-law is a really beautiful woman. She's always had a great deal of admiration. And Tony worships her father. I—well, I thought there might be some one in love with her and Tony knew it. But nobody calls her up, so far as I know, and I don't see her mail. As a matter of fact"—she looked embarrassed—"I don't even know if she sees all of it. Tony watches for the postman and gets it first."

She came to a full stop. Her hands were moist with nervousness, and she got a handkerchief from her bag and wiped them.

"I hate doing this," she said. "It—this part of it really isn't a police matter. I just need advice. But one of my friends wrote asking Nina to lunch and bridge. She got a telephoned regret from Tony. Later I spoke to Nina about it. I thought she looked very queer, as if she hadn't known about it."

"But she accepts all this—attention?"

"She's used to being looked after. My brother spoiled her. If she and Tony disagree I wouldn't know about it. Since the accident with the car Nina's been in bed a good bit. Dr. Winant says it's merely shock, but she has some neuritis too. In her arms."

"When did this shooting take place?"

"Two months ago. I really do think Tony was walking in her sleep then. She was very unhappy. She'd broken her engagement, just when everything was ready for the wedding. That was probably the reason." She wiped her hands again. "Such a nice boy, too. Johnny Hayes. He's a lieutenant in the Army. I suppose he's gone now, or on his way."

"Did Mrs. Rowland object to the marriage?"

"No. She was delighted. We all were."

"Did Tony ever say why she broke her engagement?"

"No. She simply said it was all off. She was quite definite about it. She sent back the presents and took her trousseau up to a closet on the third floor. It's still there, her wedding dress and everything."

"About the shooting. Did she say she'd been walking in her sleep?"

"She didn't say anything. She never has, since. But the gun was under some clothes in a drawer in Nina's room. Charles had given it to them after the attack. It was loaded, and none of us knew how to unload it."

"Can you remember that night, Miss Rowland? You heard the shots, I suppose. What then?"

"I ran in, in my nightdress. Nina's room is behind mine, and Tony's is across the hall. I found Tony on the floor just inside her mother's door, with the gun beside her. She had fainted, and Nina was trying to get out of bed. She didn't seem to know what had happened."

"She wasn't hurt? Your sister-in-law, I mean."

"No, but she was badly shocked. It was late at night, and with the house being detached only the servants heard the shots. They ran down and helped put Tony to bed. Nina wasn't any use. She never is in an emergency. But she said Tony had often walked in her sleep as a child, especially if she was worried."

"And Tony? How did she react?"

"She seemed dazed. When we put her to bed she just lay there. I tried to find her pulse, but she had hardly any. I called Dr. Wynant, and he gave her a hypodermic of some sort. I told him a little. I didn't say she'd fired at her mother, but she had, Inspector. I found one bullet in the head of the bed. The other must have gone out the window. It was open."

"This was two months ago?"

"Yes. She was in bed for a week or so. But I'm very anxious. You see, she fired twice. That's the part I don't understand. You'd think, if she were really asleep, one shot would have wakened her."

About the car accident she was more vague. She had not been there, and Nina had said something had gone wrong with the steering gear. After all the car was old, and few mechanics were available. What she couldn't understand was where it had happened.

"We have very little gas," she said. "I can't imagine Tony going out in the country at all with things as they are, or Nina going with her. Yet she did, and it happened on a remote road. Only Tony was the one who was injured. She hurt her arm, and it's still stiff. Nina isn't much good in an emergency, but Tony walked a mile or two, holding her arm and not making any fuss about it. Nina says she was very pale but quite calm."

"Then all this has been in the last two months? Things were normal before that."

"Yes."

"Was there anything else to worry her, outside of breaking her engagement?"

"I don't know. I don't know why she broke it. And Nina doesn't either."

"Didn't she explain at all?"

"I don't know what she told Johnny. She merely told her mother the bare fact, as she did me. But she's very unhappy. She doesn't sleep or eat. She's dreadfully thin."

"Have you talked to young Hayes?"

"Once. He's bewildered like the rest of us. He doesn't know what it's all about. He had to go back to camp of course. We haven't seen him since. He'll be going to the Pacific any time now."

Fuller was thoughtful.

"Of course I'm no psychiatrist," he said, "but certainly there's an emotional upset there. Some sort of mental conflict, I imagine. If we knew why she broke off with young Hayes . . . You're sure there was nothing else?"

"I can't think of anything to worry her. In fact, there was good news. My brother wrote that he was probably coming back on some military business."

"Was this before or after she broke her engagement?"

"After. Why would that affect her anyhow, Inspector? She worships her father. But even that's rather strange. She . . ."

She hesitated, as if unwilling to go on.

"Yes?" he prompted her.

"Well, ordinarily I'd have expected her to be pleased, or at least excited. She hasn't seen him in more than three years. She wasn't. She acted—well, as though she didn't want him to come. It worried Nina. She couldn't understand it either."

She got up then and laid a package on the table.

"I brought the gun," she explained. "None of us knows anything about guns, and it seemed better to have it out of the house. You know how Honolulu was after the attack, with so many Japanese around. Charles gave it to them—Nina and Tony—and told them how to take the safety catch off. But we were afraid to unload it."

He opened the parcel. The automatic was lying in a bed of cotton in what looked like a shoe box, and he took it out and examined it. It was a heavy Colt automatic, which had been fired and not cleaned.

"There were two shots fired?"

"Yes."

"Close together?"

"I think so. Yes."

"How far from her mother's door was she when she fired? How many feet?"

"I don't know. The bed is at the side of the room. Perhaps

ten or twelve feet. Maybe more. Our rooms are large."

"That's pretty close. How could she miss?"

But Alice Rowland did not know. She stood there, nervously clutching her bag, not relaxing until he had emptied the magazine and put the gun down. Then she opened the bag.

"I brought one of the bullets," she said. "I dug it out of the bed. I don't know whether you want it or not."

She produced it, wrapped neatly in tissue paper, and laid it in front of him.

"I do hope you understand." Her voice was unsteady. "I don't want Tony to suffer. I don't want the police around. What I need is advice. What am I to do, Inspector? I can't talk to Nina about it. She is convinced Tony was walking in her sleep."

"And you are not?"

"I don't know what to think," she said evasively.

She was preparing to go, but Fuller pushed a pad and pencil across the desk to her.

"Suppose you draw a rough sketch of Mrs. Rowland's room," he suggested. "Make it of the second floor, showing the general layout. I'll get you a chair."

He had done so, and Alice had drawn a shaky outline. It showed four main bedrooms, with a center hall; her own room at the front, her sister-in-law's behind it, a guest room—also at the front of the house—across from hers, and a wing extending beyond Nina Rowland's room, containing a room she called the sewing room, a servants' staircase, and some storage closets. Nina's bed was to the right of the door from the hall, and there was no window beside it. The two windows shown were oppposite the door.

Fuller examined it carefully.

"If the second shot went out the open window she was pretty far off the mark," he observed. "You're sure it's not in the room?"

Alice was positive. She had examined every part of the room carefully. The screens had been taken out, and the window was wide open. There had been two shots and only one bullet. Therefore . . .

It was after this that Fuller had suggested the psychiatrist, and the family doctor, Wynant, had agreed. It had not been easy. Tony had at first refused entirely. She hadn't walked in her sleep for years. If they were afraid of her they could lock her in her room at night. In the end however she had gone, only to remain stubbornly non-co-operative.

"I never even chipped the surface," the psychiatrist had reported to Fuller. "It was like working on a china nestegg. She was polite enough, but she simply wouldn't talk. However she's got something in her mind, Fuller, and I'd say it isn't healthy. She's—well, she's unnatural for a girl of twenty. Too quiet, for one thing. I had an idea she was hating me like the devil all the time."

"Maybe she was afraid of you."

"She's afraid of something. That's certain."

But he had noticed one reaction. Her hands began to shake when he mentioned Honolulu.

"I don't like guessing," he said, "but I'd say something happened to her there. They got out after the attack, didn't they?"

"Yes," Fuller said. "And why wait almost four years for it to send her off?"

The psychiatrist shrugged.

"The mind's a curious thing. The more I work with it the less I seem to know! But I'd say she's heading for trouble."

Alice Rowland's story had stuck in the Inspector's mind. One day he went around to the garage where the car had been taken after Tony wrecked it. It was still there, waiting the delivery of some new parts. He looked it over carefully.

"Got quite a bump," the garage man said. "Smashed the radiator, for one thing. It's a wonder the gal and her mother didn't go out through the windshield."

"How did it happen?"

"Well, you know how some women drive. Turn their heads to talk to the person with them and socko, they're off the road."

"Then it wasn't the steering gear?"

The garage man stared at him.

"Is that the girl's story?" he inquired. "Well, take it from me she's lying. The insurance people were here almost as soon as the car was. They know what happened."

That was as much as Fuller knew. He had had one other talk with Alice Rowland. She had been frightened, both for and about Tony, but any suggestion to her mother that a rest in one of the institutions for nervous cases would help had only met with furious resentment. However, nothing had happened, and Fuller had stopped wondering about the case and devoted himself to a crime wave near one of the Army camps. Then, the morning of the day he saw Hilda Adams, Dr. Wynant had called him up.

"I have a message for you, Inspector," he said. "Alice Rowland fell down the stairs today and cracked some ribs. It's all right, according to her. Purely accidental. There was no one near her at the time. But she asked me to tell you."

"Tony's not involved?"

"So Alice thinks, but I wondered if that nurse you use sometimes is available. What is it you call her?"

"Miss Pinkerton. Her name's Adams, of course."

"Well, nurses are scarce, and I think Alice is uneasy. She's going to be flat in bed for a few days. Pretty helpless too."

"You mean she's afraid of the girl?"

"I don't know. But her sister-in-law isn't much good in a sickroom. As a matter of fact she's laid up herself. Don't ask me what's wrong. She won't see me. Seems I offended her after the automobile accident. I asked her if she thought it was deliberate and she blew up. I suppose it's a combination of her old neuritis, plus shock and resentment. Tony's looking after both of them now."

"It's all right, I suppose. Safe, I mean?"

"Tony's never shown any animus against Alice, but that's as far as I go."

Which was the state of affairs when Fuller mixed himself another drink that night after his appeal to Hilda and went to bed. He slept rather badly however, and was awake at six when his telephone rang. He was not surprised to find Hilda on the wire.

"I've been thinking about that girl," she said. "What's all this about desperation? Can't she be manic-depressive or dementia praecox or something simple like that?"

"Could be."

"Well, what do you think?" she asked impatiently.

He yawned.

"I'm not at my best at this hour," he said. "I think she's in trouble. I don't think she wants her mother to know, and that it's bad enough for murder and suicide—in her own mind anyhow."

"You think she meant to kill herself too?"

"Why try to wreck a car and hope to escape yourself? I thought you were going to raise chickens. The market's good these days."

She ignored that.

"Where's the house, and who's the doctor?"

"Wynant. You know him."

"All right. I'll call him," she said and rang off, leaving Fuller smiling to himself.

III

It was half after seven that morning when Hilda got into her taxi and perched her small suitcase on the seat beside her. She looked washed and ironed, as Fuller always said, but also she looked slightly starched. Her childlike face was rather set. Jim, the local taxi driver who usually drove her on her cases, took a quick glance at her in his rearview mirror.

"Thought you were going to the war," he said. "My wife said she'd be glad to take your canary if you did."

Hilda's face stiffened still more.

"I'm too old, and I've got a bad heart," she said sourly. "I can work my legs off here at home, but I can't do the same thing overseas."

"Bad heart! You sure look well enough."

"I *am* well. If I'd dyed my hair I dare say I could have made it."

He helped her out with the suitcase when they reached the address she had given. The Rowland house stood by itself, a large four-square brick structure with handsomely curtained windows and an air of complete dignity and self-respect. It was a civilized house, Hilda thought, eying it as she went up the cement walk to the porch across its front; the sort of building which implied wealth and security rather than—what was Fuller's word? Desperation. That what had been a handsome lawn around the building showed neglect meant nothing. Men were scarce, as indeed was all sorts of help.

This was borne out when an elderly maid admitted her. She

looked as though she had dressed hastily and she was still tying a white apron around her heavy waist. Hilda stepped into the hall and put down her bag.

"I'm Miss Adams," she said. "Dr. Wynant sent me. If you'll show me where to put on my uniform . . ."

"I'm surely glad you've come," the woman said. "My name is Aggie, miss. I'll take your bag up. Would you like some breakfast?"

"I've had mine, thanks."

"We're short of help," Aggie said, picking up the bag. "The chambermaid's gone, and the butler left for a war job two years ago. Of course Miss Tony helps all she can."

Hilda said nothing. She was surveying the long hall, with its heavy carpet, its mirrors and consoles, and the big square rooms opening off it. The effect was handsome but gloomy. The stillness too was startling, as though nothing lived or moved in the house save the heavy figure of Aggie noiselessly mounting the stairs. The stairs, she thought, down which Alice Rowland had either fallen or been thrown the day before. She had a feeling of surprise too. A Tony who helped with the housework was hard to reconcile with a neurotic or possibly insane girl who had twice tried to kill her mother.

Her surprise was augmented when she met Tony in the upper hall, a slender girl in a skirt and pull-over sweater, with shining dark hair loose over her shoulders, and looking about sixteen. What was even more important, a friendly girl, with a charming sensitive face and a sweet but unsmiling mouth.

What was all this about, Hilda thought resentfully. She's a child, and a nice child. Before she knew it she was shaking hands, and Tony was saying, "I'm so glad you could come. I can do housework, but I'm not much good with sick people. Would you like to see your room? It's old-fashioned, but comfortable."

It was both, the large guest room Alice had shown on her diagram, and facing the street. The furniture was obviously of the nineties or earlier, but some hasty attempt had been made to prepare it for her: a bunch of flowers on the bureau, a magazine on the table. It had its own bathroom, too, and Hilda heaved a sigh of relief.

The whole layout looked better than she had expected, and the hard core of anxiety which had brought her there began to relax. Then she got her first real look at Tony herself. The hall had been dark. Now in the bright morning light of the bedroom she had to revise her first impression of the girl. She was certainly young and attractive. But the friendliness had been forced, and the lines around her mouth were too tight. Also she looked tired, tired to the point of exhaustion, as though she had not slept for many nights, and there was a silk sling around her neck, although she was not using it.

Aggie had brought in the bag and gone out, and rather unexpectedly Tony closed the door behind her.

"I hope you don't mind," she said, her eyes anxiously searching Hilda's face. "My mother isn't very well. She's nervous, and she likes me to look after her. Anyhow, I expect Aunt Alice will take all your time."

Hilda took off her neat black hat and placed it on the closet shelf. Casually as it had been done, she had been warned off Mrs. Rowland, and she knew it. Her face was bland as she turned.

"I suppose your aunt's accident has been a shock, too," she said. "Just how did it happen?"

"We don't know. She doesn't know herself. It might have been the cat. She lies on the stairs sometimes, and she's dark like the carpet. She's hard to see."

"Does Miss Rowland think that?"

She was aware that the girl was watching her, as if she were suddenly suspicious.

"It doesn't really matter, does it?" she said coolly. "She fell. That's bad enough. If you'll come in when you're ready—it's the room across—I'll give you the doctor's orders."

She went out, her slim body held rather stiffly, and Hilda felt she had made a bad start. Yet after seeing Tony Rowland the whole story lost credibility. She thought again of Fuller and his statement about desperation as a motive for crime. There was something unusual about the girl, of course; that statement that she would herself look after her mother, for one thing. But she did not look like a psychopathic case, and on the other hand the house, Aggie, even Tony herself in her short skirt and pull-over sweater and with her hair sweeping over her shoulders, seemed the very antithesis of tragedy. Only the girl's eyes . . .

She got into her uniform, pinning her cap securely to the top of her head. One of the first things she observed to Fuller when she took her first case for him was about her cap. "I don't want it like a barrel about to go over Niagara Falls," she said. "I wear it where it belongs." It was where it belonged as she crossed the hall to her patient's room.

Alice Rowland lay in the big double bed where she had almost certainly been born. She was only a name and some cracked ribs to Hilda at this point, and she surveyed her without emotion. She saw a thin middle-aged woman with a long nose and a fretful mouth, now forcing a smile.

"Good morning," Hilda said briskly. "Have you had your breakfast?"

"Yes, thanks. I wasn't hungry. So stupid of me to fall downstairs, wasn't it? I've gone down those stairs all my life. To be helpless just now . . ."

She didn't complete the sentence, and Hilda wondered if she suspected her identity. Apparently she did not, for she lay back looking more relaxed.

"I don't remember having had a nurse for years," she said. "But two of us were really too much for the servants."

"Two of you?"

"My sister-in-law is not very well. Nerves, largely. She's in bed a good bit of the time. They were all in Honolulu during the raid, and she hasn't got over it yet. Then of course she worries about her husband, my brother Charles. He's a colonel in the regular Army. He's in the Pacific somewhere."

So that was to be the story, Hilda reflected as she got out her old-fashioned watch and took her patient's pulse. Everything was to be laid to the war. Mrs. Rowland was worried about her husband and still suffering from Pearl Harbor, after almost four years. Her daughter had shot at her twice and tried to kill her in a car, but the trouble was still to be the Japs.

"Tony looks after her," Alice said, as Hilda put her watch—it had been her mother's, an old-fashioned open-case one with a large second hand—back in her bag on the bureau. "He left Nina in her care." She looked sharply at Hilda. "I suppose she warned you off, didn't she? She's a jealous child, you know. She was frightfully upset when I told her you were coming."

"That doesn't make sense," Hilda said brusquely. "Why should she mind?"

"I wish I knew," Alice said, and submitted to having a bed-bath and to having her linen changed. She did not revert to Tony, and Hilda, moving her skillfully, saw that her adhesive-strapped body was thin and angular. She was a spinsterish fifty, certainly unattractive and as certainly worried. But she was evidently not going to discuss her niece.

"How did you happen to fall?" she inquired, as she drew the last sheet in place.

"I caught my heel near the top and stumbled. It was awkward of me, wasn't it?"

"Were you alone when it happened?"

"Quite alone," Alice said rather sharply. "Why? I'd have fallen just the same."

"I asked because I noticed your niece had hurt her arm. I thought perhaps—"

"That was some time ago. She bruised it."

As this was evidently all Alice intended to say Hilda went on with her work. She finished the bed, brushed her patient's thin hair, and then carried out the soiled linen. The hall was empty, the door into Nina Rowland's room closed and no one in sight. On her way back she went to the staircase and starting at the top examined it carefully. There was always the possibility that some trap had been laid, a string stretched across to catch a heel perhaps. She found no sign of anything of the sort however, and she was still stooping over, her back to the lower hall, when she heard Tony's voice behind her.

"What on earth are you doing?" she asked.

Hilda was startled out of her usual composure.

"I dropped my class pin," she said, rather too hastily. "It's all right. I've got it."

Tony stood watching her as she went back to Alice's room, but Hilda felt a wave of almost palpable suspicion and distrust. And she had made a mistake. Since she had been on the stairs she should have gone on down, to see the cook about the patient's diet, to use the telephone, almost anything but her ignominious retreat.

The case was already getting on her nerves, she realized. Of the two women she had seen, Alice Rowland seemed far more the neurotic type than the girl. She began to question whatever story Fuller had heard. After all people did walk in their sleep. There were automobile accidents too without any implication of murder and suicide. Yet the girl's face haunted her.

She saw her only at a distance after that until lunchtime. Once, glancing out, she saw her meet the postman on the front walk and take the mail from him. The other time she was dressed for the street, returning later with what looked like the morning marketing. She looked older for she had rolled her hair back and had used lipstick and rouge. But she walked slowly, as though she dreaded coming back to the house again.

At noon Hilda went downstairs to the kitchen to discuss Alice's lunch. The cook was there alone, a thin little woman who said her name was Stella, and who seemed to carry a perpetual grouch.

"I've got a chop for Miss Alice," she said unsmilingly. "You'll have to eat fish, like the rest of us."

Hilda was accustomed to dealing with obstreperous cooks. She did so now.

"I don't care for fish. You can boil me an egg. Four minutes, please."

Stella stared at her and Hilda stared back. But Stella had met her match. Her eyes dropped first.

"All right, miss," she said. "Four minutes."

This being settled Hilda went to the kitchen door. There was a brick walk outside, leading a hundred feet or so to a garage and an alley. The next houses stood some distance away, the grounds separated by low privet hedges. Behind her she could hear Stella banging pans about. She turned and looked at her, and the noise ceased.

"Been here long?" she inquired pleasantly.

"Thirty years."

"Always have a cat?"

Stella glanced at her.

"What's the cat got to do with it?"

"Miss Rowland thinks her aunt tripped over it."

"That cat was right here when she fell. I've told Miss Tony that. Miss Alice don't like cats. She says they carry germs.

She's fussy about things like that. Anyhow it's my cat. It stays with me."

And as if to answer a black cat emerged stretching from behind the range. Hilda stooped and stroked it, and Stella's face softened.

"That fall was an accident," she said. "Don't you go thinking anything else."

"Why should I?" Hilda asked, simulating surprise. "Of course it was an accident."

Stella however had tightened her mouth and said nothing more.

Alice was dozing when she went back to her, so she ate her lunch alone with Tony in the big square dining room with its sideboard crowded with old-fashioned silver. The girl had evidently abandoned her suspicions. She even made an effort to talk, the difficulty of buying food with two invalids to care for. Her mother was not sick, of course, but she was very nervous. She didn't like to see people, and she slept badly.

She ate very little, Hilda noticed. She smoked through the meal, taking only a puff or two of a cigarette and then crushing it out on an ash tray, while Aggie agitatedly hung over her.

"Just a bite of this, Miss Tony. It's caramel custard. You always liked it."

And Tony taking a little and pushing it around on her plate but only tasting it.

It was toward the end of the meal that she put down her third cigarette and asked Hilda a question, her eyes curiously intent.

"How long have you been nursing?"

"Twenty-odd years."

"You must have had all sorts of cases in that time."

"I have indeed. Everything from delirium tremens to smallpox and nervous breakdowns."

Tony's eyes were still fixed on her, but if she meant to say more Aggie's entrance stopped her. Was she about to ask about somnambulism, she wondered?

She was puzzled as she carried Alice's lunch tray up to her. It had been Fuller's custom when she took a case for him more or less to lay the situation before her, with all its various angles. The night before however she had cut him off before he could really discuss it with her and her own decision to come had been sudden. So now she wondered what Tony had not said, and at the look of anxiety in her eyes.

She was twenty or so, Hilda thought. Then she must have been not more than seventeen, probably less, when she left the islands. Too young for a love affair, very likely, certainly for one to last so long. And what would that have had to do with two attempts to kill her mother? If indeed she had made such attempts at all.

She was to be increasingly bewildered as she passed Mrs. Rowland's door. A plaintive voice beyond it was speaking.

"Tony," it called. "Is that you, Tony?"

Hilda stopped.

"It's Miss Rowland's nurse," she said. "Can I get you something?"

She shifted the tray to one hand and put the other on the doorknob. To her astonishment the door did not open. It was locked. She stared at it.

"I'm afraid it's locked," she called.

There was a short silence. Then the woman inside laughed lightly.

"Good gracious," she said. "The catch must have slipped. Don't bother. I only wanted to tell Tony I'd have tea instead of coffee."

Hilda became aware then that Tony had come up the stairs with her mother's tray. She had stopped abruptly when she saw Hilda, and this time there was no mistake about it. She was frightened. She whirled and set the tray on a hall table.

"I forgot something," she gasped, and ran down the stairs again.

Hilda was baffled. Why did Mrs. Rowland lock herself in her room? Was she afraid of something in the house? Whoever it was, certainly it was not Tony. Then who, or what? When she went back to her patient she found her watching the door.

"I thought I heard Nina calling," she said. "Is—is everything all right?"

"Tony forgot something for her mother's tray," Hilda said placidly. "I could have carried it up for her if I'd known. With her arm. . . ."

"There are still two servants in the house," Alice said shortly. "It's perfectly silly for her to do it."

IV

If Hilda had hoped that Alice Rowland would talk to her that day she was mistaken. Beyond saying that her sister-in-law was what she called delicate she did not refer to the family again. But there was certainly tension in the house. That evening, when Hilda prepared for her usual walk before settling down for the night, it became obvious that Alice did not intend to be left alone and helpless in her bed.

"I have some things to talk over with Aggie," she said. "She's been here for years. In a way she's more of a housekeeper than anything else. Do you mind asking her to come up?"

So Aggie was there when Hilda left, and she was still there, with the door into the hall closed, when she came back.

She came back, as a matter of fact, rather shaken.

She was in the corner drugstore when it happened. She had been in the booth trying to locate Inspector Fuller, and coming out she saw a good-looking young man in uniform with a first lieutenant's insignia staring at her over the Coke he held in his hand. She had thrown her cape over her white nurse's uniform, and at first she thought this was what had interested him. As she started out however she saw him paying hastily for his drink. He was on her heels when she reached the street, and he spoke to her before she had gone a dozen feet.

"I'm sorry to bother you," he said, "but I saw you coming out of the Rowland house. Is anything wrong there?"

There was a sort of sick anxiety in his voice. Hilda halted and looked up at him. He was a tall young man, and just then with the pleading eyes of a whipped dog.

"Who are you?" she asked.

"I'm John Hayes. I'm—I used to be a friend of Tony Rowland's. She's not ill, is she?"

"She's perfectly all right. Her aunt fell downstairs and hurt herself yesterday. That's why I'm here. It's not serious."

It was not like Hilda to explain, but she felt confident she knew who the boy was. Also she liked what she could see of him. He was not too handsome, for one thing. She had a vague suspicion of all handsome men. And his uniform entitled him to consideration.

He did not leave her. He walked along beside her, trying to fit his long steps to her short ones and then abandoning the idea. At first he did not speak, nor did she. When at last he did it was to surprise her.

"Why have they kicked me out?" he inquired. "Do you know? Have they said anything?"

"I only got there this morning. No one mentioned you—unless you are the man Tony Rowland was to marry."

"That's right," he said morosely.

"I'm afraid I don't know anything about it, except that the wedding was postponed."

"Postponed!" His voice was incredulous. "So that's what they say. Postponed! Tony gave me the complete brush-off two months ago, without any warning. I'd got leave, the plans were all made, I'd . . ." His voice broke. "She sent back her engagment ring. We'd even got the license. And then—good-bye and be a good boy and take it nicely. Hell," he said thickly. "I don't know why I'm still hanging around."

"Well, why are you?" Hilda asked.

He took this literally. He seemed to be a literal young man.

"I got the measles," he said. "Missed my outfit when it sailed. I'll be going soon, of course."

This seeming slightly anticlimactic, Hilda smiled in the darkness.

"What explanation did she give?" she asked.

"Said she'd changed her mind. Said it was all over. Said she didn't care for me as she'd thought she did, which was a damned dirty lie." He stopped and shakily lit a cigarette, offering Hilda one which she refused. "It's her mother," he said sullenly. "Her mother or that aunt of hers. I've got a mother too. She thinks I'm good enough. Plenty. What's the matter with them?"

"What about Tony herself?" Hilda said. "Young girls do queer things sometimes. They are neurotic, or they get odd ideas."

He laughed without mirth.

"Tony's twenty," he said. "She's no neurotic kid, Miss . . ."

"Adams is my name."

"Well, if she's neurotic she got it pretty suddenly, Miss Adams. She was as normal as any girl I ever saw. She visited my sister Nancy, and the whole family fell for her. They still can't understand it. They think I must have done something."

"When was all this?"

"A year ago last summer. That's when I met her. I had thirty days' leave. We have a summer place in Massachusetts, and if she was having any queer ideas she darned well hid them. She swam and sailed and danced—" He stopped abruptly and stood still. "I suppose I'm making a fool of myself," he said. "Thanks a lot, Miss Adams. Good night."

He gave her a stiff-armed salute, wheeled and left her standing in the darkness, rather open-mouthed with astonishment.

She did not see Fuller until the next night. Nothing had happened in the interval, and on the surface everything was normal in the Rowland household. Alice, still strapped with adhesive, was fretful but comfortable. Dr. Wynant paid a hasty visit, said she would be up in a few days and hurried away. Tony seemed to have accepted Hilda, with reservations. The house ran smoothly, with Tony doing the marketing and helping with the housework.

Then, on that second day, Nina Rowland asked to see her. Tony brought the message, looking resentful as she did so.

"She's worried about Aunt Alice," she said. "It's silly. I've told her she's all right." And she added, "She's very excitable. Please don't stay long. All sorts of things upset her."

"Is it only nerves?"

"She has a touch of neuritis in one arm," Tony said unwillingly.

"What does the doctor say?"

Tony moved abruptly.

"She's fed up with doctors," she said. "All she needs is rest, and to be let alone. Is three o'clock all right?"

She might, Hilda thought wryly, have been making a call on royalty. Nevertheless at three o'clock precisely by her old-fashioned watch she knocked at Nina Rowland's door. Tony admitted her and she stood blinking in a blaze of autumn sunlight. Her first impression was one of brilliant color, of flowers everywhere and bright hangings and chintzes.

Then she saw the woman in the bed. Hilda was startled. What she had expected she did not know, but what she saw was a very beautiful woman, not looking her forty-odd years, and with a breath-taking loveliness that even Hilda—no admirer of feminine good looks—found startling. She was dark, like Tony, but there the resemblance ended. She knew Tony was watching her, but so great was her surprise that it was Nina who spoke first.

"It seemed rather unneighborly not to see you, Miss Adams," she said. "My little girl takes almost too good care of me. I'm much better today."

Tony said nothing, and Hilda did not sit down. She stood rather stiffly near the foot of the bed.

"I'm glad you're better," she said. "If there is anything I can do . . ." She felt awkward.

Tony was still watching her, and now she spoke.

"We won't take you from Aunt Alice," she said quickly. "She needs you. We don't."

Nina Rowland smiled pleasantly, showing beautiful teeth.

"No, of course not. How is poor Alice? Of all things, to fall down the stairs. It's so—undignified."

"She's more comfortable today. The doctor says she will be quite all right."

But now she was aware that Nina too was watching her. She was still smiling, but her eyes were sharp and wary.

"What does she think happened?" she asked.

So that was it. Hilda had been brought in because the woman

in the bed was uneasy. But she had no chance to answer. It was Tony who spoke.

"I've told you all that, mother. She stumbled. I was in the kitchen when I heard her fall."

"She's lived here all her life. I don't understand it."

She did not look at Tony, but obviously the remark was made for her. For an instant Hilda wondered if there was some buried resentment there; if the girl and the woman were on less friendly terms than Alice had indicated. It passed quickly however. Nina Rowland put her arms up and fixed a pillow under her head, and Tony moved quickly to help her. She was too late, however. The sleeve of Nina's bed jacket had fallen back, and showed a heavy bandage on the arm nearest the door.

Hilda glanced away hastily.

"What lovely flowers," she said. "May I look at them?"

When she turned back the bandage was hidden again, but Tony was very pale. She stayed only a minute or two after that, but she left with a firm conviction that one of the two shots Tony had fired at her mother had struck her arm, and it had not yet been healed.

She told Fuller that night when she found him outside the house as she left for her evening walk, and he seemed impressed.

"Although I don't know why the secrecy," he said. "Dr. Wynant knows she shot at her mother, and if the bullet's still there it may cause trouble."

"I don't understand it." Hilda was thoughtful. "Miss Rowland isn't the sort to keep quiet about a thing like that. I imagine she's been spoiled and petted all her life."

"Well, mother love, my girl!" he said drily. "If Tony actually shot her she may be keeping her mouth shut to save the girl."

"I don't think she's as fond of her as all that."

He eyed her.

"What would you expect? She's tried to kill her twice."

"But she doesn't know that, does she?"

He stopped abruptly.

"Now look," he said. "What's on your mind? Did Tony push her aunt down the stairs?"

She shook her head.

"I think not. She was in the kitchen when it happened. Alice seems pretty positive she stumbled. It's just—it almost looks as though Nina is suspicious of the girl. Why should she be?"

That was when he told her in detail the story as he knew it from Alice Rowland, the flight from Honolulu, the quiet years, the broken engagement, the shooting, the automobile accident, the psychiatrist's failure, as well as his statement that Tony had something on her mind and might be heading for trouble. She listened attentively.

"So that's the layout," he finished. "Now you've seen them all. What do you make of it?"

"None of it makes sense," she said testily. "The girl's certainly devoted to her mother. Maybe she's protecting somebody else."

"Who?"

"I don't know. Alice Rowland perhaps. If Alice wanted to throw dust in your eyes she might have done what she did, gone to you saying Tony's crazy. She's no crazier than I am."

"You don't like Alice, do you?"

"I take care of my patients. I don't have to love them."

He laughed a little as they walked on. Hilda's sharp tongue and warm heart always amused him.

"What motive would she have had? Alice, I mean."

"Well, look at it," Hilda said more reasonably. "She's lived alone all her adult life. She's had servants and money. Her house was her own, and her time. Then what happened? She finds her brother's family parked on her, some of the servants leave, her whole scheme of living is changed, and she's—well, she's at a time of life when women are not always responsible. On the other hand. . . ."

She stopped. Fuller eyed her curiously.

"On the other hand what?" he inquired.

"Tony locks her mother in her room when she has to leave her."

Fuller stopped and stared down at her.

"That's fantastic," he said. "Are you sure of it?"

"I don't usually make statements I'm not sure about," Hilda said stiffly. "I found it out yesterday. Last night I put the light out in my room and watched her go down to dinner. She looked around to be sure I wasn't in sight, took a key from the neck of her dress and locked the door from the hall."

"Then the mother knows?"

"I'm not sure. She's in bed most of the time. Tony's been doing it only since I came."

"Hell's bells, Hilda!" he said, exasperated. "Why don't you tell me what you know, without my having to get it bit by bit? How do you know she's afraid of you? Not that I blame her," he added. "That baby face of yours never fools me. You're as dangerous as a rattlesnake, and even it rattles before it strikes."

Very properly, Hilda ignored that.

"Aggie's bunions," she said succinctly.

He stopped.

"Aggie's what?"

"Aggie's the housemaid. She has bunions. I told her what to do for them, so she talks. Are we walking or standing still? I need exercise."

He went on and she explained. When Hilda had gone out the night before Tony had gone out too, and when Aggie tried to take fresh towels to Nina's room the door was locked, and no key inside it.

"She said it scared the daylights out of her," Hilda said reflectively.

"Now just why," Fulelr inquired, "did that scare the daylights out of her?"

"Because it hadn't happened before. Because she doesn't think Tony fired those shots at all. Because she thinks Nina Rowland tried to kill herself and Tony got the gun from her and took the blame."

"Could be," Fuller said. "So now she locks her mother up. What sort of woman is she anyhow? The mother."

"I've told you. Beautiful, spoiled, and self-indulgent. Scared too about something. Maybe about Tony. Maybe about her sister-in-law."

"So now it's Nina who's crazy!"

Hilda was silent for a moment.

"I don't think any one of them is crazy," she said finally.

"Something has happened, either to them all, or to one or two of them. Personally, I think it happened to Tony."

"But it's bad enough to set them all on edge? To put it mildly," he added smiling.

Hilda did not smile.

"We have only Tony's word that she was driving the car when the accident happened," she said. "Maybe the mother did that too. But I'd say she's pretty fond of her pretty self. She likes lying in bed, with flowers all around her and Tony waiting on her hand and foot."

"Not the suicidal type, eh?"

"Definitely not."

They had almost reached the Rowland house. Hilda stopped, and Fuller put a hand on her shoulder.

"Look," he said. "I want you to take care of yourself in that house. I'm beginning to wish you hadn't gone. This isn't a question of crime. No real crime's been committed, according to the way I see it. But one may be. There's tension there, and it may snap. Keep out of the way, Hilda. Watch yourself."

He left her then, and Hilda walked on. She was quite sure she saw a masculine figure lurking in the shrubbery across the street and wondered if it was Johnny. He did not approach her, however, and looking back from the porch she realized that whoever it was was not in uniform.

V

That night Alice Rowland asked Hilda to sleep in the room with her. Hilda had given her an alcohol rub and the tablet the doctor had ordered to make her sleep, and Alice held the pill in her hand and looked at it.

"I suppose it's all right, isn't it?" she said, with a bleak smile. "I mean—one or two odd things have happened, and—I suppose I'm being childish, but will you look at it?"

Hilda examined the pill.

"It's all right. That's the way they're always marked. What do you mean by odd things, Miss Rowland?"

Alice did not answer directly. She took the pill with a swallow of water and put her head back on her pillow.

"You've been here a day or two," she said. "I wonder what you think of us."

"I haven't seen much of the others," Hilda said calmly. "Miss Rowland seems very fond of her mother. I've only had a glimpse of Mrs. Rowland."

"I'm thinking of Tony. You've seen her quite a bit. Do you think she's worried about anything?"

"She seems rather serious, for a girl of that age," Hilda said evasively.

"That's all? You think she's perfectly normal? Please be honest, Miss Adams. I'm anxious about her. She broke her engagement a couple of months ago, and she hasn't been the same since."

"It may have upset her more than you realize. Unless she

didn't care for the man."

"Care for him! She was quite shamelessly in love with him."

Hilda raised the window for the night before she made any comment. The man across the street had apparently gone. She was more and more sure it had not been Johnny, but her face was bland as she went back to the bed and pulled up an extra blanket.

"I may have seen him last night," she said. "A young officer saw my uniform and spoke to me. He was afraid Tony was sick."

"I don't see why he would care," Alice said, her voice sharp. "She treated him outrageously. Everything was ready. His people were coming to stay here, and the presents were lovely. Then all at once it was over. I felt like a fool. It was too late to do anything but announce the postponement in the newspapers, and people kept calling up. All I could say was that he had been moved unexpectedly. I didn't say he'd gone overseas, but I let them think so."

"I see," Hilda said. "Was that when she started walking in her sleep?"

Alice looked startled.

"Who told you that?"

"Aggie said something about it."

"What else did she tell you?"

"Just that Tony was inclined to sleepwalking, and not to waken her suddenly."

Alice's suspicions were lulled. She settled back on her pillows.

"It was about that time," she said. "Things were pretty confused here, what with calling off the wedding and everything. Her mother went to bed in a sort of collapse, and Tony looked like a ghost. Then she walked in her sleep one night and—I suppose you'll hear it sooner or later—she found a loaded gun and almost shot her mother."

Hilda registered the proper surprise and horror.

"Perhaps she was remembering the Japs," she said. "Where did she find the gun?"

"Nina had it in her room. Tony knew where it was, of course. You see, don't you, why I'm worried about the child?

And now I'm afraid she's sleepwalking again. I thought if you didn't mind the couch here tonight—you'll find it quite comfortable."

"What makes you think she's walking in her sleep," Hilda persisted.

"She came in here last night after you had gone to bed. It must have beeen about two o'clock. I wakened to find her standing beside the bed looking down at me, with the oddest look on her face. She—I spoke to her, and she gave a start and shot out without saying a word."

"You're sure it was Tony?"

"She'd left the door open into the hall, and the light was on there. I saw her plainly."

"Maybe she merely wanted to talk to you, and then decided against it."

"Why should she go like that? I was awake, and she knew it."

"Then you don't think she was walking in her sleep?"

Alice looked annoyed.

"I don't know," she said fretfully. "I don't know anything about girls. I certainly don't know anything about Tony these days. She's changed. She's not herself at all. I'm half afraid of her."

Hilda slept on the couch in Alice's room that night. Or rather she lay there, keeping an eye on the door and trying to think things out. That Fuller was right, and that the tension in the house was building toward a crisis of some sort she felt confident, but what such a crisis might be she did not know. The vulnerable person was Alice, comparatively helpless in her bed. Yet she could see no rational reason for any danger unless she was involved in the shooting episode. Someone had fired the shots. According to Fuller's story Tony had been found in a faint just inside her mother's door, with a gun beside her and Nina trying to get out of bed. If Nina had been wounded she had managed to conceal it in the general excitement. Would that be possible, she wondered? Still, as Fuller said, if she was protecting her own child . . .

It would have required considerable stoicism, she thought, but it could have been done, the bloody sheets rinsed out in the bathroom, a self-applied tourniquet to stop the bleeding, and perhaps the assistance of one of the servants. Not the garrulous Aggie. Stella, possibly. She determined to talk to Stella the next morning.

Alice had had her tablet and slept soundly. Because the night was warm Hilda had left the door open, and at two o'clock she heard a faint noise in the hall. It sounded like a door being stealthily opened and closed again, and unconsciously she braced herself. Nobody came into the room, however, and she got up quickly and looked out.

Some one was moving quickly and quietly down the staircase. She could not see who it was. The lower hall was dark, but whoever it was below was moving toward the back of the house, with the ease of long familiarity.

Hilda caught up her kimono and put it on as she went. For a woman of her build she could move rapidly and quietly, and she did so now. She was at the foot of the stairs almost before the door into the service wing at the rear had closed. After that however she went more cautiously. The back hall was dark and empty, but someone was in the kitchen beyond. She heard the lifting of a stove lid and the striking of a match. There was a brief interval after that, practically noiseless. Then, so rapidly that Hilda had barely time to get out of the way, the unknown was opening the door in the darkness and on the way upstairs again.

Hilda had to make a split-second decision, whether to follow and identify the figure or to see what had been put in the stove. She chose the latter and went quickly to the kitchen.

It was quite dark, save for a small gleam of something on fire in the range. She made her way to it, striking her shins on a chair and making considerable noise as she did so. There was no indication that she had been heard, however, and she limped to the stove and managed to pry up the lid. The fire beneath was low, and whatever was burning had not been entirely consumed.

She found a box of matches by fumbling over the top of the plate heater where she knew Stella kept them, and lit one. The mass slowly charring was a surgical dressing of cotton and gauze bandage. Only an end of the bandage remained. The cotton was practically gone, but she had no doubt whatever as to what it was. Some one had burned a dressing from Nina Rowland's arm.

She felt a little cold as she went back to her room. Any one in the house except Alice could have crept downstairs, but why the secrecy? There seemed to be no question that Tony had fired the shots at her mother. But if she had really injured her why run the risk of infection now? Could there have been another gun in the case, and Tony's shooting a cover-up, perhaps for Nina, perhaps for Alice Rowland? Had the story as Alice had told it to Fuller been a clever device to protect someone, possibly herself?

Yet if it had been Tony the night before in the kitchen, she seemed entirely natural the next morning at the breakfast table. She was wearing again the sweater and short skirt, with her hair loose about her face, making her look about sixteen again. And she ate a normal breakfast, to Hilda's relief. In fact she looked as though she had had a reprieve of some sort, which was the more surprising because of what she said.

"We've had a letter from my father," she observed. "He's not coming home after all. Things in the Pacific have changed. Everything is moving fast now."

"That must be rather a blow," Hilda said dryly, and saw Tony flush.

"It *has* rather upset mother," she said. "She was counting on seeing him soon. But he's a soldier. He wouldn't want to miss anything even if he could."

Hilda made her way upstairs. To her surprise Nina's door was open and her room empty. And as she reached the upper hall she heard voices in Alice's room. Evidently Nina was there, and equally evidently the sisters-in-law were quarreling. Nina's voice was raised and shrill.

"You're having her watched," she said stormily. "That's why the nurse is here, isn't it? First a psychiatrist, now a nurse. What are you trying to do? Prove she's crazy?"

Alice's voice was hard.

"I think you're hysterical," she said. "You can't blame me because Charles isn't coming home. As for Tony, if you think it's normal for a girl to shoot at her own mother . . ."

"She never shot at me, and you know it. She had the gun and it went off in her hand. She'd never fired one in her life before."

"She did pretty well, in that case," Alice said drily.

"Just remember, *you* found her. She doesn't remember anything about it. It's your story, not hers. And I'm no fool, Alice." Nina's voice was still high. "I know you don't want us here. I begged Charles to make other arrangements, but he said you would be hurt if he did. If he'd only come home . . ."

Hilda heard Tony coming up with Nina's breakfast tray and had only time to duck into her own room. When some time later she went back to her patient she found her indignant and highly nervous. She looked up at Hilda resentfully.

"Nina's been here," she said. "She thinks I'm trying to have Tony put away."

"And are you?" Hilda asked bluntly.

Alice looked shocked.

"Certainly not. But I am worried. She may do someting dangerous, to herself or some one else."

"I suppose," Hilda said, "there's no chance Mrs. Rowland had the gun that night and Tony tried to take it from her?"

Alice laughed.

"To shoot herself?" she said bitterly. "With looks like that? And a husband who adores her? I assure you she likes to live, Miss Adams. She likes clothes and money. She's fond of herself, too. She's had a wonderful life. While I . . ."

She did not finish, and Hilda, going methodically about her work that morning, realized that there were undercurrents in the house which were being carefully concealed from her. Nevertheless in spite of the quarrel between the two women the day was better than the preceding one. After she had settled her patient with a book that afternoon she wandered down to the kitchen.

Tony was out, and Stella was pouring milk out of a bottle for the cat. She gave Hilda a curt good afternoon. Hilda merely nodded and sat down.

"I want to ask you about the night of the shooting," she said without preamble. "What do you know about it?"

"Me? Nothing. I heard the shots and came down. So

did Aggie."

"Is that all?"

"I don't know what you mean, miss."

"Who attended to Mrs. Rowland's arm that night?"

"Her arm? I never heard anything about her arm. What was wrong with it?"

Hilda watched her, but Stella's thin face was impassive. She tried again.

"How often do you find that something's been burned in your stove when you come down in the morning, Stella?"

This time Stella gave her a sharp look and turned away.

"My stove's the way I leave it, miss. If you don't mind my asking, what business is it of yours?"

Hilda knew defeat when she faced it.

"All right," she said resignedly. "Who put Mrs. Rowland to bed the night this shooting took place?"

Stella looked relieved. "She never really got out of it. She was faint, as well she might be. Miss Alice helped get her settled after the doctor came for Miss Tony. Or maybe it was Aggie. That's all I know."

It was possible, Hilda thought as she got up. Alice might have tried to avoid scandal by dressing Nina's arm herself. The story that one bullet had gone out the open window had been hers. She could have washed the sheets too, and ironed them in the sewing room where an electric iron was kept ready for use. But when she followed Dr. Wynant down the stairs later and put the question to him in the library he merely laughed at her.

"Nina shot!" he said. "You don't know her. If she banged her finger she'd rouse the neighborhood."

"Her arm is bandaged."

"My dear girl," he said pontifically. "Don't ask me why she wears a bandage. Don't ask me why she lies up there in bed either. She's a perfectly strong healthy woman who likes to be coddled, that's all. And that," he added, "is one of the reasons why she doesn't have me any more. I told her so."

Hilda eyed him coldly.

"So that's all?" she said, her blue eyes icy. "It's easy, isn't it? Tony has tried twice to kill her mother, but her mother likes to be coddled, so it's all right with you."

"My dear Miss Adams . . ."

"Don't dear Miss Adams me," she said tartly. "They don't have you any more. You think none of this is your business. Well, I'm sorry, but it is mine."

"I suggested that you come here. You might remember that," he said, highly affronted.

"Then I have a right to know certain things." She watched him put down his bag and look at her resignedly. "How were they—Tony and her mother—when they first came here from Hawaii? You saw them then, didn't you?"

"Certainly. Nina was complaining, but all right. Tony didn't adjust very well. In the sense that a neurotic cannot adapt himself to a change of environment. I suppose you can say she was neurotic. She avoided me, for one thing. I thought she was rather afraid of me. We became good friends later, of course."

"And Mrs. Rowland? What did she complain about?"

"Oh, just small things. The cold weather, a personal maid she'd been fond of had to be left behind, Alice's rather rigid housekeeping. Nothing serious."

"And Miss Rowland herself?"

"She did her best. It was rather hard on her. She and Nina are not very congenial, but as Nina spends most of her time in her room it hasn't mattered much. It has helped since Tony came back from school, of course. She's a friendly child, even if she does walk in her sleep."

He picked up his bag. He was not young and he looked very tired. Hilda felt rather sorry for him, although she stiffened at his parting words.

"Don't let your imagination carry you away, Miss Adams," he said. "There's nothing wrong with Nina Rowland except a chronic case of inertia and an occasional neuritis in the arm. You'll find that's the trouble now, and Tony has merely tied her up as usual."

VI

Hilda found Alice asleep when she went upstairs, and an Aggie with the face of a conspirator waiting for her in the hall.

"Miss Tony's gone," she whispered. "The car's back and she's trying it out. Would you like to see the wedding dress and her other things? I'm going to pack them away tomorrow, so if you care to look."

Hilda agreed. Nina's door was closed, and she had nothing to do for the moment. She found that the trousseau had been relegated to the third floor, a floor she had not seen, and she surveyed it with interest. In general it followed the pattern of the second, with the servants' quarters in the rear. The wedding clothes were in closets in the room over her own, and Hilda cautiously opened the door and going across raised a window shade.

"The dresses are in the closet," she said. "Such lovely things! And the wedding dress is a dream—wait until you see it."

But it became evident after a moment that Hilda was to wait some time to see it, if ever. Aggie moved the sheet which had covered it and turned a bewildered face to her.

"It's gone!" she whispered. "Look, here's where it was. Whoever could have taken it?"

"Maybe she took it herself."

"Why? Where is it? It's not in her room." She poked around among the things hanging there. "Her cocktail dress is gone too. Do you think—maybe she's changed her mind.

Maybe she's going to marry him anyhow. Everything was here yesterday. I showed them to Stella's sister."

"Did you see her going out today?" Hilda asked practically.

"No. I didn't. Maybe Stella did."

But Stella had not seen Tony leave the house. She had been upstairs changing her uniform after lunch, and after cautioning both women to silence Hilda went back upstairs.

Tony's room was still empty when she went along the hall, and after ascertaining that Alice was still asleep Hilda went back to it and stepped inside. It was the usual girl's room, feminine with its pale blue carpet, its white curtains, and its rose-colored bedspread and silk quilt neatly folded at the foot of the *chaise longue.* There was a tennis racket in a frame, and on the toilet table the photograph of a man in uniform, evidently of her father. Hilda inspected it carefully. He was a fine-looking man with a strong nose and jutting jaw, but with Tony's sensitive mouth. It was inscribed "To Tony, my own girl, from Dad."

But the wedding dress was not in the closet, and the small desk by a window yielded nothing. The only incongruous thing, in fact, was the doorstop. It was Volume XIII of the *Encyclopedia Britannica*, and she was stooping over it when she heard Aggie behind her.

"Is it here?"

"Is what here?"

"The dress. I'm scared, Miss Adams. I was responsible for it. Only yesterday Miss Alice asked me about it and I said it was all right."

"They won't blame you," Hilda said soothingly. "I imagine she took it herself. She may be giving it to someone."

"Giving it away!" Aggie screeched. "It cost a fortune. Her father sent her the money for it. She'd never do that."

There was no use asking Aggie about the *Encyclopedia.* She was running around like a wild woman, looking under the bed, frantically opening bureau drawers and moaning to herself. Her search was only interrupted by the ringing of the front doorbell. She tried to smooth her hair as she went down the stairs, and Hilda watched her as she opened the front door.

Standing on the porch outside was a woman in the early

fifties, gray-haired and handsomely dressed.

Aggie stood as if stunned, staring at her, and the woman smiled faintly.

"I want to see Miss Tony, Aggie," she said. "I know she's at home. I just saw her driving back to the garage."

Aggie found her tongue.

"I'm sorry, Mrs. Hayes. Maybe she's in, but I don't think . . ."

Mrs. Hayes however showed grim determination. She walked into the hall and stood there, planted with dignity and firmness.

"Either she sees me now or I'll wait until she does," she said flatly. Then she saw Hilda in her uniform at the head of the stairs. "Is someone sick? I didn't know . . ."

Aggie explained, her voice bleak, and when she had finished, Mrs. Hayes walked with deliberation into the living room, leaving Aggie staring at her.

Behind her Hilda heard Tony's voice.

"Who is it?"

She turned. Tony was standing near her door, her hand holding to the frame of it as if for support. Her face had lost all its color.

"I think it's Mrs. Hayes."

Tony said nothing. She seemed to be bracing herself. Then with her head held high and a strange look of determination in her face she passed Hilda and went down the stairs. The living-room door closed behind her, and an agitated Aggie came up and sat down abruptly on a hall chair.

"I couldn't help it, Miss Adams," she said wretchedly. "You saw how she walked in. Right over me, so to speak. It's his mother."

"So I gathered," Hilda said. "Don't worry. You couldn't stop her. Aggie, how long has that book been holding back Miss Tony's door?"

"What book? I didn't notice. She does her own room these days."

"Will you do something for me? Get another volume from the encyclopedia set in the library, and put that one in my room. Hide it in a drawer. I'd like to look at it."

She went back to her patient's room, and a few minutes later she saw from the front window Mrs. Hayes going down the walk to her waiting taxicab. She walked slowly and almost unsteadily, and before she got into the cab she looked back at the house with her pleasant face bleak and incredulous. It was some time before Tony came up again. She did not go into her mother's room. She went into her own and closed and locked the door.

There was no sign of her that night at dinner. To Hilda's surprise Nina was there, in a flowing housecoat with long sleeves, and with a troubled look on her face.

"Tony won't be down," she said. "She's not well. She said she didn't want a tray. I wish she would eat more," she added as Hilda sat down. "She's so very thin lately. Perhaps I don't understand girls any more. It's a long time since I was one myself."

"Why not have Dr. Wynant go over her?"

"She won't let him. She's been very odd the last few weeks. She used to be so gay, Miss Adams. I don't understand it at all."

Hilda saw that she was using both arms, but the left one rather stiffly. And she did not mention Tony again. She chattered amiably through the meal. It was nice to be out of her room again. And wasn't it sad that her husband was not to get back after all. She missed him dreadfully. And she missed the personal maid she had had so long in Honolulu. In fact of the two, Hilda considered as she ate stolidly, the husband's absence was a grievance, but the maid's was a grief.

"She gave such a wonderful massage," Nina said, and sighed. "And she was so good with hair. I have never looked the same since."

Not receiving the expected comment on this she went on. The maid's name was Delia, and she was to have sailed with them to the mainland. Only at the last minute she didn't show up. Her brother came instead, with some story about Delia's being suspected of working with the Japs. Of course it was all nonsense. Colonel Rowland never kept any papers in the house.

There was more, of course; her resentment of losing Delia, the inability to get the beauty treatments she was used to, and

Alice's niggardly housekeeping "with only two servants." Hilda ended her meal with the feeling that Nina was a completely self-centered self-indulgent woman, and a little puzzled too about Delia, the paragon, who was suspected of working with the Japanese.

"This maid of yours," she said as she got up. "What does she say about the accusation?"

"I don't know." Nina's voice was resentful. "She's never even written to me. As good as I'd been to her, too."

"But you think she is innocent?"

"Maybe she had her price. Most of us have, haven't we? Only I don't see how she could know anything important, when we didn't even know it ourselves."

Neither one of them had mentioned Mrs. Hayes's visit, and after dinner Nina went upstairs again. Hilda heard her rapping at Tony's door, but there seemed to be no answer.

At Alice's request Hilda again left Aggie in her patient's room that night when she went out for her evening walk. Alice was nervous, either because of the scene that morning with Nina or because she had learned of Mrs. Hayes's visit. Evidently she had, for she was querying Aggie as Hilda in the room across got her cape and her bag.

"What did Tony tell her?"

"I don't know, Miss Alice. I don't listen at doors."

"You do when it suits you," Alice said petulantly. "Now, when I need to know you go virtuous. How did Mrs. Hayes act when you let her out?"

"I didn't let her out. She just went."

They were still bickering when Hilda left the house. And after what had happened she was not surprised to find young Hayes waiting for her across the street. He angled over and caught up with her, and under a street lamp she saw that his young face looked set and stern.

"I've been waiting for you," he said without preamble. "What goes on in that house? What sort of song-and-dance did Tony give mother this afternoon?"

"I haven't an idea," said Hilda mildly.

"You're sure you don't know?"

"I don't usually listen at doors." Hilda recalled Aggie and

smiled faintly. "Why? What happened?"

"All I know is that mother is in bed at her hotel, the Majestic. She won't talk, but she's in poor shape, crying and carrying on, and I've been across the street here for hours. What's wrong anyhow? It must be pretty bad. Mother's got plenty of guts usually. All she says now is that I mustn't try to see Tony again, or bother her."

Hilda was silent. Had Tony told Mrs. Hayes about shooting her mother? Was that it? Or was there something else, something which went deeper, of which the shooting was a result? Whatever it was she was confident it was not over. But she could not say that to the boy beside her.

"I'll tell you this," she said at last. "Tony didn't do whatever she did easily, Lieutenant. She's still shut in her room."

He drew a long breath.

"I've been over everything," he said. "There may be insanity in the family. Mother would be terrified of that. It must be something," he added naively. "She did care for me, you know. We were frightfully in love. She wrote me every day in camp. I have her letters and I keep rereading them. They're wonderful."

"You never did anything to make her change her mind? Or cause this change in her?"

"Never. There's nothing in my past either. I've been around a bit. Who hasn't? But nothing that matters. Certainly not since I knew her."

He left her soon after, a sadly perplexed and dejected young man, and Hilda turned back to the house. She was as bewildered as he was, and she was still debating the situation when she approached the house. In her rubber heels she walked lightly, and the street lamps left a small oasis of darkness at the foot of the walk. She roused suddenly to see two people there, a man and a girl, and to realize the girl was Tony. She was confident they had not noticed her, and she turned sharply and crossed the street, stopping in the shadows to watch.

She could not hear much that they were saying. The street was wide and their voices low. That there was an argument of some sort going on was evident, however, for once Tony tried to break away and the man caught her by the arm and raised his voice.

"Maybe you'd like me to report it," he said. "It would make a nice story, wouldn't it?"

"You wouldn't. You don't dare to." Tony's voice was raised too.

"Oh, wouldn't I? Wait and see."

Hilda heard no more. A moment later Tony had rushed back to the house. Hilda thought she was crying. But her own eyes had turned to the window of Alice's room upstairs. Someone, probably Aggie, had been standing there.

VII

The scene had roused Hilda's quick curiosity, and as the man started down the street she trailed him at a safe distance. At the end of two or three blocks he stopped, evidently waiting for a bus. The street however was dark. He was only a vague rather sinister figure as he stood there, and as the bus rumbled along she decided to follow him. He paid no attention to her. He got on first, throwing away a cigarette as he did so and swinging on easily. Even then she could only get a general impression of him, a man of probably forty, in a shabby blue suit and a well-worn brown hat.

If he had noticed her he gave no indication of it. He seemed to be absorbed in thought, and Hilda decided to find out his destination. But he stayed on the bus almost to the end of the line and she began to worry about her patient. Then abruptly he got up. Two or three other passengers alighted also, and Hlida was the last to leave. He was some distance ahead of her when, drawing her blue cape around her, she set out to follow him.

He stopped once to light a cigarette, and so far as she could tell he was still unaware of her. She was in a part of town she did not know, but he seemed at home in it. The streets were empty, the buildings dark and forbidding, and his own figure not so distinct. She began to feel uncomfortable. Then she lost him altogether, in front of one of a row of small dilapidated houses. So far as she could tell they had no numbers, and she began counting from the end of the block. She had lost him at either six or seven, and she went on past, making a mental note of the location.

Which was the last mental note she made of anything for some time.

When she came to she found herself lying on the pavement of a narrow dirty alley between two houses, with her purse gone and her head aching wildly. It was a number of minutes before she could get to her feet, and then it was to find herself retching violently and her legs almost unable to hold her.

There was no sign of her assailant. The street was empty and quiet when she staggered to it, and she sat down on a doorstep and tried to reconsider her situation. She was miles from the Rowland house or from her own apartment, she had no money, and what was even worse she had fallen for what was the cheapest and most obvious of tricks.

It was some time before she could think coherently. Evidently he had known who she was all along. Probably Tony had seen her and told him when he tried to hold her.

"My aunt's nurse is watching you across the street. Let me go or I'll call her."

It had been easy enough after that, she thought sourly. Her uniform, her hatless head, and the long wait for the bus. When she had followed him . . .

She felt better after a few minutes. Her head still ached but her legs would at least obey her. She managed with several stops to reach a drugstore, and the man behind the counter looked startled when she more or less stumbled through the door.

"I'm sorry," she gasped. "I've been knocked down and robbed. May I use the telephone? I have no money."

"Sure," he said. "Don't bother with the booth. Use this."

He put the instrument out on the counter and she sat down gratefully. It was a moment or two before she felt able to use it, however, and she looked up to see him putting a glass in front of her.

"Aromatic ammonia," he said. "It may help."

She drank it and before long was able to call Fuller at his apartment.

"It's Hilda," she said. "I'm at . . ." The man supplied the

address and she gave it. "I've had a little trouble. Been knocked out and robbed. Can you send for me?"

"I'll come myself. What the hell are you doing out there?"

"It's a long story," she said, and hung up abruptly.

When at last he arrived she had lost the aromatic ammonia and divers other things in the gutter outside, and the man from the drugstore was standing on the pavement beside her, offering paper tissues in lieu of handkerchiefs. He looked surprised when he saw the police car with its uniformed driver.

"Lady's in poor shape," he said when he saw the Inspector. "Guess you'd better take her to a hospital."

"I'm all right," Hilda said disgustedly. "Just a plain damned fool, that's all. Do I get in the car or do I stand here all night?"

Fuller smiled. Hilda was herself again, he realized. She might look like the wrath of God, as indeed she did, but she was practically normal. He made no fuss over her as she got into the back of the car. He simply followed her, rolled up the glass to cut off the men in front, and lit a cigarette.

"Talk when you're ready," he said cheerfully. "That bump may ache but it won't kill you."

"I wish you had it. You wouldn't be so happy."

"All right. When one of my best operatives lets herself be lured to this part of town and is knocked out, either she isn't smart or she had a good reason. Which is it?"

"He fooled me. He didn't pay any attention to me. I ought to know better, at my age."

Fuller eyed her.

"Very clear. Very lucid," he said. "Maybe we'd better go to a hospital after all."

"I'm going back to my case," she said firmly. "It all started there. He was talking to Tony Rowland on the street. That's why I followed him."

She told her story as briefly as she could, describing the man and the method by which he had disposed of her. Especially however she related Tony's crying, her attempt to escape, the man's threat to report something or other, and the likelihood that he had then been told who and where she was, and that she might overhear.

"He put on a good act," she said. "But then everybody's

doing it in the house. Tony or some one else burns a surgical dressing at night in the kitchen stove. Today her wedding dress is missing. It cost a fortune, and it's gone. She uses the *Encyclopedia Britannica* for a doorstop, and this afternoon she saw Johnny Hayes's mother and sent her back to her hotel in hysterics."

"Good God," Fuller said. "Are you sure you're all right? It sounds like delirium."

"It's all true," Hilda said, trying to lean her head back against the car cushion and deciding against it.

"And after all that you still think the girl is normal?"

"I'm not sure I'm normal myself."

She was determined to go back to her case, and it was useless to argue with her. Fuller tried it, only to meet with stubborn silence. Finally he turned on the top light and surveyed her. Some of her color had come back, although her face was dirty, her short gray hair standing in every direction and her white uniform smeared. But her eyes were cold and hard and very Hilda-ish at her most obstinate.

"All right," he said resignedly. "If you can take it I can. It's your head and your headache."

Before he left her however he got a description of her assailant and was thoughtful for some time, trying to assort the various items. The surgical dressing he did not bother about. "If she shot her mother and doesn't want it known that's their affair." But the wedding dress puzzled him.

"Would she burn it?" he suggested. "After all it couldn't have been a pleasant thing to have around."

"The furnace isn't going. She may have sold it."

"I see. You think this man was after money?"

"He was after mine," she said drily. "He got my mother's watch too. That's all I care about."

He got a description of the watch, in case it was sold or pawned. Then he sat back and looked at her again.

"Now see here," he said. "What we want to know is why the girl shot at her mother, if she did. Why they had the car accident, and if there may be another one. That's why you're there. You must have some idea by this time."

"Ideas!" she said bitterly. "I'm filled with them. One thing

I'd like to know is why Tony is consulting Volume Thirteen of the *Encyclopedia Britannica.*"

He eyed her with annoyance.

"See here," he said, almost violently, "if you've got any theory on this case I want it. It's no time to hold out on me."

But Hilda merely shook her head, a gesture which proved disastrous, and remained silent.

VIII

It was one in the morning before they reached the house, and some time later before Aggie in a dressing gown opened the front door an inch or two and gazed with terrified eyes at the two of them. Hilda was urbanely calm.

"Sorry to bother you," she said. "I was knocked down and my bag taken. This gentleman found me and kindly brought me home. Is everything all right?"

Aggie had found her tongue.

"I've been scared to death about you," she said. "Yes, they're all asleep. Maybe I'd better stay with Miss Alice tonight."

"I'm perfectly all right," said Hilda, staggering slightly. "Go to bed, Aggie, and don't worry." She turned to Fuller formally. "And thank you very much. You've been most kind."

The Inspector took the hint, mumbled something and departed, while Hilda sat down on a chair in the hall and watched the walls rotate and finally settle back to where they belonged. Aggie was still looking startled.

"Who did it?" she asked. "I declare, the amount of crime since this war makes a body wonder. Did you see him?"

"I caught a glimpse of him," Hilda said cautiously. "A man about forty and very well dressed. He had a dark skin. That's all I saw."

Aggie stared at her.

"Him?" she said. "Why should he be knocking you down?"

"You know who he is?"

But Aggie pursed her lips.

"No, miss," she said stolidly. "I thought for a minute it was somebody I'd seen around. But it couldn't be."

If she knew more she was not talking, and with her help a dirty and exasperated Hilda climbed the stairs. Alice had taken her sleeping tablet and was quiet, and Aggie followed Hilda into her room.

"I put the book in your bureau," she said, with the air of a conspirator. "She never noticed the change. She was out for a while and when she came in she looked queer. I feel kind of worried about her."

Hilda sat down dizzily on the edge of the bed.

"I haven't told Miss Alice about the dresses," Aggie said, still cautiously. "I've been everywhere. They're not in the house. I'll take my Bible oath on it."

Hilda got up and began to take off her filthy uniform. She was not listening to Aggie's account of the wedding dress. She was back in the car, talking to Fuller and he was saying it sounded like delirium. So it did, but it had a definite beginning, if not yet an end.

"Try to think back, Aggie," she said. "How were things here before Miss Tony broke her engagement?"

"Just the way they'd always been, miss. Except for the excitement, packages coming and clothes and all that. The florist in to see about the flowers for the reception, and the caterer about what they were to eat.

"How about Miss Tony?"

"She was singing all over the place. Very happy she was, miss, and that crazy about the Lieutenant it would make you want to cry."

"When did that stop?"

Aggie thought.

"Well, about ten days before the wedding. I remember Stella saying her breakfast tray hadn't been touched. The next day I saw her coming downstairs, looking sort of sicklike. She went into the library and stayed there a couple of hours. I guess she'd used the telephone, for when she came up she went to her Aunt Alice's door and said there wouldn't be any wedding at all."

"How did they take it? Her mother and Miss Alice?"

"They acted like they thought she was out of her mind. But she wouldn't budge an inch. Her mother about had a fit. She hasn't really been the same since."

"What reason did she give?"

"I don't know as she gave any, miss."

"And how long after that did Tony walk in her sleep?"

"On her wedding night," Hlida said impressively. "Can you blame the poor child, miss? She'd been queer all day. She did her room and her mother's. Then she locked herself in and I never saw her until that night, when I heard the shots."

"Just what did you see then?"

"Stella and I both heard the shots. We didn't wait to put anything on. We ran to the stairs, and down below Miss Alice was bending over Tony on the floor, just inside her mother's door. Mrs. Rowland was screaming in her bed. When I got there she was trying to get out of it."

"What happened to her afterward?"

"Mrs. Rowland? Well, she looked kind of faint and I made her get back. She was shaking all over."

"You didn't think a bullet had struck her?"

Aggie started.

"You mean she was shot!" she said incredulously. "And said nothing about it? Not her, Miss Adams. She'd have raised the roof."

"There was no blood about?"

"Not that I saw. I wasn't there but a minute."

"Then why does she wear a bandage on one arm?"

Aggie looked relieved.

"Oh, that," she said. "She has neuritis. It's been worse the last few weeks. That's why she's in bed so much."

"How about the lights that night, Aggie? You say you saw Tony on the floor. Was the hall light on?"

"It always is. Miss Alice is the nervous sort."

"And Mrs. Rowland's room? Was that light on too?"

Aggie hesitated.

"Well, now I come to think of it it wasn't. I could see well enough though, with the door open. I didn't turn it on until later, after we'd got Miss Tony to bed and kind of settled."

She went up to bed after that, and Hilda washed and took another look at her patient. Alice however was still comfortably asleep. Hilda went back to her room and took the heavy volume Aggie had left from her bureau drawer. It was Volume XIII, Jere to Libe, and she put it on her bed and examined it. If there were any markers in it she could not see them, and no part of it appeared to have been used more than any other. Finally she picked it up and shook it. A small piece of blank paper fell out, and she was annoyed at her carelessness. She should have gone through it page by page, she reflected, and in a very bad humor and with a worse headache put herself to bed on Alice's couch.

She had not yet gone to sleep when Tony came carefully into the room. She stood in the doorway as if she was uncertain for a minute or so. Then she came directly to Hilda and stood looking down at her. She had been so quiet that had Hilda not been awake she could not have heard her. She was not walking in her sleep, however, and she seemed relieved when she saw Hilda was awake.

"I wonder if I may have a sleeping tablet," she whispered. "Mother's are all gone, and I've been awake for hours."

In the half light from the hall she looked young and rather pathetic. Evidently she did not know what had happened. She was shaking however and Hilda reached out and caught her wrist. Her pulse was fast and irregular. On impulse she drew her out into the hall and closed the door.

"What's wrong, Tony?" she said. "There is something, isn't there? I'm a nurse. I'm used to all sorts of tings. Maybe I can help you."

Tony gave her a thin smile.

"That's kind of you," she said. "There isn't anything really." Then, as if she had just thought of it, "When I'm nervous I sometimes walk in my sleep. I don't want to tonight. That's all."

"If you're worried about your mother . . ."

"What about my mother?" Her voice had changed, was sharp and challenging.

"I saw the bandage on her arm, you know. I don't want to worry you, but if she's had an injury—"

"What on earth are you talking about?" Tony asked coldly.

Hilda lost patience at last.

"Don't be a little idiot," she said sharply. "I'm saying that if your mother has been shot in the arm it ought to be properly cared for."

Tony gasped.

"Who told you that? About the shooting?" she demanded.

"My dear child, it's not a secret, is it?" Hilda said practically. "People do queer things in their sleep. I had a patient once who almost choked her own baby to death. She thought she was choking a burglar."

Some of the suspicion died in Tony's face, but she looked ready to collapse.

"I see," she said. "The doctor and the servants. Especially Aggie. And Aunt Alice, of course. But I didn't shoot my mother, Miss Adams. You can ask her yourself."

Hilda was certain Nina would deny it with her last breath, no matter what the fact. She said nothing, however. She brought the tablet and Tony swallowed it with a sip of water and handed back the glass.

"That man I was talking to tonight," she said. "He's the brother of a maid we had in Honolulu. He's out of work, he says. But there are plenty of jobs. I don't want mother to be bothered about him."

Hilda nodded. She was not to mention this man, evidently. And she had been right. Tony had seen her across the street, had probably used her as a threat too. But she could have no idea of what had happened since, or that the police were after him; that Fuller had inaugurated a citywide search for him.

Hilda felt better the next morning. Her neck was stiff, and she had bruised a knee and torn a stocking in falling. Otherwise she was all right. She was uneasy, however. The case would not last much longer. Alice was much improved. She was to sit up in a chair that day, and she was no nearer the solution of the problem than when she came. Rather less, in fact. It had looked at the start like a neurotic or unbalanced young woman, desperately determined to kill her mother, even if she finished herself in doing so.

But she was convinced now that Tony Rowland was not

psychopathic. She was a desperately frightened and unhappy girl with a trouble she was refusing to share with anyone. Her thoughts were busy as later on she got Alice up in a chair by the window and turned her mattress. What was the secret? And as if she had read her mind Alice spoke.

"You've seen Tony now for two or three days," she said. "How does she impress you?"

"She seems worried," Hilda observed.

"Worried?" Alice smiled her thin smile. "That's a polite word for it. She's not herself at all. She really ought to be in a sanitarium, but what can I do?"

"You have no idea what the trouble is?"

"None, unless it's in her own mind. We did send her to a psychiatrist, but she wouldn't talk to him. He was furious. You see, she may have been asleep the night she fired those shots. She certainly wasn't asleep in broad daylight when she wrecked my car."

"I don't think you've told me about that," Hilda said.

"Well, perhaps I shouldn't now. Only I keep thinking about it. That accident when Tony hurt her arm. At least they say it was an accident. Something about the steering gear. But the steering gear was all right, Miss Adams. The garage says so, and Tony won't even talk about it."

"That would look as though she meant them both to—to have the accident," Hilda said thoughtfully. "It doesn't sound like her, does it? She's a devoted daughter. If she wanted to kill herself why kill them both?" Alice shrugged her thin shoulders.

"She loves her father too. Then why was she relieved when she found he wasn't coming to America? She was, you know."

Hilda smoothed the spread over the bed, and eyed it. The effect was sufficiently geometrical to satisfy her.

"I've been wondering," she said, giving a pillow a final pat. "The attack on Honolulu must have been quite a shock. Did she lose anyone in it? Anyone she cared about?"

"I don't know. After all she was only sixteen. If you mean a man . . . There is one strange thing. Nina likes to talk about the Islands. She hopes to go back there when the war's over. She's done her room here much as it was there, and Tony keeps it full of flowers. But Tony hates the place. In the almost four years she's been here she's hardly ever mentioned it. She seems to hate the thought of it."

Hilda considered this. She was no moving picture fan, but she had seen the films of Pearl Harbor. Even when the attack was over they could not have felt safe there. Colonel Rowland had given his wife a gun, had sent them to the mainland as soon as possible. And with the lights out everywhere . . .

"Something must have happened to her there," she suggested. "Something Mrs. Rowland doesn't know. Something nobody but Tony knows. There are such things as psychic scars. If she had been attacked—"

"I'm sure it was nothing of the sort," Alice said, flushing. "And she got over it, Miss Adams. She was perfectly normal after the first month or two."

"Does she get any letters from the Islands?"

"I never see her mail. She gets it first."

While Hilda straightened the bathroom Alice had evidently been thinking, for when she emerged she threw her first words like a bomb.

"What was Herbert Johnson saying to Tony last night, Miss Adams? Aggie says you were across the street."

Hilda managed to keep her voice smooth.

"She was talking to a man. I didn't know who it was."

"You didn't hear anything?"

"I was pretty far away."

Alice looked disappointed.

"I think he's been bothering her off and on for the last four years," she said fretfully. "His sister Delia was Nina's personal maid in Hawaii, and he comes from there too. He's no good and I've told them so, but they were fond of Delia." She eyed Hilda. "Would you think Tony gave him any money last night?"

"I don't know, Miss Rowland. I didn't see it if she did."

Alice was obviously disappointed. She was silent for some time. Then what she said was apparently a *non sequitur*.

"My sister-in-law is a very attractive woman," she observed drily. "I imagine a good many men have envied my brother. It's just possible that Nina—"

But she didn't finish and Hilda made no comment.

IX

That morning Fuller saw Commissioner Bayard. They were old friends. The Commissioner offered him a cigar and Fuller sat down. Bayard had a cold, and was using a paper towel as a handkerchief. He crumpled it up and threw it in the wastebasket.

"Dab the thigs," he said. "Bight as well use a dutbeg grater. Why dod't they bake theb out of cottod? South's full of it. What's wrog with you? You look as though you hadn't beed to bed."

"Hilda Adams had a narrow escape last night."

"Od a case for you?"

Fuller nodded.

"Knocked out and her bag taken. Luckily it had an old-fashioned watch in it. If the fellow tries to sell or pawn it we've got him. But I'm not very easy. I'd like to have a man or two to keep an eye on the house where she's working. There's some sort of trouble there."

The Commissioner sneezed.

"Good God," he exploded. "Dod't you know we're dowd to less thad two-thirds of the force? What's the matter? The Adabs wobad cad take care of herself. She always has."

"She's never had a case like this," Fuller said, and proceeded to tell what he knew. The Commissioner listened grimly.

"So we watch a girl who's god batty!" he said with disgust. "What good is a cop across the street? To call the Bedical

Exabiner after it's all over?"

"It's going to be done, if I have to do it myself."

"Don't be a fool. You've got a job to do."

In the end however Fuller got what he wanted, or a part of it. A plain-clothes man would watch the Rowland house at night, and follow Hilda if she persisted in her evening walks. But Hilda did not go out that night.

She chose the afternoon instead.

"I'd like to get some fresh uniforms," she told Alice after lunch. "If you'll be all right I won't be long."

Alice yawned.

"I'll take a nap," she said. "Go right ahead. Just tell Aggie to look in now and then."

So Hilda went downstairs. In her neat black suit and hat and in her comfortable flat-heeled shoes. As usual she walked quietly, and in the lower hall she saw Tony in the library at the telephone. She hung up hastily when she saw Hilda, and the expression on her pale face was one of shocked alarm. Hilda saw it and ignored it.

"I'm going out for an hour or two," she said. "Miss Rowland will try to sleep."

Tony did not answer at once. She stood staring at Hilda, and when she spoke her lips seemed stiff.

"Aggie says you met with an accident last night."

"I was knocked down and robbed," Hilda said cheerfully. "I'm all right today. It takes a lot to kill me."

She thought Tony went even whiter, and she was puzzled as she went out to the street. Did Tony suspect what had really happened to her, she wondered? And what was the truth about the man last night? What hold had this Herbert Johnson had on her? A hold of some sort he certainly had. He had shown it when he caught her arm and jerked her back. And what was it he had threatened to report? To report to whom?

She was still thoughtful as she took a bus downtown. For contrary to her statement to Alice she did not go at once to her apartment. She went instead to the Majestic Hotel and inquired for Mrs. Hayes. Mrs. Hayes, it appeared, was not well and seeing nobody. However on the mention of Tony Rowland's name over the telephone she was told to go up.

The door was open into the sitting room, and when she knocked a voice called her to come in. She found Johnny's mother in bed, still pulling on a bed jacket and looking exhausted and pale.

"You're Alice Rowland's nurse, aren't you?" she said. "I saw you in the hall yesterday."

Hilda agreed and sat down. She had no bag, so she folded her hands in her lap and eyed Mrs. Hayes serenely.

"I came because your son told me you were worried about Tony Rowland," she said. "I don't mind saying I am too, Mrs. Hayes. I thought if we could get together . . ."

Mrs. Hayes' mouth tightened.

"I'm afraid I can't discuss her, Miss Adams. I am seeing you to ask you to talk to Johnny. He might listen to you. He won't—to me. I don't want him ever to see Tony again, or to try to."

Hilda raised her eyebrows.

"That's rather drastic, isn't it?" she said politely. "Unless you have a very good reason."

"I can't discuss the reason." Mrs. Hayes' voice was frozen. "It's not my secret. I've sworn not to talk about it. But any marriage, any engagement, is out of the question. Tony knows that herself. If she sent you . . ."

"No. She doesn't know I'm here. I wondered—did she tell you there was insanity in the family? Because if I'm any judge she's as sane as I am."

Mrs. Hayes remained stiffly silent, and Hilda went on. "There *is* something wrong, Mrs. Hayes. I know that. Tony Rowland is pretty close to desperate. I'm only afraid . . . She may try to take her own life, you see."

"I'm sorry, Miss Adams. I'm fond of her, or I was. But I assure you there is nothing I can do."

Hilda eyed her, her handsome flushed face, reminiscent of Johnny's masculine one, the platinum wedding ring and large square-cut diamond on her hand. The sort of woman, she thought, who would be a good homemaker, a good wife and mother. But also a woman without imagination.

She got up.

"It's just possible," she said, "that by keeping this secret to yourself you may actually cause trouble. How can I help Tony if I don't know anything?"

"I'm afraid I'm more interested in my son. There must be no marriage, Miss Adams, if I have to sacrifice everything I care for to prevent it. And Tony knows it."

On that note Hilda took her departure, feeling frustrated and more anxious than she had since she had taken the case. Her apartment when she reached it looked orderly and peaceful, and she sat down for a minute or two to try to assort her ideas. Mrs. Hayes had had an air of finality in everything she said. That she had been profoundly shocked by her talk with Tony was certain. Then what had Tony told her?

She was rummaging for a bag to replace her stolen one when her landlady puffed up the stairs to give her a message relayed from the Rowland house. It was to call Fuller, and she was tempted not to do it, to sit down for an hour or so in her comfortable easy chair and rest her head, still sore from the attack. Instead she took two aspirins and picked up the telephone.

Fuller was in a bad humor. He snapped a hello at her, stated that she ought to be in bed, and then said he wanted to know what sort of monkey business was going on in the Rowland house.

"I don't know what you mean. If it's because I saw Mrs. Hayes—"

"Oh, you thought of that, did you? No. It's about your watch. It was sold this morning to a pawnbroker downtown who is known to traffic in stolen jewelry, and bought this afternoon. I'll give you three guesses who bought it."

"How would I know?"

"Tony Rowland," he said. "Your nice gentle little friend. The girl who tried to kill her mother. Remember? She walked in there as bold as brass an hour or so ago, asked to look at watches and selected yours. Did you tell her you'd lost it?"

"No."

"Then you see where that leaves it. She knew the fellow had it. He got word to her, describing it. He was probably scared we'd trace it. So she protects him by getting it first."

Hilda was very still. It looked as though, instead of using her the night before to protect herself, Tony had warned him against her. She found her hands shaking.

"That's your angel child," Fuller said. "Now maybe you'll change some of your ideas. Find out if she got a note or a telephone message some time today. It can help if we can trace it. We've got a good description of the fellow. It's your man all right."

"She did get a telephone message. I know that."

"When?"

"About half past two. I was on my way out."

"That's it, then. She hot-footed it down to the shop, getting there at three. What do you bet you'll find it in your room when you get back?"

"I think it's the last place I'll find it," Hilda said curtly. "She's no fool. She'll send it here or hide it, if she hasn't dropped it in the river. The man's name is Herbert Johnson, if he's using it. He came from Honolulu after Pearl Harbor, and his sister was Nina Rowland's personal maid. I think he's blackmailing her."

"That's my girl!" He was pleased with her. He always was when she came out coldly with important bits of information. "Fellow a Hawaiian?"

"No, and they'd cut me off the wire if I told you what I think he is."

She hung up and, after looking in at the landlady's quarters to see her canary, made her way stolidly back to the Rowland house. There was no Tony in sight, and she met the postman on the pavement and took the mail from him. There was a letter for Alice from Honolulu, and Alice looked triumphant when she took it.

"Maybe I'll know something about Herbert now," she said as she ripped it open. "I wrote to a friend of mine out there." She glanced up at Hilda. "Did Tony see you get it?"

"No. I met the postman on the pavement."

She was reading the letter when Hilda went back to her room to change into uniform again. As she had expected the watch was not there. The room was as she had left it, except for one thing. Volume XIII of the *Encyclopedia* in her bureau drawer had been changed to XIV, Libi to Mary, and a heavy china elephant with large pink roses painted on it was now propped against Tony's open door.

When she went back to her patient there was no sign of the letter, and Alice had got out of bed and was standing in her nightgown in front of a chest of drawers, with a key in her hand. But something had happened to her. She had lost all her color, and she staggered as she turned to look at Hilda.

"I'm sorry," she said. "I'm not as strong as I thought I was."

Hilda had to help her back to her bed, and she lay there for some time, not speaking and with her eyes closed. It was some time before she spoke, and then it was not to explain anything.

"I'm all right now," she said. "Just some bad news from Honolulu."

A little later however, as her color came back, she said: "So it was Herbert Johnson who knocked you down and robbed you last night! I know you followed him. It's the sort of thing he would do. Why didn't you tell me?"

"I don't bother my patients with my personal troubles," Hilda said stiffly. "Why is he blackmailing Tony, Miss Rowland? If that's what he's doing?"

But Alice did not answer, and Hilda went down to dinner confused and in a bad humor. Except that Tony was present the meal that night was more or less a repetition of the night before. Nina for some reason chose to talk about Hawaii, and her hope to go back there eventually. Tony ate almost nothing, said even less, and smoked one cigarette after another. But there was something wrong with Aggie. She was clumsy and nervous and Hilda suspected that the *Encyclopedia* was involved.

She had a sudden desire to break the polite veneer of the meal, to destroy the illusion of well-dressed civilized people eating a highly civilized meal, to see the mask of Nina's beautiful face change, if it ever did. She even made an attempt at it.

"I saw a rather dark-skinned man loitering on the pavement last night," she said. "He looked as though he might be waiting for someone."

If looks could have killed Tony's would have slain her. Nina however was only politely interested.

"Was that Herbert again?" she inquired. "I thought you'd got rid of him, Tony." She turned to Hilda. "He's the brother of the maid I told you about in Honolulu," she explained. "He's no good, Tony. I wish you wouldn't see him."

Tony got up, her face set.

"I'm sorry," she said. "I have some things to do," and left without further explanation.

So Herbert was not to be discussed, Hilda reflected. He had taken her bag, suspected the police were after him and it, and got Tony to salvage the watch. But he was not to be suspected. What was the hold he had over the girl? Did it involve her alone, or was she protecting her mother. After all, four years . . .

With Tony gone, Nina looked at Hilda.

"I didn't like to ask before Tony," she said. "She's very nervous these days. Aggie says you had some trouble last night. I hope it wasn't serious."

Hilda glanced at her. If she suspected Herbert it did not show in her face.

"I did a silly thing," she admitted. "I took a bus ride, and got out in a low part of town. Some one knocked me down and robbed me."

"How dreadful! Are you sure you ought to be up and around?"

"I'm quite all right, thanks."

"Did you lose much? If that's too personal, forget it. I just thought . . ."

"I never carry much money. I lost my mother's watch. I valued that, of course."

"What a pity! Have you notified the police?"

Hilda looked at her, but she was eating her chocolate souffle calmly and with enjoyment.

"I believe they're trying to trace the watch," she said warily. "They seem to have located it, but someone bought it today. I'm afraid it's gone."

But Nina had dismissed the watch. She waited until Aggie brought in the fingerbowls. Then she showed the first real emotion Hilda had seen since her arrival. She leaned forward and lowered her voice.

"I'm worried about Tony, Miss Adams. She's not herself at all. And she does such strange things. I'm quite sure she reads my mail before I get it, for one thing. She steams the letters open in the sewing room, and once or twice since you came I know she has locked my door. I hate telling you this, but Alice thinks she's not—well, that she has some mental condition. The way she broke her engagement, for one thing, with everything ready."

It was Hilda's chance.

"You have no idea why she did that?"

"Not the slightest."

"Of course Pearl Harbor was a shock. Sometimes these things are late in developing, Mrs. Rowland."

But Nina shook her head.

"She got over that very soon. Only a couple of months. It was terrible, of course."

Hilda was silent. Whatever had happened Nina obviously had no idea of it.

"Sometimes these nervous upsets come from something held over from childhood," she said after the pause. "Can you recall anything of the sort?"

Nina reached over and took a cigarette from Tony's package on the table. She was thinking back, her handsome face troubled.

"She was a very happy child," she said. "She had a nurse she adored, a Hawaiian woman. Then when she was ten we had to let her go. The nurse, I mean. It was dreadful. Tony fretted for a long time. But it was necessary to send her away. You see she—"

The sentence was not finished. Tony came back. If she had heard what Nina had said she made no comment. She was very pale, although her voice was gentle.

"You've been up a good while," she said to Nina, avoiding Hilda's eyes. "How about bed and a game of gin rummy?"

In her room that night after Alice was settled for the night Hilda went over the situation. Since the conversation with Nina she was confident that the secret Tony was guarding was hers alone. And that whatever it was, up to a short time before Tony had been a happy normal girl, falling in love, getting her trousseau together, writing daily letters to her *fiancé*, and opening and exclaiming over the wedding gifts as they arrived. Then something had happened and it was all over.

Hilda was no prude. She knew the temptations of beautiful women, and Nina was all of that. Had there been a lover, and had Herbert knowledge of it? But Tony was a modern girl. She might resent such knowledge bitterly, but she would not try to kill her mother for such a lapse.

She considered the maid, Delia Johnson. What was it Nina had said about every one having his price? Had she, Nina, had her price? And had Delia known it?

But that was absurd. Selfish she might be, and self-indulgent she certainly was. But to attempt to connect her with the Japanese was preposterous. All in all Hilda knew that night that she had failed, and that her case was almost over.

But how nearly over she had no idea.

X

Later Hilda was to try to bring the events of that night into some sort of order, and to find it difficult.

She remembered the walk with Tony, of course. She had found the girl in the lower hall, looking lonely and lost, and for once the woman in her triumphed over the detective.

"Why not come out and get some air?" she asked. "I'd like company anyhow, after last night."

The girl's face was pitiful as she looked at her.

"I'm afraid I haven't been very nice to you, Miss Adams," she said unexpectedly. "You see, I've been in sort of a jam. And I had no idea . . ."

She hesitated, and Hilda thought she might bring up the matter of the watch. She did not, however.

"I'll get a coat," she said, and ran quickly up the stairs.

They had not had their walk after all, of course. They started companionably enough, after Tony had shot a quick glance up and down the street. But neither Johnny Hayes nor Herbert was in sight. Only a man in plain dark clothes who began suddenly to whistle for an invisible dog, and they had reached the corner of the block before a tall uniformed figure detached itself from the shadows and confronted them.

Tony stopped and caught her breath.

"Just what," said Johnny Hayes sternly, "did you mean by upsetting mother the way you did yesterday?"

Hilda thought she was about to turn and run. So evidently did Johnny, for he caught her by the shoulder and forced her to face him.

"No, you don't," he said. "You're staying right where you are. We're having this out, here and now."

"Let go of me," Tony gasped.

"Not yet," he said. "Not ever, if I can help it. You crazy little fool, what notion have you got in your head anyhow? I'm not going to the Pacific with some fantastic bit of nonsense between us. What if you did walk in your sleep? Hell, yes, I know about that. Aggie's a friend of mine. D'you think I care?"

He dropped his hand, but Tony did not move. She was trembling. She put out a hand and reached blindly for Hilda, as though to steady herself. The man across the street was walking toward them. Hilda recognized him. He was a plain-clothes man named Rogers from headquarters, and she wished furiously that he would mind his own business.

"Anyhow, you gave me the brush-off before that," Johnny was saying. "What was it? What did I do?"

"It has nothing to do with you, Johnny," Tony said, her voice shaking. "Only if you ever cared for me you'll let me alone now. I couldn't go on with it. That's all. I can't go on with it. Ever."

"Why? That's all I want to know. Why? You did love me. I think you still do. What crazy idea have you got in your heart?" Then, still ignoring Hilda, he put his arms around Tony and held her. "Tell Johnny, darling. Let me help. You know I'll do anything, everything. Tell Johnny, won't you?"

Tony shook her head, but her composure suddenly broke. Against his uniform she began to cry, great heavy sobs which shook her whole body, and he was wisely silent. He let her cry it out, while Hilda saw that Rogers had turned back and was the plain-clothes man once more whistling for his imaginary dog.

When it was over Tony released herself.

"Give me a little time, Johnny," she said brokenly. "Maybe things will be better soon. I'm sorry about your mother. I just tried—I do care, Johnny. Always remember that, won't you?"

"What do you mean, remember?"

"When you're overseas I'll write. I promise I'll write," she said, her voice feverish. "There's nobody else. Just you. You can be sure of that."

She turned and started back toward the house, and young Hayes stared gloomily after her.

"Now what the hell do you make of that?" he asked.

Hilda was cautious.

"I don't know," she said. "She's in some sort of trouble. I may learn about it before long. Why not give her time? That's what she asked for."

"Time's the one thing I haven't got," he said, and turning on his heel left her abruptly.

Hilda found Rogers waiting for her on her way back, a middle-aged man with shrewd intelligent eyes.

"Nice little scene," he observed. "Only what did it mean? Boy's been waiting for a couple of hours. Not the fellow who got you last night, I gather?"

"No," Hilda said absently. "He used to be engaged to her. He's sailing soon, and she's worried."

He let that go. "I'll be around," he told her. "Just watch your step," and went back to his lonely vigil in the shadows.

That matters were approaching a crisis of some sort Hilda felt in her very bones that night as she put on her dressing gown over her long-sleeved nightdress and placed her slippers under Alice's couch. But tired as she was she did not go to bed at once. She carried up Volume XIII of the *Encyclopedia Britannica* and went through it page by page in her room. At one place it had apparently been laid face down on something which had smeared it slightly, and she stopped at one rather brief article. Was it possible, she thought? But she dismissed the idea and put the book away, yawning. She had had little real rest the night before, and because she was still bruised she had taken a couple of aspirins. After an hour or so she went to bed and dozed off.

She wakened some time after two in the morning, to find her neck stiff and to try to rearrange her pillow. There was some light in the room from the hall, and after her custom she glanced at her patient's bed. The first intimation she had that anything was wrong was that the bed was empty.

She looked at the bathroom, but the door was open and there was no one in it. Still she was not apprehensive. Alice had not been able to sleep and was wandering around somewhere in her new freedom. Nevertheless she put on her slippers and went out into the hall. Everything was quiet. Nina's door was closed and locked. Tony's door was closed too. And of Alice there was no sign whatever.

When she looked downstairs the front hall was dark and empty, and for the first time she began to feel anxious. She tried to reassure herself. Alice had been hungry and had managed to get down to the kitchen, and because it was nearer she made her way to the back stairs. She stopped sharply as she approached them.

Below her someone was coming up, or trying to. All she could see was a dark huddling figure near the foot of the staircase, a figure which seemed to be on its hands and knees, and which was making small painful noises as it scrabbled at the steps.

"Miss Rowland!" she said sharply. "Wait there. I'll come for you."

She could not find the light switch, and so it was not until she had reached the figure and stooped over it that she realized it was Tony; a Tony who gave a small gasp as she touched her and then fainted dead away. Hilda reached down and felt her pulse. It was slow and feeble, and she hardly knew what to do. In the end she decided to get her down rather than up, and getting below Tony's body she half carried, half dragged it to the floor below. There she laid her out flat and felt for the light switch. The glare almost blinded her as she went back to the girl. She had not moved. Her face had no color whatever, and there was blood on her hands and on the front of her white blouse.

Even in the shock of this discovery Hilda realized that Tony was fully dressed. She had changed from what she had worn at dinner to her usual skirt and blouse, but she had discarded the sweater. The blood was coming from a deep cut on the palm of one hand. Otherwise she seemed uninjured.

There was no sign of Alice as she straightened and looked about her. The door from the small back hall to the kitchen was closed, and when she opened it she thought at first that the kitchen itself was empty. On the table, however, there had been set what was the making of a light meal; a loaf of bread with a knife beside it, a small pat of butter and some sliced cold meat and mustard. At the edge of the table was a bloody print as though some one had laid a hand flat on it.

Tony had not moved when she glanced back at her, and she moved into the room. Only then did she see Alice Rowland, face down on the floor beyond the table, with the back of her head crushed and the fragments of a milk bottle on the floor beside her.

She was dead, beyond a hope.

Hilda stood over the body, with a sense of helpless rage which fairly shook her. She had come on this case to prevent further trouble, and she had not only failed. She had slept while a murder was being committed. Worse than that, it was her patient who had died. Only once in her long experience had such a thing happened, and the picture was too plain to be ignored. Whatever she thought—if she was thinking at all—she knew the police would be sure Tony had done this thing; the Tony who was now lying with blank open eyes on the floor in the hall, staring at the ceiling but seeing nothing at all.

That was when she saw the envelope. It was lying a few feet from the body. She picked it up almost automatically. It was addressed to Alice Rowland, and it was quite obviously the one she had taken from the postman that day. She thrust it hastily inside her uniform and leaving Tony where she was ran upstairs to Nina Rowland's room. It was still locked, and she pounded on it furiously. If Nina had been awake she gave an excellent imitation of shocked arousing.

"What is it?" she called, her voice frightened. "Who's there?"

"Open the door," Hilda shouted. "It's locked. And hurry. Please hurry."

Nina unlocked her door. She was in her nightdress, her feet bare and her hair in curlers with a net over them. In her short-sleeved gown the bandage on her arm showed plainly. She was very pale.

"What's wrong?" she managed. "I was asleep. What's happened?"

Hilda surveyed both Nina and the room. It looked like any

normal bedroom where a sleeper had been disturbed, the windows open, the bed clothing thrown back and a jar of skin cream with some tissues on the toilet table. The memory of the quarrel between Alice and the woman in front of her was strong in her mind, but she had no time to investigate.

"Tony's all right," she said. "She's cut her hand. I . . . Maybe you'd better get your clothes on, Mrs. Rowland. There's been some trouble, and Tony's fainted."

She did not wait. She ran down the front stairs, stopping only to turn on a light. Across the street Rogers was sitting on a low stone wall smoking a cigarette. When she called to him he came over on the run.

"We've had a murder here," Hilda said breathlessly. "Come in and call the Inspector. I'll be in the back hall downstairs."

She showed him the telephone in the library and went back to Tony, still lying where she had left her, and with her eyes still open. They were less blank, however. They moved slowly from Hilda to the stairs and then to the green-painted walls.

"How did I get here?" she asked slowly.

"Don't you know?"

"No. I . . ." She began to remember then, for she lifted her injured hand and stared at it. "Aunt Alice?" she said, with an effort. "Is she . . . ?"

"Can you sit up?" Hilda put an arm around her and raised her, but it seemed to make her dizzy. She let her down again. She could hear Rogers in the front hall, coming back, and went quickly to meet him. He began to speak, but she silenced him with a gesture.

"Tony Rowland has fainted back here," she said hastily. "Don't talk about what's happened before her. I want to get her out of the way. The other's in the kitchen."

"Tony the little girl with the officer?"

"Yes. You'll have to carry her."

He picked Tony up easily, to be confronted by Nina at the head of the back stairs, a Nina who had thrown on a dressing gown but had not removed her curlers, and who only stared when she saw what he held.

"What's the matter?" she said shakily. "She isn't hurt, is she?"

But Tony did not move or speak. She lay back in Rogers' arms with her eyes closed, and she did not open them even when she had been put in her bed and Nina bent over her. She saw the blood and gave Hilda a horrified look.

"She's hurt, Miss Adams. Badly hurt."

Hilda on her way out stopped in the doorway.

"I told you. Her hand's cut. That's all. Call the maids, won't you?"

But Nina was calling no maids that night. She sank into a chair, evidently on the verge of collapse, and turned a desperate face to Hilda.

"Who found her?"

"I did," Hilda said quietly. "I might as well tell you, Mrs. Rowland. Miss Alice has had an accident. I'm afraid it was fatal."

That was when Nina Rowland fainted, and Hilda had two patients on her hands. Not until the two maids had come and they got Nina to her bed across the hall did Hilda get downstairs again. She found Rogers in the kitchen, staring down at the body and looking rather shaken.

"Who did it? The girl?" he asked.

"I don't know," she said shortly. "You got Inspector Fuller, I suppose. I'll get the doctor."

"Little late for that, isn't it?"

"The family doctor. The girl's cut her hand."

"On the bottle? Or on the knife?"

She saw the knife then. She had hardly noticed it before. It was on the table, and there was blood on the long blade. He gave her a forced grin.

"What was it anyhow?" he asked. "A duel? The one with a knife and the other a milk bottle? Where were you while all this was going on?"

"Asleep," she said bitterly and went forward as the doorbell rang.

Two police officers stood outside, their squad car parked at the curb. She sent them back to the kitchen and ran up the stairs, to meet both maids in the upper hall. She felt incapable of coping with them just then. She brushed past them and into Tony's room. The girl had not moved since Rogers had carried her up, except that now her eyes were closed.

"You're not asleep, Tony, and you're not fainting," she said firmly. "You can hear what I say perfectly well."

There was no movement, but Tony opened her eyes. There was such misery in them that Hilda felt like an executioner. She bent over the bed.

"Listen, my dear," she said, her voice one Inspector Fuller had never heard. "You must tell what you know. The police are here. You can't help anybody now by hiding things."

"Is she . . . ?"

"Yes, Tony."

The eyes closed again. "I'm tired," she said. "Please let me alone. I want to sleep."

Aggie had followed Hilda into the room. Now she spoke.

"Why don't you let her alone?" she said sharply. "She's sick. What happened to her anyhow? What are those policemen doing downstairs?"

Hilda straightened.

"Miss Alice is dead, Aggie," she said. "Somebody killed her, down in the kitchen. And Tony here either saw it done or found her there."

Aggie gasped.

"Dead!" she said. "But why? Who would do a thing like that?"

"Ask Tony," Hilda said briefly. "I think she knows."

But there was no time to ask Tony anything. Dr. Wynant came into the room, and downstairs Fuller had arrived and was asking for Hilda. She went down, to find him in the front hall. He surveyed her dourly.

"Well, what do you make of this? Still holding out for the girl?"

He did not wait for a reply. He stalked back to the kitchen and she followed him. The two men from the cruise car and Rogers were standing near the kitchen door. They stood back to let him survey the body, but he did nothing more than that.

"The Half-Truck will be here soon," he said. "Just hold everything until it comes."

The Half-Truck was the humorous name given by the force to the Police Mobile Laboratory. It carried everything from pulmotors to a sound-amplifying device for bombs, and its crew consisted of print experts, several technicians, a photographer, a chemist and a variety of tools. Fuller was proud of it, but now he wanted Hilda's story. She told it to him in the library.

She gave him only the bare facts as she knew them, and he listened attentively.

"All right," he said when she finished. "You don't claim the girl was sleepwalking this time, do you?"

"I don't claim anything."

"You saw the kitchen table. One of them came down to get something to eat, and the other followed. They quarreled, and perhaps the aunt got scared. She picked up a knife, so the girl took it from her and then got the milk bottle. That's the way it looks from here, anyhow."

"What would take Alice Rowland downstairs? She was barely able to walk."

"Yet she did go down. She's still down. Don't forget that, Miss Pinkerton."

Angry color rose in Hilda's cheeks.

"So Tony killed her!" she said. "What about the other people in this house? What about that open kitchen door, and the man who attacked me last night?"

He was not obliged to answer. The Half-Truck arrived just then with its crew, and Fuller followed it back. But Hilda did not go with him. She knew the ritual too well, and there was nothing she could do anyhow. When some time later he came forward again he found her sitting on the stairs, her head buried in her hands and her whole small body dejected and hopeless. She looked up at him as though she did not see him.

"What took Tony downstairs?" she said, her voice unsteady. "And why did Alice follow her? If I knew that . . ."

"It might have been the other way."

She shook her head.

"Alice was still far from well. She'd never have gone down alone anyhow, with me there. She followed Tony. I'm sure of that. If she thought she was sleepwalking—"

"Cutting bread and butter in her sleep! And I suppose she's still asleep when she picks up a milk bottle and brains her aunt."

Hilda got up slowly. She felt drained of all vitality.

"It's just possible she'll say exactly that," she said drearily.

Fuller's look at her was fond but exasperated.

"Why?" he said. "Don't act the sphinx with me. You're no good at it. Why would she say that?"

"She probably thinks she has to," she said.

XI

She followed him stiffly up the stairs to the girl's room. The doctor was in the bathroom preparing a hypodermic, while Aggie hovered over the bed. Tony's hand had been neatly dressed by that time. There was no sign of Nina, but both servants were in the room. Fuller cleaned it of every one except Wynant.

Tony lay with her eyes closed, and he went to the bed and stood looking down at her.

"I want you to tell me what happened downstairs tonight," he said sternly. "Everything. Why you were there. How you cut your hand. And what happened to your aunt."

"I don't know," she said weakly, not opening her eyes. "I went down to get something to eat and she followed me. I went into the pantry for something. I was still there when I heard—when I heard her fall," she shuddered. "I found her—like that."

"How did you cut your hand?"

She raised her hand and looked at the bandage, as though she had not seen it before.

"I don't know," she whispered. "Maybe the knife slipped."

"Did your aunt have the knife? And did you try to take it from her?"

"No," she said, and began to cry, slow tears which rolled unnoticed down her white cheeks. "She never touched it. I was fond of her. We didn't quarrel, if that's what you mean. She was good to me."

"Were you in the habit of going down for a night supper?"

She shook her head, without replying.

"You saw nothing? Or nobody?"

But here the doctor intervened. Tony was badly shocked. The questions could wait. Just now she needed rest and quiet. And Fuller too realized that the girl had said all she intended to. After Dr. Wynant had given the hypodermic both men left, and Hilda alone with her at last, went quietly to the bed. Tony lay very still with her eyes closed, but Hilda knew she was conscious. There was no softness in her voice now.

"Was Herbert in the kitchen tonight?" she asked. "You'd better talk, Tony. I'm warning you."

"Herbert!" Tony gasped, trying to sit up. "What do you know about him? He hasn't anything to do with all this. He wasn't even here. He . . ." She gulped and stopped. Hilda's face was stony.

"I think he was here tonight," she said gravely. "I think he came here tonight to hide from the police, and that you were getting food for him. That's when your Aunt Alice discovered him, wasn't it?" And when Tony said nothing: "He's been blackmailing you, hasn't he? And today your aunt got a letter from Honolulu. She had it in her hand when she followed you to the kitchen."

"Oh God!" Tony lay back in her bed, shivering. "Please don't tell any one about it. It—it hasn't anything to do with what happened."

"What became of it, Tony?" Hilda said, her voice still hard. "I want it. Where have you hidden it?"

"I haven't got it. I never did have it."

"But you know what was in it, don't you?"

Tony however only shook her head and closed her eyes. She refused to speak again, and Hlida stood looking down at her, divided between anger and pity. Any psychiatrist would say she was a mental case, she thought. But she did not believe it.

It was imperative, she realized, to see Nina. But the Nina she found in the bed across the hall was a wild-eyed, hysterical creature, entirely beyond reason, who dared her to think Tony had done anything wrong and tried to order her out of the house. She was not prepared however for Nina's rage when she told her she had been working for the police, and still was.

"So that's it!" she said furiously. "You've been here snooping all the time, and my poor Tony . . ."

Hilda listened as long as she could. When Nina stopped she spoke quietly.

"I would like to see that arm of yours, Mrs. Rowland," she said. "I assure you it's necessary. If you have been wounded and infection has set in, it needs attention."

Whatever she had expected it was not what followed. For Nina almost immediately went into a fit of screaming hysteria, laughing and crying wildly. It was necessary for Dr. Wynant to give her a hypodermic before she quieted, and after it had taken effect he followed Hilda out of the room.

"I don't know whether you are staying here or not, Miss Adams," he said. "I do advise you to keep away from her. Let the maids look after her. She's pretty badly shocked. What set her off this time?"

"I asked to see her arm."

"Still harping on that?" he said indulgently. "Well, keep away from her anyhow. It's *her* arm."

Tony lay in a drugged stupor the rest of the night, while the usual reporters crowded the grounds and used various devices to get into the house, while late as it was a crowd gathered on the pavement and in the alley back of the house, to be held in bounds by the police, while flash-bulbs burst, measurements were taken, the bottle fragments carefully gathered up and while at last Alice Rowland left her home for the last time.

Hilda, not needed elsewhere, spent the time in a search for the letter which she was confident Alice had carried downstairs with her. It was not in Tony's room, and if it had been burned the kitchen stove showed no sign of it. The kitchen was quiet again, and by daylight only the smear on the floor remained to remind her of the tragedy. The police and the crowds had gone, the Half-Truck had departed, the grounds had been examined, and only a policeman outside, a guard in the lower hall and Fuller drinking coffee in the dining room with Dr. Wynant remained.

They paid no attention to her when she joined them. The doctor put down his cup. He looked tired and unhappy.

"I can't believe it," he said. "I like the girl. Always have. It was a fine family—until lately, at least."

"When did you notice a change?"

"Only recently. Mind you, I'm not saying Tony's abnormal even now. She's not been herself since she broke her engagment, of course. But a thing like this . . . !"

Fuller lit a cigarette and surveyed the doctor over it.

"How do you get around the other facts? She did try to shoot her mother, didn't she? And there was the automobile accident later. Why all that? Does she hate her?"

The doctor looked shocked.

"Hate her!" he said. "Hate Nina! She is and has been devoted to her. Perhaps like most girls at her age she cared most for her father, but as for hate—that's absurd."

"Then you do think she was walking in her sleep when she fired the gun?" Fuller persisted.

"Something of the sort."

"It wasn't possible Alice did it, I suppose? And that last night was the result of Tony's knowing it?"

"I'd consider it highly unlikely," the doctor said gravely. "Alice Rowland had her faults. But she took in her brother's family and looked after them. Not too amiably, perhaps. As I say, she was pretty difficult at times. But she did it as well as she could, I imagine."

Fuller looked thoughtful.

"The boys think they have a case against Tony," he said. "That story of hers won't wash. They got her prints on the knife and the table, both bloody. If they find any on the pieces of the milk bottle and they turn out to be hers we'll have to take her in for questioning. Hilda's going to fight that, I suppose."

He looked at Hilda and smiled.

"Why?" The doctor was puzzled. He too stared at Hilda, who said nothing. She had poured herself a cup of coffee and was slowly sipping it.

"Don't ask me. Ask her. One of her hunches probably. Something she's got in her head about Honolulu. But four years is a long time." He got up and, picking up his hat, set it carefully on his head. "I have a great deal of respect for her hunches," he said, and went out.

The doctor looked at Hilda.

"What's all this about Honolulu?" he said gruffly. "I don't believe in hunches, but if you know anything . . ."

Hilda did not reply directly. She put down her coffee cup and looked at him stonily.

"When you see Nina Rowland again will you examine her arm?" she inquired.

"What the hell has her arm got to do with Alice's murder?"

"That's what I want to find out."

He was irritated. He got up and gazed down at her with extreme distaste.

"I'll examine her arm when and if she asks me to," he said. "Not before."

"You may be sorry," she told him. But he picked up his bag and flung it out of the room without replying.

She did not see Fuller again that morning. Now that it was daylight he wandered around the lawns surrounding the house. But he found nothing and at last he got into his car and drove to his office. He found a message there from the Commissioner and discovered that gentleman surrounded by morning papers and a distinct aura of unpleasantness. His cold was better, however, so he was articulate. Very completely articulate.

"What sort of a mess is this?" he demanded. "I give you one of my best men to watch the house, you put the Pinkerton woman in it, and under both their noses we have a murder." He eyed Fuller coldly. "At least you saved Hilda Adams. That probably pleases you."

"It does," Fuller said. "I'm very fond of Hilda."

"Well, goddammit, she was there. How did she let this happen?"

"She was asleep," Fuller said serenely. "She'd been knocked on the head the night before, and she was about all in."

"And who the hell did that?" said the Commissioner. "Not that I haven't felt like doing it myself every now and then. And to some other people I could name," he added darkly as Fuller grinned.

When he got back to his office, having left his chief in a state bordering on apoplexy, he found a young officer waiting for him, a tall boy with a white face and a pair of desperately clenched hands holding his cap.

"Lieutenant Hayes, sir," he said. "I've just come from the Rowland house."

"I see," Fuller said politely. "Sit down, son, and relax. No use getting into a dither about it, you know. Easy does it."

The lieutenant did not sit down. He stood stiffly, staring at Fuller.

"Are you going to arrest Tony Rowland?" he asked. "Because if you are—"

"We don't arrest people as easy as you seem to think, Lieutenant. This isn't the Army."

If he had hoped his last words would distract Johnny Hayes he failed. That single-tracked young man ignored them.

"Then why did you take her prints?" he demanded. "Aggie—one of the maids—says you did."

"We print everybody in a case like this."

Hayes however refused to relax.

"I got the story from Aggie," he said. "You're going to pin this on her, aren't you? Because she got hold of a gun once in her sleep and it went off . . . What sort of evidence is that? She never killed anybody, or tried to. I know her."

"She hasn't been accused yet, Lieutenant." He pushed a box of cigarettes across the desk. "Have one and get hold of yourself. I'd like to ask you a question or two. Just why did she break her engagement to you?"

Hayes sat down. He did not take the proffered cigarette, however. He got a leather case from his pocket and lit one of his own. His hands were not steady.

"That's a private matter, sir," he said.

"Rather sudden, wasn't it?" And when there was no reply to this: "I understand all the plans were made. Then out of a blue sky—"

"Oh, for God's sake. If she changed her mind that's her business."

Fuller studied him. He looked like a nice boy, the clean-cut type the Army either produces or discovers.

"Is that all? Did she merely change her mind, or did

something happen between you?"

"Nothing happened."

"There was no quarrel?"

"No, sir."

"You realize, of course, that she isn't in a very happy position, Lieutenant. I'm not referring to the shooting a couple of months ago. I'm speaking of last night. On the surface it looks as though she and her aunt had quarreled, that Alice Rowland picked up a knife, that Tony took it from her—her prints are on it—and then struck her aunt with a milk bottle which was on the table. On the surface, I say. If her prints are on any of the glass from the broken bottle it won't look very good."

"But you haven't got them?"

"The bottle broke, and the milk hasn't helped any. They're working on them now."

The telephone rang at his elbow. He picked it up, aware of the boy's eyes on him. He listened for a minute or so, then said thanks and put down the receiver. Hayes was standing by that time.

"A good many blurred prints on the glass," he said. "Some that seem to be hers. They're still working on it. I'm sorry, Lieutenant. It isn't decisive. Not yet."

Hayes however was not listening. He jerked his cap on his head, gave a halfhearted automatic salute and departed. Fuller sat for some time after he had gone. He had liked the boy's looks, and damn it all, with what was ahead of him . . . He picked up the telephone again.

"Work on those other prints," he said. "If we haven't got them try Washington. Maybe they are the milkman's, but maybe they're not. That's what I want to know."

XII

At the house Hilda had had a trying day. The uniformed officer still patrolled outside the house, and another one remained in the lower hall, looking bored and now and then slipping into the library for a surreptitious cigarette. Nina's door was locked and Tony was still only semiconscious. Hilda ate her lunch alone, feeling useless and inadequate. Before she went upstairs she went back to the kitchen.

Stella was alone there. She had mopped the milk from the floor and cleaned up generally. Now she was at the table drinking strong black tea to settle her nerves. She was not cordial, but she seemed glad to see anybody.

"You've been here a long time, Stella," Hilda said. "Was it usual for Miss Tony to get a night lunch for herself or her mother?"

"No, miss. I said that to Aggie today. I've known her to get a piece of cheese or something like that. But that's all, and only once in a while. As for that milk bottle, she never touched milk." Stella's face crumpled. Unexpectedly she began to cry. "The poor child!" she said. "So nice and kind and then breaking her engagement and now this. When I think of her carrying out her wedding dress yesterday—"

"Are you sure of that?" Hilda asked sharply.

"Well, Aggie says it's missing. Another dress too. And she had the car out. I saw her come back."

Hilda was puzzled.

"Why on earth would she do a thing like that, Stella?"

"I suppose she just wanted to get rid of it. Couldn't bear to have it around, poor dear. And so crazy she was about it when it came!"

Hilda digested this in silence. When Stella had wiped her eyes and regained some of her composure Hilda opened the door to the basement staircase.

"I suppose the police were down there?" she asked.

"They were all over. The dirt in this place you'd hardly believe. They even went into the butler's room! It's empty, of course, has been since we got rid of that Herbert Johnson."

In spite of herself Hilda started.

"Herbert Johnson?" she said. "What was he here?"

"Miss Tony found him somewhere. They knew him in the Islands. He wasn't rightly a butler. More of a houseman really. And he wasn't any good. Always sort of snooping around. Miss Alice fired him, and not too soon if you ask me."

"When was this?"

"Oh, two—three months ago. We really got him because of the wedding. His sister Delia used to be Mrs. Rowland's maid. If she wasn't any better than he was . . ."

"Where is the butler's room?"

"Off the back hall, so he could answer the doorbell. It's closed now. Nothing there."

Hilda left the kitchen, but she did not go upstairs. She found the door to the room, slipped inside and closed it carefully behind her. The window was closed and the shade down, but a glance told her that some one had been in it briefly and recently. Possibly the police too. But certainly the police had not put a blanket on the dismantled bed, or a fresh cake of soap and a towel on the stationary washstand in the corner. Both soap and towel had been used, and the under side of the soap was still moist.

Some one had made hasty preparations to sleep there the night before. To get a supper of sorts and then to sleep, and she had no doubt whatever as to who it had been. When she went back to the kitchen Stella was pouring milk into a saucer for her cat and looking rather sulky.

"I guess I talk too much," she said. "But if that Herbert was here last night he'd be the one who did it. Him and his goings-on, scaring Miss Tony half to death and getting her little bit of money from her."

"How do you mean he scared her?"

"I wouldn't know. Something about that sister of his—as if anybody cared! And Tony slipping him into her mother's room when she thought nobody was around! I didn't draw a full breath until Miss Alice fired him."

Hilda went back upstairs. She had not told Fuller about the envelope from the kitchen floor, and she had no real doubt as to why it had been where she found it. To make certain however she went into Alice's room and to the chest where she had locked the letter the day before.

The chest was not locked now. The keys were hanging in the upper drawer and Hilda opened it. It contained nothing however but neatly arranged piles of stockings and gloves, and the other drawers were equally innocent. If she had had any doubt that Alice had had the letter in her hand when she went downstairs that night the doubt was gone.

Just to be certain she searched the rest of the room. The letter had definitely disappeared, however, and the picture of the murder grew clearer in her mind; of Alice, letter in hand, following Tony to the kitchen, of her telling or reading its contents, and of a Herbert, hiding from the police and seeking sanctuary in his old room, overhearing her. Coming up behind her maybe and picking up the milk bottle.

Still, in the light of what she already knew, why had he killed her? Either he had only meant to knock her down and escape, or she had some knowledge which made it necessary for her to die.

Somewhat grimly, Hilda picked up the telephone on the bedside table and called Fuller.

"Can you talk to Honolulu by wire?" she inquired.

"I can. I'll be monitored, of course. Why Honolulu?"

"Herbert Johnson came from there.'

"Herbert Johnson?"

"The man who knocked me down and robbed me. You may recall that," she said drily. "He was butler or something of the sort here two or three months ago. Tony got him, but Alice Rowland fired him."

He whistled.

"I think he was here last night," she went on. "Tony seems to have hidden him here, or someone did. He comes from Hawaii. He may have a record there. You'd better find out all you can about him. About his sister too. You might see what you can find out about the Rowlands at the same time."

Fuller was duly impressed.

"You think this Herbert's the killer, don't you?" he inquired. "Anybody but Tony Rowland, eh?"

"I'm only saying he's been hiding out, and Tony was probably getting him something to eat last night. If Alice came in and recognized him . . . She may have known him. Or she may have written to someone in Hawaii about him. She got a letter from there yesterday and I can't find it."

"If he was there why didn't Tony say so?"

"She probably has a reason," Hilda said drily and put down the receiver.

He sat back and considered this after he had put in the Honolulu call. He had in fact some hours to consider it, due to wartime delay. He went back to the beginning of the case and Alice's story to him when she brought the gun. Getting out the rough sketch she had drawn of Nina's room he studied it again, the doorway, the bed, the location of the open window. Suppose this Herbert had been the one who shot at Nina and missed her? Hilda was laying emphasis on him. Was he in the house as butler at that time?

He looked over his notes. No. Only the family and the two women servants, he saw. Of course someone might have admitted him. Tony, by choice. In that case why had she protected him? As she was still doing, he thought irritably; getting Hilda's watch before the police found it, and hiding him the night before. Unless it was blackmail, and of a serious sort. Not of Tony probably. Very possibly of her mother. What he had seen of her had shown him a beautiful and not too intelligent woman, the sort who expected admiration from men and undoubtedly received it. What did Herbert have? Letters and photographs were the usual stock of the blackmailer. Outside of those . . .

At five o'clock he called Hilda on the phone.

"We've picked up a dozen or so fellows who more or less answer your Herbert's description," he said. "Can you come down?"

She did not answer at once, and when she did she was doubtful.

"I can," she said. "I'd rather not, of course. Tony's beginning to rouse. I don't like to leave her."

"Put Aggie there. How's the mother?"

"Still shut away. Perhaps I ought to tell you she's sent one word. I'm fired."

"You seem to be still there!"

"What do you think?" she inquired.

She agreed to come however, leaving Aggie with Tony and before six she was viewing a sorry-looking line of men in the glare of the line-up. None of them was Herbert and Hilda, looking them over much as she would a row of Christmas turkeys, rejected them in much the same businesslike manner and prepared to go. He followed her to the door.

"If Tony's coming out of the hypo I'd better talk to her," he said. "It's time she spoke up."

Hilda stopped and turned chilly blue eyes up to his.

"You're not going to question her until I get the bandage off her mother's arm," she said coldly, and walked out.

So Hilda still thought Tony had shot her mother, he reflected. Well, what if she had? And once more his mind turned to a possible lover, to blackmail, and the girl's probable resentment at both. But it was Alice who had been murdered, not an attractive but certainly an inoffensive onlooker. Or was she?

He went back to his office to wait for his call and—he thought grimly—for Hilda to get the bandage off Nina Rowland's lovely white arm. How had they managed it, he wondered. After all a bullet wound was a serious matter, even if it only plowed through the flesh. There would have been blood to hide, and pain to conceal. Not for the first time he wondered if Hilda had not got off on the wrong foot. But long experience had taught him to respect her methods.

He decided to give her a few hours more, which turned out to be a mistake. And an almost fatal one at that.

XIII

When Hilda got back to the Rowland house she found the young police officer in the hall below staring up the stairs.

"Say," he said. "I thought the girl was sick."

"So she is. What's wrong?"

He scratched an ear reflectively.

"I don't know as it's anything," he said. "I just saw somebody up there out of the tail of my eye. Looked like a young lady. Maybe I'm wrong."

Hilda scuttled up the stairs, but everything was quiet. Tony was in bed, awake but not moving. Aggie, however had disappeared, and Hilda was immediately suspicious. Nothing seemed to be wrong, but she was confident Tony had been in the hall for some purpose of her own.

"How long have you been alone?" she demanded.

"Only a minute or two." Tony's voice was flat. "She went to get me some soup."

Hilda glanced around the room. Nothing was apparently changed. Colonel Rowland's picture still stood on the toilet table. The few drops of blood on the blue carpet from Tony's cut hand had been washed up, her slippers and dressing gown were in the closet as before. But Tony was watching her with the eyes of a sick child. She walked over to the bed.

"What have you been doing?" she asked bluntly. "You've been up to something, haven't you? That policeman downstairs saw you."

"Can't I even see my own mother?"

"Not at the head of the stairs. Where were you? What were you doing?"

Tony however refused to answer, and Hilda felt vaguely uneasy. She looked down at the girl.

"Now you're awake," she said, still bluntly. "I'd like my watch again. It belonged to my mother, and I know you have it."

"It's in the toe of a shoe in the closet," Tony said indifferently. "When are they going to arrest me?"

"Why do you think they *are* going to arrest you?"

"Because I did it," she said, with that strange new indifference. "They needn't look any further. You can tell that man downstairs. Or maybe I'd better tell him myself."

"You killed your aunt? With a milk bottle?" Hilda inquired blandly, "and that stiff arm of yours?"

"I did it. That's enough, isn't it?"

Hilda's patience gave way.

"Now listen to me," she said crossly. "You're behaving like a child. You're too old to go on dramatizing yourself. Who are you protecting? Herbert Johnson? Did he kill your Aunt Alice?"

"I told you I did it."

Hilda wanted to shake her.

"Has it occurred to you," she said, "that you've done more than your share of damage? That if you'd acted like a sane person your Aunt Alice might be alive now?" And when Tony only shuddered and closed her eyes—"And that you haven't helped anybody or anything? Suppose I tell you that the police are looking up Herbert Johnson's record in Honolulu right now."

To her horror and dismay she realized that the girl had fainted again. She was still not conscious when Aggie came in with the soup, and to turn a blistering tongue on her.

She went back to her room after Tony was better, but she was uneasy. What had the girl been doing in the upper hall? And why had she fainted when she learned about Herbert's record in Honolulu? She felt defeated and deflated as she changed from her street clothes into her uniform again. Nina's door was still obstinately closed and probably locked. There had been no sound from it. And there was still no word from Fuller.

She went downstairs to her supper in an unhappy frame of mind. Even the theory she had been slowly evolving seemed far-fetched and unlikely. After all why kill Alice? If anyone had to be killed it should have been Herbert Johnson. Unless . . .

She ate very little. She was still too uneasy to be hungry. Outside in the hall she saw Aggie carrying a supper tray to the library for the police officer, and saw him eating it as she went up the stairs again. Nothing suspicious had happened, however. Tony was not asleep, but she refused to talk, and there was no sound from Nina's room. She located her watch where Tony said she would find it, and wound and set it automatically by the bedside clock.

It was eight o'clock, she was to remember later.

For two hours she sat in the dim light in the bedroom, aware that Tony was watching her. But she made no effort to speak or to get out of bed, and at last Hilda got stiffly to her feet and prepared to go to her room and get ready for the night.

Tony asked for a glass of water then, the first time she had spoken. Hilda placed it beside the bed and stood watching her. But she did not drink it. She lay there looking up with tired sunken young eyes.

"Don't worry," she said. "I won't get up. And I'm sorry I've given you so much trouble, Miss Adams." She smiled faintly.

"That's a promise, is it?" Hilda looked down at her.

"Absolutely. I'm going to sleep." She yawned, and turned on her side.

That was at ten o'clock. As she went out Hilda heard Aggie and Stella going up to their rooms on the third floor, and she looked down into the front hall for the officer there. Rather to her surprise he was not in sight, and she suspected him of being in the kitchen searching for food or in the library smoking.

One of her profoundest beliefs being that men were all right in their place but seldom in it, she made her usual systematic preparations for the night. She took a short bath, brushed her teeth and her hair, began to wind her watch and remembered she had already done so, put on her nightgown and a warm dressing gown over it, and then having switched out her light went to her door.

To her astonishment it did not open. She pulled at it vigorously, but nothing happened. And when she found the switch and turned on the lights again she saw the key was not in it.

For the first time she felt terrified. She stood staring at it incredulously. This could not be happening, not to her, Hilda Adams. It happened to people like Nina, but not to her. She shook it violently and called.

"Officer!" she said. "Officer, some one has locked me in."

There was no reply however, and she looked around her helplessly. She could open the window and shout, she thought. But she hesitated to do it. Anyhow the house was a detached one, and the patrolman was not in sight on the pavement outside. What had happened to the guard in the hall? Was he dead? Had some one knocked him out?

It was wrong. All wrong. Something was going on in the house, and she was helpless. The nearest telephone was across the hall in Alice Rowland's room, and it chose that moment to ring violently. It kept on ringing for some time, while she looked around for a method of escape. She glanced up at the closed transom over the door. She had no illusions that she could get through it, but at least she could look out, maybe call so some one would hear her. It took some time to move the table under it, and to mount by means of a chair. The transom too had apparently not been opened for years. She managed it at last, to realize that the light in both upper and lower halls had been extinguished, and that if the guard was there he was either unconscious or dead.

She called without result, and as she was getting down from her perch the chair slipped and fell. She sat on the floor for a minute or two, a small and ignominious figure of defeat. A frightened one, too. For almost the first time in her life she felt helpless and desperate.

To add to her confusion the telephone across the hall was ringing again, and she realized that something would have to be done, and done soon.

She limped to the window and looked out. The policeman

was still missing, but a man was walking along the pavement. He had a dog on a leash, and he stopped sharply and looked up when she called.

"Do you mind ringing the doorbell?" she asked.

"Doing what?"

"Ringing the doorbell. I'm locked in my room and can't get out."

He let the dog go and came up the walk. He was middle-aged and carrying his hat. He seemed to be quite bald.

"There's nothing wrong, is there?" he asked. "I mean—this is the Rowland house, isn't it?"

"Yes. I don't know what's happened. Do try the bell. I think it rings on the third floor too. The servants will hear it."

He climbed the steps and put a thumb on the porch button. The dog had followed him, looking interested. Through the open transom Hilda could hear the bell far away, and after an interval Aggie's heavy steps coming down the stairs from the third floor. She exclaimed when she saw the dark hall, and evidently turned on a light, for it was reflected in Hilda's room. Hilda called to her.

"You needn't go down," she said. "I'm locked in here. It's Miss Adams. See if you can find the key and let me out."

"Whoever did that?" said Aggie. "Maybe the door's stuck. There's no key here."

Hilda went back to the window and leaned out.

"It's all right," she said to the man below. "Thanks a lot. One of the maids is here now."

He went away looking vaguely disappointed, as though he had expected something more dramatic. But Hilda wasted no time on him. She was back at the door.

"Try Miss Alice's key," she said urgently, "and see if that policeman is around. I don't know what's happened to him."

It took some time to find a key which fitted. Aggie moved slowly, and her hands fumbled as she tried one after another. Hilda was on the verge of shrieking hysteria when at last the door opened and she shot out into the hall.

Somewhere not far away the engine of a car had started to roar, then settled down to a purr. The telephone had stopped ringing, and save for the guard missing from the lower hall everything seemed quiet. But she saw that Tony's door, which she had left open, was now closed. She felt her throat tighten as she ran back to it.

It was not locked, however. She threw it open and stepped inside to find the bed empty and no sign of Tony in the room.

Alarmed as she was, even then Hilda had no idea of the extent of the calamity. With Aggie at her heels she crossed to Nina's door and banged on it. It took a long time to rouse her, but at last she came to the door and Hilda asked rather wildly if Tony was there.

"Tony?" Nina said thickly. "Why no. What's wrong? Where is she?"

Hilda did not wait. She scurried forward to Alice's room, and from there down the front stairs. In the library the young police officer was heavily asleep on the leather couch. He was breathing noisily, and a cigarette had fallen from his hand and burned a small hole in the carpet.

There was no sign of Tony anywhere. In the back of the house the lights were out, but the kitchen door was standing wide open, and she ran frantically outside. Back along the alley the garage was closed and locked, and by the light of a nearby street lamp she could see that the car was still there. But there was no sound of the motor running, and she drew a long breath of relief. If Tony had only run away, and not . . .

She was dripping with perspiration, although the night was cool. Her one fear had been that the girl had found herself facing an insoluble problem and had killed herself. It was still possible, of course. She could have made her way to the river, or there were a dozen other sickening possibilities. But in that case she would have had to dress. Had there been time enough for that, she wondered. How long had she been locked in her room?

She never even heard the doorbell as she ran back to the house, and she only realized Aggie had admitted Fuller when he caught her by the arm and held her.

"Why the hell don't you answer your telephone?" he demanded angrily.

She looked at him, her face blank.

"Tony's disappeared," she said.

"Disappeared?" he said incredulously. "Where's she gone?"

"How would I know? I've been locked in my room, and the policeman on the street probably went to the drugstore for cigarettes. All she had to do was to walk out."

He followed her up the stairs. The servants had roused Nina and she was standing in the door of her room. Dulled as she was by the opiate she had been given, there could be no doubt of her bewilderment.

"Where could she go?" she was saying, her eyes staring in her white face. "She wasn't even dressed, was she?" She caught Fuller by the arm. "You've got to find her, for God's sake. Before it's too late. Before she does something dreadful."

Hilda did not wait. She caught Aggie's eye and went into Tony's room.

"You know her clothes," she said. "Look and see if anything is missing."

But nothing was missing. Aggie inspected the closet and the bed.

"Her clothes are all here," she said, her voice flat. "But there's a blanket gone from her bed. And her slippers aren't here."

Hilda reported that to Fuller as he came in, followed by a terrified Nina. He ignored the matter of the clothing, however. He looked from Aggie to Nina, his face dark with anger.

"The officer downstairs has been drugged," he said sternly. "What do you women know about it? Did you drug him so your daughter could escape, Mrs. Rowland?"

She stared at him blankly.

"Me!" she said. "Why would I do a thing like that?"

"Somebody did," he said, his voice gruff. "Someone in this house. And someone has taken your daughter away. What do you know about that?"

"I don't know anything," she said. "And I wouldn't tell you if I did. At least you can't arrest her now."

"We had no idea of arresting her," he said, his voice grim. "We've got Herbert Johnson, Mrs. Rowland, if that means anything to you."

She looked even more pale, if that was possible. But there

was no doubt of her surprise.

"Herbert?" she said unbelievingly. "But what has Herbert got to do with this?"

He was compelled to believe her. Whatever had been going on, at least she did not connect Herbert Johnson with it. He sent her back to her bed, to comfort a Hilda who for once had lost her composure. She was coming from Alice's room, a small empty bottle in her hand, and she held it out to him, her face a frozen mask.

"Sleeping tablets," she said. "I'm afraid she's taken all of them."

Fuller stiffened as he took the bottle and examined it.

"How long do you think it is since she took them?"

"It can't be more than an hour and a half. She was awake when I left her. But I was locked in for a good while, and before that I was getting ready for the night."

"How many tablets were there?"

"Plenty. If we don't find her soon it will be too late."

Neither of them had noticed Aggie, standing by. The first warning they had was a heavy crash behind them as she fainted and fell to the floor.

XIV

No one paid any attention to her. At some period she must have revived and got up, have gone upstairs to her room and packed her clothing, sobbing bitterly as she did so. At some time later too she must have crept down the back stairs and left the house by the kitchen door. But by that time Fuller had been to the garage and seen the car still there.

For once in his life he was thoroughly at a loss. Obviously Tony had not gone of her own volition. She had been carried away, wrapped in a blanket, and she might easily die before she was located. He had an idea what had happened, but that was all, and the likelihood that they could locate her before it was too late was small indeed.

When later on he decided to talk to Aggie she was gone, bag and baggage.

That Tony had been taken away in a car was evident, but the policeman who belonged in front of the house had seen none. He appeared as Fuller went down the stairs.

"I saw the lights on," he said. "Is anything wrong, sir?"

"Only a kidnaping," Fuller said shortly. "A girl's been stolen out of this house, the nurse was locked in her room and you weren't around. Where the hell were you?"

He looked astonished. He had heard a window break somewhere near, he said, and saw a man running down the street. He had followed him for two or three blocks, but he was pretty fast. He had lost him near the bus stop.

"Funny thing, sir," he said. "He could have dodged into any

of the places around here and got away. He didn't. He—just kept going."

He had no description of him, except that from the way he ran, he was young. And that he was without a hat. Kind of a light-colored suit, he thought. As to the broken window, he'd located it across the street and notified the family.

Fuller went into the library. The young guard was sitting rather dazedly on the couch in the library.

"I don't know what happened to me," he said, his voice shaken. "I got sleepy all at once. I couldn't even stand up. I came in here and—well, that's all I remember. I just passed out."

Fuller's face was grim as he turned to see a stiff-faced Hilda pushing Stella down the stairs.

Stella looked frightened. Her thin body was trembling.

"It's about Aggie," she said. "She didn't take a bath."

"What the hell's that got to do with it?"

"She said she was. I heard the water running. But she wasn't. She was downstairs."

"What Stella means," Hilda interposed, "is that Aggie locked me in my room and turned out the lights. In that case she probably doped Price's supper tray. You see what that means, of course."

"Are you saying that Aggie took the girl away?"

With a magnificent gesture Hilda deplored the stupidity of all men, pushed into the library and picked up the telephone book. After that, with Fuller's baffled eyes still on her, she dialed a number.

"Hotel Majestic?" she said politely. "Give me Mrs. Hayes. Mrs. Arthur Hayes. It's urgent."

She waited. The room behind her was filled with faces: Fuller's, Nina's, Stella's, the two police officers'. So far as she was concerned they were not there.

"Mrs. Hayes?" she said. "I'm sorry to disturb you, but it's important. Have you a car in town?"

Mrs. Hayes's voice, surprised and not too pleasant, could be heard by everyone.

"In town? No. What on earth . . . Is it Johnny? Has he had an accident?"

"I imagine he's quite well," Hilda said, rapidly but still politely. "What sort of car is it, Mrs. Hayes?"

"A black limousine. But I don't really see—"

"Do you mind giving me the number of the license? And your home telephone too. We want to call up and see if it's there. And hurry, please. It's a matter of life and death."

But Mrs. Hayes was firm. She was giving no information until she knew what the trouble was, and Fuller—finally seeing the light—took the phone himself, using his best authoritative manner.

"This is Inspector Fuller of the Police Department," he said. "Please give me the license number of the car at once. I think it's been used to kidnap Tony Rowland. If it goes over the State line it's a capital offense."

"Johnny?" she gasped. "You mean Johnny has done that?"

"It looks like it."

Her reaction surprised him. She was indignant and terrified.

"You can't mean he is going to marry her? It's impossible. It's dreadful. You must find him, Inspector."

"I've got to find him, and soon. Or the charge may be murder."

She gasped for breath, but she gave both numbers, and at Hilda's suggestion the location of the summer place in Massachusetts. "But he can't go there," she protested. "It's closed. There's nobody there."

"There might be an excellent reason," he said drily, and put down the receiver. After that he spent a busy quarter of an hour over the phone. He augmented his earlier orders with the license number of the car, and after a long wait Mr. Hayes in Connecticut reported the limousine gone.

"The chauffeur says a sergeant—a young fellow—came here late this afternoon with a note from my son John. He wanted to borrow the car for overnight. As I use a coupe myself he let it go. What's wrong? John in trouble about it?"

"Very definitely," said Fuller, and put down the receiver.

Aggie was gone by the time they looked for her, sitting red-eyed and terrified in a jolting bus. She had nowhere to go, after thirty years in the Rowland house. When the bus reached the end of the line she was still there. The driver looked back at her.

"What's the idea?" he said. "Just taking a ride?"

She said nothing. At the end of the trip she was back where she had started, and she picked up her bag automatically and got out. She walked doggedly back to the house and up the stairs, to confront a Hilda remarkable in her dressing gown and magnificent in her fury. Aggie did not give her a chance to speak.

"It was to be only for a minute, Miss Adams. Just long enough to get her out," she sobbed, her heavy shoulders shaking. "How could I know?" she protested, tears rolling down her cheeks. "He called me on the telephone this afternoon. He didn't want her to be arrested. He knew she didn't do it. All he wanted was to get her away until they found out who killed Miss Alice."

"So you locked my door. You doped that guard downstairs, too. Where were you when he carried her out?"

"Up in my room. I was to wait and when the car drove off in the alley I was to unlock your door again. I didn't mean any harm. I was trying to help."

"Help her to die, you mean," Hilda said bitterly. "If they don't find her in time that's what will happen, Aggie. Think that over. Then go up to your room and pray. She needs it."

It was some time before she went downstairs again. Fuller was once more hanging up the receiver, after issuing orders, statewide and including near-by states as well, to pick up any car answering the vague description he had, and containing a girl, probably asleep and wrapped in a dark blanket. It was pretty hopeless, he knew. Tony might be on the floor in the back of the car, or the car might already be garaged and hidden somewhere. But it was a fight against time. Something had to be done.

When he turned from the telephone he surveyed Hilda with his usual mixture of pride and irritation. He did not notice that she looked on the verge of collapse.

"The Honolulu message is in," he said. "Johnson's wanted for murder out there. Nothing on the sister yet. Your hunch was good, Hilda."

She still said nothing. There was, as a matter of fact, no time for her to say anything. A car drove up to the curb, and two young men got out. One of them carried a figure wrapped in a dark blanket. The other ran ahead and rang the bell. Both men were in uniform, one of them a sergeant, and it was Johnny Hayes who brought Tony into the house, a Johnny pale to the lips and visibly shaking.

"Look, for God's sake!" he said hoarsely. "We can't wake her up. There's something wrong."

He attempted to carry her up the stairs, but Fuller blocked the way.

"Get her back into the car you young fool!" he shouted. "She's had a poisonous dose of sleeping tablets. The hospital's not far. You two damned idiots may have killed her."

They did not resent it. They were scared and pitiful. They did not even notice Hilda—still in dressing gown and slippers—as she got in with them. It is doubtful if they realized that Fuller was grimly telling them they were under arrest for abduction, or that kidnaping was a capital crime. The other boy drove while Johnny sat in the rear holding Tony, his face filled with despair. He spoke only twice. Once he said: "I couldn't let her be arrested. I only meant to hide her for a while." And again: "Who gave her the poison?"

"She took it herself," Fuller said grimly.

XV

Hours later, with a cold October sun shining into the hospital windows, Fuller roused himself from sleep in the straight chair outside Tony's room. He felt stiff and hungry, and the sight of Hilda, in a borrowed uniform and a cap set uncompromisingly on top of her head made him also feel guilty.

"See here," he said roughly, "how about home and bed? She's all right, isn't she?"

She looked worriedly at him.

"She'll live. I don't think she wants to."

"She's young, Hilda. She'll get over it. And we have Herbert. Don't forget that."

She looked up at him. He seemed relieved and self-confident. She made a move toward the pocket of her dressing gown, then abandoned the idea. In an endeavor to cheer her Fuller laughed.

"I don't want a night like that again," he said cheerfully. "Quite a plan those youngsters had, wasn't it? The sergeant to break a window and call off the man in front, and Johnny to grab the girl. Then when it was all over to see the sergeant topple over in a faint! I hope to God the Army doesn't hear it."

Hilda however refused to be cheered. She sat staring ahead of her, her eyes blank, and his gaze grew more intent.

"What's wrong with you, Hilda?"

She stirred then, but she still did not look at him.

"Nothing," she said, and got up heavily. "I meant to tell

you. I got the bandage off Nina Rowland's arm last night."
"And Tony had shot her?"
"No. Nobody had shot her." She reached up and took off her cap. "I'd better go home. I'm not needed now."
He felt confused as he took her down to a waiting police car, still in the ridiculous borrowed uniform, with her bathrobe over her arm. She had refused to say anything more, and he thought she walked as though she felt slightly dizzy. He was still puzzled as he went back to his vigil outside Tony's door.
To his disgust Johnny Hayes was there again, prowling the hall, with a face which needed a shave and could have stood a washing.
Fuller groaned when he saw him.
"Why don't you go somewhere else?" he said irritably. "Get a bath and go to bed, for instance."
Johnny looked astonished.
"Bed, sir?" he said. "I thought I was under arrest."
"Oh, for God's sake!" Fuller said sourly. "Get out of my sight. Go and get some breakfast. Get that sergeant of yours and beat it. Let the Army take care of you. You're its baby. Not mine."
Johnny made a gesture which threw the Army at least temporarily overboard. He stood in front of Fuller, rocking slightly on a pair of excellent shoes, and with his unshaven jaw set.
"I'm entitled to some information, sir," he said, not without dignity. "Why did she take that stuff? If she did take it."
"I imagine she blamed herself for her aunt's death."
"But that's ridiculous!"
"Not entirely," said Fuller gravely. "She was sheltering a fugitive from justice, a man named Herbert Johnson. Alice Rowland must have found him there and threatened to call the police."
"It doesn't sound like Tony, Inspector."
"I expect she had her reasons," Fuller said, his voice dry. "Let her tell you herself when she's able to. Now go and get some breakfast and a shave. And take that window-breaking sergeant of yours with you. I have other things to do."
Which proved to be more true than he had anticipated. For one thing when he was finally admitted to Tony's room at first

she would not talk to him. She looked small and young in the high hospital bed, with her shining hair spread over the flat pillow. But she only shuddered when she saw him and turned her head away.

He sat down beside the bed and took her hand.

"I'm glad you're better, my dear," he said. "It's all over now. And you needn't be afraid of Herbert any more. He's under arrest. It's all right."

He felt her hand give a convulsive jerk. Then she said the only thing she said while he was there.

"Why didn't you let me alone last night?"

"Let you die?" he said lightly. "My dear child, with a long happy life ahead of you, and a young man ready to break down that door at any minute! Don't be foolish."

But although he tried questioning her as to the events leading to Alice Rowland's death she said nothing more. When the nurse came in she was apparently asleep, her sensitive mouth set and her eyes closed. He went out feeling frustrated and slightly bewildered, to go back to his office, put his feet on his desk, and sleep peacefully for several hours.

It was afternoon when the telephone wakened him. . . .

Hilda was alone in her apartment that night when he arrived. She had been sitting in the dark, her hands folded in her lap and her eyes gazing out at the roof and chimneys beyond the window. She was still sitting there when, receiving no answer to his knock, he opened the door and walked in. He did not see her at first. Then he made out her smallish huddled body and put his hat down on the table.

"I've been thinking things over," he said coldly. "Perhaps you'd better raise chickens. You won't mind cutting their heads off, will you?"

"What's the difference between using an ax and breaking their necks?"

"That's no excuse for what you have done. And you know it."

"There were only two alternatives."

But this was not the old Hilda. There was defense in her voice, and resentment. He lit a cigarette and pulled up a chair. He was still furiously resentful.

"How long did you know this thing?" he demanded.

"What thing?"

"The secret Tony Rowland was trying to keep. The hold Johnson had over her."

"I didn't know it. I only suspected it. I kept trying to have somebody look at Nina's arm. Nobody would do it." She was still indignant. "Last night I made her show it to me. It wasn't what they were afraid of, and I told her so."

"I see. And that's the reason she—"

"I had nothing to do with that," she said hastily.

"But you suspected something wrong from the start?" he persisted.

She moved in her chair.

"If I had I'd have saved Alice. All I was sure of was that Tony Rowland was not a psychopathic case. I didn't think she'd shot her mother in her sleep, either."

"But you thought she had shot her?"

"What was I to think? At first, anyhow," she said defensively. "I hadn't been in the house five minutes before she told me to keep away from her mother's room. And she locked the door at first, too, until she saw I was minding my own business."

Fuller smiled rather wryly. The idea of Hilda on a case minding her own business amused him.

"All right," he said. "You were attending strictly to your job. Then something set you off. What was it?"

It was some time before she answered. The room was still dark. Over her head the canary chirped sleepily. That and the cries of children playing in the street below were all that broke the silence. When she did speak her voice was tired and dispirited.

"I don't know much about girls," she said. "But it isn't usual for them to lock their mothers in their rooms, is it? And there was Herbert, of course. He had to fit in somewhere."

"Don't tell me you suspected him because he knocked you down and robbed you?"

Some of the resentment was gone from his voice.

"I wasn't within a mile of the truth at that time," she confessed. "Tony had a secret of some sort. I knew that. And the Johnson man was involved in it. But it seemed queer for her to be using the *Encyclopedia Britannica* for a door stop."

He looked astonished.

"The *Encyclopedia*! What on earth did that have to do with it?"

She sighed. "Did you ever go through a whole volume of it page by page? It's horribly tiring. But one page had a smear on it, as if it had been put face down on something."

"I see. Of course that explained everything!"

She ignored the irony in his voice. Probably she never noticed it, engrossed as she was in what she knew.

"It simply suggested something. Why for instance Tony burned the bandages from her mother's arm at night. And I never was really certain even then. It was just a possibility—until the end."

"Why for God's sake didn't you take me into your confidence?" he demanded. "You could at least have told me what you suspected."

"Why should I? Nobody had been killed then. If Tony had a secret like that it was hers, not mine. But if she had Herbert knew it too. There had to be some reason why she bought my watch. Apparently she didn't want him arrested. Then she'd sold a couple of dresses, so she evidently needed money, probably for him. But I began to suspect something very serious after I talked to Stella, the cook. She said he had been in the house as a butler just before Tony broke her engagement and tried to kill both her mother and herself. You gave me the clue to that yourself before I even took the case."

He stared at her.

"*I* gave you the clue! What sort of clue?"

"In the park that night. You said there was one motive for crime usually forgotten. That was desperation. Tony Rowland was desperate. Any idiot could have seen that."

Angry as he was Fuller grinned in the darkness. This was Hilda again, not the cowering creature he had found on his arrival. And a Hilda ready to talk, to justify the thing she had done.

"I suppose I began by wondering why Tony locked her mother's door. She relaxed later, but it was a queer thing for a girl to do. Then there was her broken engagement. No one knew why, even Nina herself. After Herbert appeared I decided it was a case of blackmail, but blackmail didn't explain everything. The queer thing was that her mother didn't seem to know anything about it. She was perfectly willing to talk about Herbert and his sister Delia, who had been her maid. She even talked about the change in Tony.

"I thought of everything from Japs to a lover for Nina Rowland. I even wondered if Alice had tried to shoot her sister-in-law, and Tony was taking the blame. Then I saw Mrs. Hayes. She worried me. She wouldn't talk, except that her son was to keep away from the girl. She looked shocked and half sick. It was more than his marrying her. She didn't even want him near her. I thought Tony had told her the truth, or what she thought was the truth, so—"

"So you went to the *Encyclopedia*?" He looked at her with a sort of awe. "Don't tell me, on the basis of what you had, you went through twenty-four volumes, including the Atlas!"

"Only one. She had been using it as a doorstop."

"Of course. Why not?" he said, his mouth twitching. "I always thought there must be some practical use for the damned things."

She remained unsmiling, however.

"Later she changed it for a china elephant, but I found it in the library. I didn't have a chance to go through it until just before Alice Rowland was killed. I should have acted at once, of course. I blame myself. After all Alice had had the letter and hidden it, and it came from Hawaii. Up to that time Tony had watched the mail, but that day she happened to be out. I took it to Alice myself."

Fuller looked baffled.

"What letter? What on earth are you talking about?"

"The letter about Herbert's sister Delia, the reason she didn't sail with them from Honolulu. Alice got the letter, and everything broke wide open."

"Where is this letter now?" he inquired impatiently.

"I have it," she said. "I found it last night. But maybe I'd better tell you how I think things happened when Alice Rowland was killed."

And this is the story of the murder, as she told it, and as it actually happened.

XVI

Tony had not been asleep that night. She was waiting for the household to settle down before she burned the dressings from her mother's arm. But also the meeting with Johnny Hayes had upset her. When she finally slipped into her mother's room Nina had been awake and irritable.

"You've been crying again," Nina said, eyeing her. "I don't understand you, Tony. It isn't enough that you spoil everyone's plans, including my own. You go around looking like a ghost yourself."

"I'm sorry, mother. I'm all right, really."

"And why all this secrecy?" Nina demanded. "Why not tell Alice and be through with it? She can't do anything about it, can she?"

"You know how she is, mother. She'd raise a row. She'd get Dr. Wynant in, for one thing."

Nina subsided. She loathed Wynant. Then too she was never certain of Tony these days. The night of the shooting, for instance. Had she been walking in her sleep? Or was Alice right after all and there was something wrong in Tony's mind?

Tony was dressing her arm by that time. It looked better, but she said nothing, and Nina lapsed into sulky silence. She lay back against her pillows and submitted glumly. Seen thus, even with her hair in curlers and a thin gleam of cold cream on her face she still looked attractive. She waited until Tony had washed her hands in the bathroom and came back.

"What happened to your wedding dress?" she said abruptly.

"I happen to know it's missing."

Tony did not answer. She was wrapping the dressings in a towel, and Nina went on petulantly.

"Don't you think you've acted the fool long enough?" she demanded. "What happened between you and Johnny Hayes? I've a good notion to send for his mother and see what she knows. She's in town. I saw it in the paper."

Tony stiffened, and her young face set in hard lines.

"If you do I'll never forgive you, Mother."

"Am I supposed to sit back and see my only child eating her heart out? No wonder Alice thinks you've lost your mind. I'm not sure she isn't right."

"I'm doing what I think is best. If that's crazy I can't help it."

She left the room, closing the door carefully behind her, and went down the stairs. The house was very quiet, and following her usual custom she deposited the dressings in the stove and set fire to them. The kitchen was dark until she lit the match, but she was startled as she replaced the stove-lid to hear some one rapping on the window outside.

She stood still, afraid to move. There was no light from the stove now and the darkness was thick. But beyond the window a distant street light showed her a figure which she all too surely recognized.

"It's Herbert," said the voice. "Let me in, quick. The police are after me."

She stood uncertain for a moment. Then she went to the door and unlocked it, and Herbert burst into the room. He sounded as though he had been running, and he was in an ugly mood.

"Who put them onto me?" he demanded. "If it was you you know what that means."

"I didn't. How do you know they're after you?"

"I've got ways of finding out," he said cryptically. "It's that damned watch. Look, pull down the shade and let's have a light. I need food and a bed. How about my old room?"

She was shaking, but she steadied her voice.

"Did you have to come here? It isn't safe, for either of us. Even if you do stay you'll have to be out of there before Stella comes down in the morning. Suppose she finds you there?"

"What if she does?" he said, impatiently. "Look, I'm hungry. How about something to eat?"

She was trapped. She was afraid of him. She always had been afraid of him. Even in Honolulu. Even when he came to the ship and taking her aside had told her about Delia.

She had never told any one about that.

Now she tried to steady herself. She got soap and towels and a blanket and put them in the bedroom off the back hall. When she went back to the kitchen Herbert was comfortably settled in a chair, smoking a cigarette and with Stella's cat on his lap. The sight made her flush with anger.

"You know your way around here," she said coldly. "Why don't you get your own supper?"

His terror had apparently gone. He grinned at her.

"You know your way too," he said insolently. "What did you do with that watch?"

"That's none of your business."

"Well, you better bury it. It won't be nice if you're found with it."

She had gone to the refrigerator and was getting out some food. Now with the milk bottle in her hand she turned and looked at him.

"I wonder why I haven't killed you before this," she told him. "I've wanted to long enough. I lie awake at night and think about how to do it."

He threw back his head and laughed.

"Killing takes a lot of nerve, Tony. You ought to know that. You've tried it twice, haven't you? Only not me."

He looked wary however as she took a long bread knife from a drawer. She did not approach him, however. She went out into the pantry, and was there at the bread box when to her horror she heard the door into the rear hall open again and Alice's voice, high and shrill with fury.

"What are you doing in this house?"

Herbert was startled. He leaped to his feet, dropping the cat. His cocksureness had dropped away, and he was trying to smile.

"Now look, Miss Rowland," he said. "There's no harm in

my bumming a little supper, is there? Miss Tony's known me for years, and when I saw her in here . . ."

Tony was in the doorway by that time, the bread knife in her hand. Herbert saw her, but Alice did not. She was holding a letter in her hand, and her face was hard.

"You're getting out of here," she said. "Right now, before I put in a call for the police. You're doing no more blackmailing. I know now what I should have known all along. Leave the house and don't try to come back, or I'll set the police on you."

He moved toward the door, picking up his hat as he went. But some of his cocky manner had come back.

"*You'll* set the police on me!" he said. "Ask your niece there about that. She won't like it."

He left then, closing the door behind him. Tony was still near the pantry, the knife in her hand. Neither she nor Alice had seen the knob turn to the back hall, or that there was a motionless figure behind the door there.

Alice sat down by the table. She looked collapsed, but the face she turned to Tony was stone cold.

"How long have you known?" she asked.

"Known what?"

"Don't try to act the innocent with me. I have this letter in my hand. Shall I read it to you? It came from the Islands today." She drew it out of the envelope. "But of course you know what it says. You've known all along, haven't you? That's why you broke your engagement, isn't it? Listen, I'm going to read this to you."

And read it she did, Alice by the table and Tony with the knife still in her hand and unconcious of it. Neither of them saw Nina open the door and stand listening, her face livid with amazement and horror. Neither of them knew she was in the room until she struggled to take the knife from Tony. And the letter was still in Alice's hand when Nina picked up the milk bottle and struck with all her strength at Alice's head.

XVII

That was the story as Fuller heard it that night from Hilda, and as he learned it in detail later. At the time he merely listened carefully, putting in a question now and then. When she had finished she reached over to the table and turned on a lamp.

"The letter's here," she said, picking it up. "Shall I read it? Or will you?"

"Carry on," he said. "It's your case, apparently. Not mine."

She made no comment on that. She put on the shell-rimmed glasses which made her look like a baby-faced owl, and under the light he saw her hands shaking. Her voice, however, was steady enough.

"My dear Alice," she read. "I was terribly shocked when your letter came. It does look like it, doesn't it? Why else the secret dressings at night and Tony burning them? And the refusal to see Dr. Wynant, or any doctor.

"After all Tony would know. She has seen it here in the Islands. I remember years ago they had to dismiss her nurse for letting her see an advanced case. And you *must* have medical advice at once. I say that because I find that Delia, for whom you inquired, has it and is at present in a leprosarium. I happen to know that she had it before they left and was not allowed to sail for that reason. The family did not know it of course.

"It sounds brutal, Alice, but you must get Nina out of the house at once. They have institutions for lepers in the States, I believe, and that is where she will have to go. I believe . . ."

Hilda stopped reading. She put the letter down.

"There's more," she said, her voice flat. "It doesn't matter."

Fuller had found his voice.

"Good God!" he said hoarsely. "No wonder Nina picked up the milk bottle!"

"No. She was hardly sane. She was a beautiful woman, and she thought she was facing exile and horror."

"And Tony thought so too?"

"Yes. She knew what it meant. Her father had told her to look after her mother, and when Herbert for his own reasons lied and told her it was what she was afraid of, she was desperate. You see, she had seen it as a child. It must have left a terrific scar on her."

"Nina never suspected?"

"No. Alice Rowland had a morbid fear of infection of any sort. She would never touch Stella's cat, for instance. When Nina's trouble developed that was how Tony kept her quiet about it. But Tony had learned about Delia before they sailed, and she'd been on the watch for four years."

When Fuller said nothing she went on rather drearily.

"You can see how it was for Tony. It was the end of the world for her. It had been ever since Herbert had lied to her about it. She must have let him see the arm somehow. And remember this, she'd been watching for trouble. And what she thought had happened to her mother was horrible beyond words."

"So she tried to kill her. Better death than what was happening, I suppose."

"She meant to kill herself too. Remember that," Hilda said defensively.

"All right," he agreed. "Now let's get to last night. Just what did you do to Nina Rowland last night to make her do what she did?"

There was a longish silence. When Hilda broke it her voice was unsteady.

"I did nothing," she said finally. "I made her let me see her arm, and I told her it was harmless skin trouble. Psoriasis, I imagine. Nasty but not what Tony had thought it was."

"I see," Fuller said, not ungently. "Only where did that leave her? It was all for nothing. She had committed a murder and Tony had tried to kill herself. All for nothing." His voice sharpened. "What could she do? What's the difference between using an ax or breaking a neck? That's it, isn't it? Don't tell me you didn't know what would happen, Hilda."

She made no effort to defend herself.

"She made her own choice. What could she expect? Disgrace and life imprisonment, or maybe the chair. If her choice was to drive the car into the river I couldn't stop her. I was at the hospital."

Fuller said nothing for some time. Then he got out his cigarette case and in the dim light held it out.

"For God's sake take a cigarette and remind me that you're merely human," he said. "And even a damned fine woman—at times."

He leaned over and lit it for her. In the lamplight he saw that she was close to breaking down. He made an effort to rally her.

"You know," he observed, "there are a good many times when you absolutely terrify me. Here you had a locked door to start with, a bandage on Nina Rowland's arm, a volume of the *Encyclopedia* as a doorstop, a bump on your head, a stolen watch returned, a lady named Hayes who registered horror, and a letter from Honolulu. That's all you had for quite a while, isn't it? Until Alice was killed. And you make a case out of it!"

She looked rather relaxed, as he had hoped. She even took a puff of the cigarette, coughed, and then put it down.

"I had Tony," she said, almost apologetically. "I liked her, you know. And what about her mother was so dreadful that she didn't want her father to come home? Or that she didn't want either the doctor or me to know about it? I—I stuck to my bullet in Nina's arm for quite a while." She smiled faintly. "I felt rather stupid about the whole thing, really. I should have known the night she burned the bandages. And there was that article in the *Encyclopedia*. Only in this country we don't think about such things."

He looked over at her, his expression one of genuine fondness tempered by exasperation.

"I wish to God you'd work *with* me on my cases," he said.

"Not against me. But I don't mind telling you you've done a damn fine job. Or advising you to go to bed for a week. Why not?" he added as she shook her head. "Tony will get over this. She's faced worse than death for her mother. And she's got Johnny Hayes. We've had to put a guard around her, to keep him out of her room. He ought to be a Commando, that boy."

"You haven't arrested him?"

He smiled sheepishly.

"I can sympathize with young lovers too," he said. "I'm not so damned old myself. Anyhow both those boys are on their way to a war. Who am I to stop them? Only by heck they're going to pay for that window they broke." He grinned. "Quite a neat little plot they hatched with Aggie, wasn't it?" he went on. "The kitchen door unlocked, and the sergeant breaking the window across the street and running like blazes while our man followed him. And you shut in your room! I'd like to have seen your face then. It must have been something to see."

"It's never been anything to see," she observed drily.

"Still and all I rather like it."

He went over and stood looking down at her.

"You don't mean this chicken stuff, do you?" he inquired. "After all, Hilda, I need you. Maybe in more ways than you know."

If Hilda flushed he did not see it.

"Oh, for heaven's sake don't go sentimental on me," she said brusquely. "I'm tired and I need a bath. So do you probably. Go home and get a night's sleep. That's what I mean to do."

And it was not until he was outside in the cool October night that he felt a faint sense of relief. He had his job and his comfortable bachelor quarters. And a policeman had no business with a wife.

He grinned as he realized that Hilda had once more saved him from a grave mistake.